Brooklyn '76

Brooklyn '76

Anthony Ausiello

A Novel

SOUTH ALLEN STREET
PRESS

Published by South Allen Street Press, Westfield, New Jersey
www.anthonyausiello.com

Edited and designed by Girl Friday Productions
www.girlfridayproductions.com

Cover design: David Fassett
Project management: Kristin Duran
Editorial production: Abi Pollokoff
Image credits: Cover © Shutterstock/Nowik Sylwia, Envato/
Moderngolf_9, Shutterstock/a katz. Image on page 273
courtesy Municipal Archives, City of New York

ISBN (paperback): 979-8-9885810-0-0
ISBN (ebook): 979-8-9885810-1-7

Library of Congress Control Number: 2023914321

First edition

JULY 4, 1976

MORNING

CHAPTER 1

Bam! Bam! Bam! Three sudden blasts startled Dee, perched as usual in front of her apartment's open bedroom window. Her fingers flew apart in surprise, and a newly lit cigarette dropped from her hand. It fell straight and fast through the dead summer air, and sparks flew silently as it collided with the concrete two stories below.

"Bastard!" She cursed her loss.

Bam! Another loud blast rattled the windowpanes, followed by the staccato of what sounded like machine-gun fire—strips of firework mats exploding in succession.

"Not even nine in the morning and it's starting already." Her grievances fell on deaf ears. The front gates and sidewalks below remained empty, for now. Dee placed her hands on the windowsill for balance, then carefully leaned her torso just past the threshold. She craned her neck and squinted, hoping to spot the culprits responsible for the racket—there was no shortage of possible suspects in this neighborhood. Oh, how she'd love to give their parents a piece of her mind. But then again, she knew full well that any parent who threw their kid out on the street this early didn't give a rat's ass. It didn't matter: only a faint trail of smoke crept into view across the street, curling around the edge of the first home on the avenue.

She fell back in her seat and reached for the pack of Pall Malls and Bic lighter resting in the window's nook. She lit a new cigarette, took a long drag, and shook her head. God, she hated the Fourth of July; that today was the Bicentennial made no difference to her. What was there to celebrate about a "holiday" where a mother had to spend every waking second worrying that one of her children might blow their fingers off, *or worse*, with those goddamn fireworks? Dee took another drag, as if in defiance. *I watch my kids,* she assured herself.

★

Around the block from their apartment, Dee's husband, Paulie Agnello, clad in his traditional Fourth of July short-sleeved polyester shirt dotted with dozens of tiny American flags, fished in his pants pocket for loose change to buy the morning paper. Gabe, a gruff bear of a man, sat atop a gray milk crate. A cigar box filled with coins and small bills balanced across his lap, and stacks of newspapers bordered him on each side. Usually, Gabe worked the weekday morning shift, wedged in the narrow space between the candy counter and a slotted wall filled with cigarette cartons. Monday through Friday, a continuous string of commuters rushed into the store, grabbed their papers, and rushed out and up the steps of the El across the street. Today Gabe seemed the one in a rush. He jutted out a plump hand, impatient for payment.

"I'm closing up soon," Gabe said.

"Closing up? You're barely open," Paulie said, nodding in the direction of the drawn-down security gates. Despite the crack, Paulie was sympathetic to the plight of many shop owners on the Fourth. Blown-out windows were a common casualty if precautions were not taken. In response, Gabe lifted his hand higher. Paulie shrugged, finally found a quarter in his pocket, and dropped it into Gabe's sweaty palm.

"Gotta drive out to my son's on Staten Island," Gabe mumbled as he peeled off the top paper from the stack nearest him and handed it to Paulie. "Need to get over the Verrazano before it gets all jammed up."

"Not the *Post*! The *News*, the *News*," Paulie protested. Gabe slapped the paper back down and snatched the top copy from the stack beside him. He mumbled something under his breath as he handed the paper to Paulie.

"What?" Paulie barked as he folded the paper and tucked it under his arm.

Gabe cleared his throat and grumbled, "Happy Fourth."

"Yeah, right," Paulie replied as he turned and walked away. "Twenty years, the guy still doesn't know what paper I buy," he muttered.

Strolling home, Paulie began whistling "Yankee Doodle Dandy." He was determined not to let anyone spoil his mood. Plus, he couldn't get the tune out of his head. It was one of his favorite films, and he had stayed up way too late last night watching it. He loved Cagney, the singing, dancing—they didn't make actors, let alone pictures, like that anymore. That one scene toward the end always choked him up, when Cohan's father is about to pass away, with Cagney, playing his son, George, at his bedside. Paulie could hear the lines in his head as clear as day: George reassuring his father that he had thanked the audience on behalf of his whole family, just as the Four Cohans act always had, with George breaking down in tears as he concluded, "And I thank you." Paulie's eyes began to grow misty, but he shook it off and continued on his way.

He looked up at the blue sky and smiled wide, confident that, at some point today, he'd get a call from his shop steward informing him that the strike was over. The latest word among the fellas at the picket line was that President Ford himself was leaning on the phone company's top brass to settle with the union. This was an election year, after all, and what better day to announce labor peace than on the Bicentennial—a proud victory for both the union and the company. A resolution couldn't arrive fast enough, as competing rumors also circulated that the company had begun to threaten layoffs.

With a pep in his step, Paulie turned the corner onto his block and sailed past the chain of three-story row houses. Most front gates were still empty, but soon each one would be bustling with block party preparations. The whole neighborhood—hell, the whole country—would be one big block party today. Paulie's whistling ceased abruptly as he arrived at his front gate and spotted Dee, framed inside the corner front window of their family's second-story rent-controlled apartment. She frowned and flicked the ash of her cigarette out the window.

"Anyone call?" he shouted up to his wife.

"No one called," Dee said dismissively.

Just wait, Paulie thought as he walked into the gate and toward the front door. *Just you wait.* Good news was coming today; he felt it in his bones.

CHAPTER 2

Neither the rumble of fireworks nor the sound of his mother's voice from the adjoining bedroom shook Tony's concentration as he masturbated furiously under the rapid fluttering of sheets. Tony oscillated between images of his new girlfriend, Maria, and stolen glances at the Farrah Fawcett poster smiling down on him.

"Tony, you okay?" Alex, his younger brother, called from the twin bed opposite his own. On the wall above, Alex had proudly hung the Mighty Marvel Bicentennial Calendar. The feature character for July, of course, was Captain America, drawn majestically against the backdrop of the Declaration of Independence, two musket-wielding Revolutionary War patriots flanking him on either side.

"Go back to bed," Tony grunted. Having just turned fourteen earlier in the week, his patience with Alex, five years younger, was thin at best.

"You having a nightmare or something?" Alex persisted.

Before Tony could respond, he heard the screen window slam shut from inside his parents' bedroom. The linoleum floor creaked as his mother rose, and her footsteps approached.

Dee slid open the vinyl accordion door that separated the

bedrooms; a cone of daylight flashed like a spotlight aimed right at Tony's bed. He lay still as a corpse.

"There's Entenmann's cake on the table. Get dressed, it's time for breakfast," Dee declared, sailing past the foot of her sons' beds. Alex bolted out of bed as Tony waited for his erection to subside so he could follow.

★

A fidgety Tony joined his father and brother at the table for breakfast. He'd been tempted to finish the job in the bathroom, but the general flurry of activity in their small apartment, coupled with the unpredictable bowels of his father, made that an untenable choice. His appetite unaffected, he carved out a large square of crumb cake with a butter knife and lifted it from the aluminum tin with his bare hands. He took a generous bite, and powdered sugar fell like snow onto the table.

Opposite Tony, Paulie bent forward over the open pages of the Sunday paper as he intently studied the day's entries for Belmont Park. He pulled the ballpoint pen from his shirt pocket and drew blue circles around the names of the jockeys and trainers he followed. Cordero in the third, Velasquez seventh and maybe the eighth. He scratched his chin for a moment and then scribbled his picks for the early daily double in the paper's margin. Never one to pass on a hunch, he scanned down the page, searching for any thoroughbred with a patriotic name and was thrilled to find several. Lady Liberty in the first was a no-brainer. Paulie was more than willing to stretch the Bicentennial connection on the late double, pairing Freedom Train in the eighth with Jefferson's Cleaners in the ninth.

"Dad, Yankees win?" Alex, seated between his father and brother, asked. "Dad? Dad?" he repeated after shoveling another scoop of Franken Berry down his gullet. (A major dustup between mother and son over Alex's shunning of the Entenmann's had only been avoided when Dee noticed the July 5 expiration date on the carton of milk. *Why spill money down the drain?*") Paulie begrudgingly flipped several pages over to the box scores.

"They won. Seven to three. Rivers hit a home run," Paulie said without looking up from the page.

Alex's dimples flashed when he smiled. Aside from the baby fat that still puffed his cheeks, he was the spitting image of his brother at the same age. Tony took some pride in his brother's joy. Alex, the antithesis of his older brother, threw like a girl and couldn't swing a bat to save his life, but Tony had successfully indoctrinated him as a die-hard Yankee fan. Tony, since grade school, had been the best player on his Little League team, an accomplishment he still held.

Newspaper pages rustled as Paulie flipped back to his horses. Abruptly he paused and sniffed loudly, like a dog catching a curious scent. A whiff of garlic roasting in olive oil teased his nostrils. He sniffed again, turned toward the wall on his left, and shouted through it. "What are you cooking for?"

"So we can eat. Who's gonna cook? You?" Dee shouted back from inside the kitchen.

"I thought we were barbecuing with next door?" Paulie scratched his head. *Next door* was code for the Bevilacqua family. Several generations of Bevilacquas occupied all three floors of the home attached to the right of their own. During block parties, Mario Bevilacqua would relocate his charcoal grill from the backyard, where the aroma of searing meat wafted up and taunted Paulie all summer long, to the front gate. Even though the two families were far from best friends, Paulie had reluctantly accepted his neighbor's offer after Dee had vetoed the invitation to spend the weekend at his brother's house on the Island. Just as long as the Bevilacquas let them chip in for the food—strike or no strike, they didn't need anyone's charity—Paulie would put up with Mario's bragging about the success of his business or his next home-improvement project. It was un-American to not eat a grilled hot dog or hamburger on the Bicentennial.

"We have our own food," Dee shouted back. "It's Sunday. I'm making sauce."

Tony watched both his father's and Alex's expressions sour. "If you want hot dogs too," his mother continued through the wall, "then go see if the butcher is open and buy them. I'll boil them on the stove." Dee made it no secret that she also believed the Bevilacquas thought themselves big shots just because they owned both their home and a small auto shop under New Utrecht Avenue.

"But I told Mario—" Paulie shouted back.

"We have our own food." Dee cut him off.

Tony watched his father shake his head and then sigh before returning his attention to his horses. Can't have a block party without a hot dog or a burger—Tony agreed, of course, but for today, his focus was on something far more thrilling than grilled meat. He swallowed his final bite of cake, completely unfazed by his parents' bickering. It was normal; this was how they always spoke to each other. Quite frankly, if he ever walked into a room and found them holding hands or locked in an embrace, he'd assume that they'd just received a call telling them someone had died.

Tony stood up, dusted some powdered sugar from his lap, and strolled toward the kitchen. He pivoted and paused in the open doorway, assuming a wide-legged stance to straddle both rooms. He stood upon the nexus of the apartment—depending on the direction he stepped, he could stride into any room in the house (except his parents' bedroom) or even out the front door. He glanced back into the living-dining room, the largest of the apartment's four rooms. Alex had hopped from the table to the paisley sectional, where he sat mesmerized opposite the Sylvania console tuned to a cartoon about a dog attending the Second Continental Congress. All regular programming was preempted today for a marathon of Bicentennial specials. Tony couldn't imagine anyone sitting inside to watch TV on a day like this. All year, on television, in school, even in church—everything was about the Bicentennial. It was finally time to celebrate.

Tony turned from Alex to his father, whose head was still buried in the paper, and then to his mother in the kitchen. An apron covered the short-sleeved forest green blouse she wore loosely over a pair of blue denim shorts that ended just above her knees. Tony watched her pivot from stove to table to sink and back to the stove, her feet never breaking the borders of the diamond linoleum tile where she seemed rooted. She yanked the latch of the Frigidaire, tugged open the heavy metal door, and extracted a yellow plastic container of ricotta. She plopped the cheese into a still-steaming bowl of ziti and sauce and began mixing with her hands. Tony took a deep breath, cleared his throat, and finally spoke.

"So, I was going to go over to Maria's around lunchtime. Can I stay for dinner, too, or . . . ?" *Bam!* He flinched as another blast from outside interrupted him, an exploding M-80 or maybe a blockbuster, Tony couldn't tell. He was about to repeat himself, but his mother cut him off.

"You think you're going where?" Dee asked incredulously, her eyebrows pinched together. Tony shifted his weight from leg to leg. He repeated, casually, "I was going to go over to Maria's for lunch. Can I stay for dinner too? Her parents invited me."

"Whose parents?" His mother's voice deepened; her tone grew ominous.

"Maria. From school." Tony then remembered that there were three Marias in his class, which was slightly below average for Bensonhurst. There was Maria Filletti, who ate tuna fish sandwiches three times a week. Maria Esposito, famous for beating half the boys in her homeroom at arm wrestling. Finally, there was Maria Tarantella, *his* Maria. So he specified, "Maria Tarantella. Her father owns the construction company—T&T." T&T vans were a common sight in the neighborhood, usually parked for weeks in front of some home renovation. In fact, one T&T crew had completed Mario's new brick face early that spring. Tony sucked in a quick breath and exhaled, satisfied he'd cleared up the simple matter. As yet unschooled in reading facial cues, Tony ignored his mother's flared nostrils and twitching left eye. Then he uttered what he'd soon realize was a poor choice of words: "She's . . . my girlfriend."

Dee's eyes widened. Despite the heat from the stove, Tony felt a sharp chill run down his neck. Dee's face flashed crimson as Tony's paled, as if some invisible vampiric force was being inflicted by mother upon son. Realizing he'd made some grave error, Tony turned to his father, hopeful for support, perhaps for male solidarity.

Paulie, who'd not said a word during the initial exchange, remained silent and motionless for several seconds more, an eternity for Tony. Suddenly Paulie tossed a hand into the air and exclaimed, "Ahhh, you're fooling around with girls now?!" He launched himself from the table, heading straight for the toilet. "This is what you do to your mother," he barked at Tony as he ran past him and into the bathroom. He slammed the door shut behind him and shouted from inside, "On the Bicentennial!"

Dee shook her head in disgust at her husband's antics, then turned her expression back on her oldest.

"This is how you act? After all you got for your birthday?" Dee accused. Days earlier, Tony had been gifted with several new pairs of dungarees and T-shirts (intended for wear in the coming school year). He'd asked for a cassette player.

"What's the big deal, I don't . . ." Tony started but again was cut off.

"Forget it," Dee yelled. "You belong with your family." She turned from her son and thrust her hands back into the mixing bowl, violently churning its contents.

"But . . ."

"You stay on the block," Dee yelled without favoring her son with another glance. "Stay on the block," she said. "Play with your friends."

Play with my friends? His mother's words cut Tony in half.

"I'm not a little kid," Tony shot back, but he sounded more distressed than assertive.

Then the doorbell buzzed, and everyone jumped, even Alex, whose attention, until now, hadn't wavered from his show. This was a rare occurrence, as most people just shouted up to the front window from the sidewalk instead of pressing the buzzer.

"Who the hell is ringing the bell?" Paulie shouted from inside the bathroom. The toilet flushed, and Paulie emerged, still fixing his pants and belt. He charged the front door, grabbed the doorknob, and froze. "Who is it?" he barked and then abruptly yanked the door open like he was trying to surprise whoever might be on the other side. The second-floor hall, however, was empty. As Paulie poked his head out the threshold for a better look, a voice echoed up from downstairs.

"Paulie, you have to move your car. The cops are towing."

CHAPTER 3

Mr. Salvatore DeMarco, or "the mayor," as the neighbors called him behind his back, stood in Paulie's front gate looking very official—clean shaven, clipboard in hand, gray pressed pants, and a white collared shirt. He was dressed more to preside over a factory assembly line than a Fourth of July block party. But this was how he dressed every day, even though he'd retired from his supervisor position with Con Edison over five years ago. At sixty-two years old, his silver hair was fading to white around the ears. Despite having two adult sons, both married and living in Phoenix, the mayor still insisted on running the block parties. Aside from filing the required permits, et cetera, he was always eager to share his talents in efficient management and logistics with his neighbors. As an additional ongoing service, he'd always offer expert opinions on topics ranging from optimal placement of garbage cans, auto repair, and aluminum siding versus brick face to the general state of affairs regarding the block, borough, state, and country.

Every night for the past six weeks, the mayor, with his trusty clipboard—the Con Edison logo embossed across its back—had trekked up and down the block, soliciting a ten-dollar donation from each household. First, he launched into a meticulous explanation of the costs that the collected funds would be used to cover. Then he made a point of reading to his neighbors, usually under duress, the entire shopping list for the celebration, always adding at the end, "And you know I don't even pay myself a dime. Not a dime." Despite the fact that Paulie had already contributed, the mayor had again approached him just days before. As he launched into the repeat performance, Paulie had shouted back, "How many times you gonna ask me?" Paulie pointed at the clipboard. "What do you carry that thing around for if you don't write nothing down?" Mr. DeMarco squinted down at the clipboard and mumbled, "Mmm, right, right." He'd turned and continued his way to the next gate. "Big shot," Paulie muttered loud enough for Mr. DeMarco to hear, had he been listening.

Now, Paulie exploded out the front door to the sight of Mr. DeMarco tapping the glass face of his Timex.

"The cops are towing," he repeated. But Paulie could see his '68 Oldsmobile, parked as usual right in front of the gate below the giant oak that shaded it from the July sun.

He turned to bark something at DeMarco, but then caught sight of the squad car, ominously the only other vehicle visible on the block. In accordance with the flyers posted on every tree and lamppost, the other residents had already moved their cars off the block last night or early that morning.

Unless forced to do otherwise, Paulie never parked the Olds off the block, reluctant to trust his car anywhere that wasn't in clear view of their apartment's front windows. The habit was a response to a trauma suffered some seven years ago. Paulie had woken for work one winter morning and discovered that his car had been stolen while parked on the avenue under the El. Two officers had responded promptly to Paulie's frantic phone call. Tony was still in his pajamas and Alex in his crib when the squad car pulled up outside. Welcomed into the apartment and seated at the living room table, the huskier of the two responding officers detached a leather-bound notepad from his belt and flipped to a clean page. Dee made a fresh pot of coffee, despite the officers' protests.

"Dope addicts?" Paulie speculated while nervously fumbling through his wallet, searching for the Olds's registration. He couldn't think straight with Alex crying for his bottle and his wife repeatedly offering them all a slice of Entenmann's cake every thirty seconds.

"Probably just a joyride," the second officer, who had bushy rust-colored sideburns, said with a shrug. Tony, seven at the time, sat quietly, watching and listening as the officers continued to collect their data.

"My uncle's a cop," Tony blurted, perking the officers' interest. They both looked to Paulie for confirmation of the boy's claim. Paulie slapped his palm upside his head. He wasn't good under pressure. "Yeah, my brother, Frank . . . where's my head? He . . ." Paulie still couldn't find the registration but did find a picture of his older brother in uniform, posing with his arm around Tony, handsome in his all-white communion suit, his hands pressed together as if in prayer.

The officers nodded at the picture. "We know Frank. Stand-up guy," the husky officer said. Paulie finally found the registration between two losing OTB slips stuffed deep inside the folds of his wallet. The officers finished their report and left without taking a sip of coffee or a bite of cake, much to Dee's chagrin. Paulie's car turned up just a few hours later, parked beside a hydrant five blocks away. Despite the quick recovery, Paulie was left blighted with a deep and festering paranoia, trusting no out-of-view parking spot. If no such spot presented itself, he'd leave the Olds double-parked for hours and perch himself at the front window, both displacing and annoying his wife, as he scanned the street below, hoping to vulture the first available spot.

★

While his father raced to save the Olds, back upstairs Alex watched his mother pour a generous portion of ziti into an orange Tupperware. She pressed the lid shut and quickly wiped the stray globs of sauce from its outer edge with a paper towel. She lifted the container from the table and walked toward both her sons. Alex eagerly reached his hands out to accept the responsibility of an errand but was quickly disappointed.

"Bring it to *her*," Dee said, standing in front of Tony. "Your father's family left her to starve today." *Her* referred to Zizi, an elderly relative of Paulie's who lived up the block. The term *Zizi* was Sicilian dialect for *aunt*, and Zizi had been referred to as such for so long that no one remembered what her actual name was.

Alex watched his brother's eyes suddenly flash bright. Tony snatched the Tupperware from his mother's hands and started for the door. Before he could exit, Dee said, "Take your brother with you." Tony stopped, head bowed in defeat, while Alex leaped up from the couch, a smile stretched across his face.

Tony and Alex exited their home onto the front gate just as their father slammed the driver's door shut and turned the Olds's ignition. The tailpipe belched a puff of black smoke, and Paulie screeched away. Mr. DeMarco, seeing a new audience, repeated to the boys, "The cops were towing people." Tony nodded absently and hurried past him, out the gate.

A wide-eyed Alex scanned the empty street as he sprinted after his brother. It looked almost exotic with all the cars gone, the sun-bleached sidewalks like two white beaches divided by a black asphalt river. He walked along the edge of the curb. Even though he could see wooden barricades at both ends of the street stopping through-traffic, he wasn't brave enough to step into the street yet without his parents' explicit permission.

Soon marching side by side with his older brother, Alex looked down at his shirt and smiled proudly. He was thrilled to finally wear his holiday flair. For several months, he'd begged his parents to order him a "Young America for '76" T-shirt—part of the Bicentennial-themed apparel line that had been heavily advertised in comic books all year. Alex was sure that, come the Bicentennial, every kid on the block would be wearing one of the three colorful designs: a white tee depicting a racially diverse representation of working-class people raising the American flag, a powder blue tee as canvas for a rocket ship blasting off in a burst of orange flame, or a yellow tee featuring an American eagle clutching a red, white, and blue ribbon in its talons. Alex wanted them all but, knowing that was out of the question, would be grateful for just one. When his mother had finally relented, Alex chose the yellow tee—he thought eagles were cool.

"Yellow isn't a good color on you. Why don't you pick the nice white or blue shirt?" His mother had tried to persuade him, but Alex held firm.

Pinned to his shirt now were two of the Bicentennial commemorative buttons he'd also collected during the year. Yesterday he'd eagerly tried on all six, only to be scolded for poking holes all over his new T-shirt.

"I didn't pay $4.75 for a new shirt so you could turn it into a piece of swiss cheese," his mother had scolded. Two buttons were the parental-imposed limit, so this morning, after some deliberation, he'd chosen the smiling George Washington button that read

"Thanks, George, You Really Started Something," and the button that featured a red silhouette of Paul Revere on horseback with the caption "Paul, We Revere You."

Trekking up the block, Alex crept a bit too close alongside Tony, who reflexively jutted out his elbows to impose an acceptable distance between them. Such a brush-off would typically make Alex frown, but today his excitement made him impervious to such trivial slights. He marveled at all the plastic streamers, the countless strings of tiny American-flag pennants strung between streetlights, telephone poles, and trees. A giant red, white, and blue banner draped over the center of the block. The block looked pretty enough for a parade. And sure, Alex was looking forward to the rides and games and riding his bike in the street, finally like the big kids. But best of all, he could finally play with his snaps. Reflexively, he felt for the outline of the small cardboard box nestled inside his right pants pocket.

The box of snaps had sat on his dresser, next to his Bicentennial buttons, for almost a month. His mother had constantly reminded him that the snaps were reserved solely for use on the Fourth. Alex dug into his pocket, extracted the box, and reverently cradled it in his left hand. He lifted the lid and stood, ready at a moment's notice to grab and fling a teardrop-shaped twist of white paper against the pavement and smile with glee. When a snap struck the ground, it made a noise that sounded more like a pop than a snap, and Alex always wondered why they weren't called pops. Regardless, they were the most powerful explosives his mother allowed him to handle. He wasn't even allowed to play with the sparklers. Other children got to wave them wildly like magic wands once night fell, carving neon slashes and spirals into the darkness. Not Alex, lest, as his mother cautioned, one of his eyeballs be plucked from his skull or, in a blink, seared by a misguided ember. Alex, a snap pinched softly between his thumb and index finger, scanned the sidewalk for a target. He was eager but also knew he had to be selective. "I'm not buying you another box." His mother's words rang in his ears.

★

As the brothers approached the police car, Tony knew instantly that it wasn't there to write tickets or tow. He just had to look at whose house it was parked in front of—Chippy's. Almost on cue, Chippy's front door swung open, and two cops escorted Frank Chipparetti, "Chippy" to everyone but his parents, out of his home for the first of his likely several trips to the Seventy-Second Precinct today. Chippy was the local fireworks dealer; he was in his midtwenties but looked a decade older with his Fu Manchu mustache and constant two-day-old stubble. He wore a camouflage T-shirt and blue jeans and threw off a Vietnam-vet vibe, even though his epilepsy had exempted him from service. Beginning around every Memorial Day, and some years as early as Easter Sunday, Chippy peddled a never-ending supply of bottle rockets, cherry bombs, M-80s, and Roman candles to half the borough. Even Alex's second cousins, who'd moved out of the neighborhood a decade earlier, would drive in all the way in from Jersey to see Chippy and return home with a large brown paper bag filled with illegal fireworks.

If Chippy knew you, or someone vouched for you, he'd hop in the back seat of your car and tell you where to drive. He kept his black Monte Carlo parked off the block, its trunk filled with enough explosives to level a small mountain. After each sale, he'd drive and park his car somewhere different and trek back toward home, often only to be flagged down by another customer in waiting. For the two weeks immediately preceding the Fourth, he was like a jackrabbit, popping up on one block only to vanish just as quickly and then pop up somewhere else.

The sight of a parked squad car in front of any other house would usually trigger the flapping open of every window shade on the block. However, no one ever batted an eye when cops knocked on Chippy's front door. It was no stranger a sight than the postman delivering mail. And since Chippy never kept any contraband on himself or in his house, the arrest was all formality; heck, half the police force were his customers. After a brief precinct visit, Chippy would soon be bopping back down the block.

Chippy chatted up both officers as they led him out the gate, strolling casually like he was off to buy a container of milk. He paused in stride, his voice louder: "So then the Black guy, his dick stuck in a bowl of ice cream, says, *'I'm fucking dis custard.'*" Chippy grinned wide and flicked his eyebrows. Both cops laughed and continued the escort. Passing Tony and Alex, Chippy stroked the tips of his mustache and winked at them. One officer opened the back door of their squad car while his partner carefully tucked Chippy inside.

Tony, in his white tank top and jean shorts, regarded the officers. He thought of his uncle Frank, his favorite uncle, recently retired from the force. He missed seeing him in his uniform. Not that he had anything against his uncle Vic, his father's other older brother who had moved out to Long Island years ago. But Uncle Vic mostly just sat silently in his leather recliner sipping Dewar's on the rocks on their rare visits to his home. Uncle Frank, on the other hand, made a point of taking his godson to a Yankee game every year. On rides out to the Bronx, he'd let Tony spin a set of handcuffs around while he drove. Uncle Frank and likely the entire extended family were at Uncle Vic's for the Fourth. Tony had initially wondered why they hadn't gone, too, but that was before Maria had invited him over, before she promised him a *special* birthday present.

Pop! The tiny blast shook Tony from his thoughts. Alex, having flung his first snap of the day, smiled back proudly. The younger of the two officers feigned surprise at the sound and jokingly reached for his holster. Tony scowled down at his brother. Alex shouted, "Happy Fourth of July!" to the officers, who nodded, climbed into the car, and drove off.

Tony shifted the container of ziti into his left hand and adjusted the charms on his gold chain with his right. He spun the chain around his neck, making sure the latch was in the back and the thin gold cross and twisted bull's horn fell appropriately between the sparse strands of his recently sprouted chest hair.

"Can I carry the tray?" Alex asked him.

"No," Tony said. He turned and glanced back at their house. No sign of their mother. He arched one eyebrow in contemplation and then flashed a quick smile as an idea struck. He resumed walking, increasing his pace, causing Alex to do the same.

Tony noted a handful of neighbors were up and about. Giovanni Verde, with his walrus mustache, sat in a plastic folding chair in the center of his gate, sipping cappuccino and smiling up at the blue sky. Both boys wished him a happy Fourth. In reply, he crooned, "Happy birthday, AAAA-mer-i-gaaaaaa." A few gates down, the aged Mr. Orsini swept little clouds of dirt and dust from his gate with his straw broom, while the missus meticulously watered the yellow and blue perennials in her window planters. From across the street, they heard loud clanging as Mr. Bonello dragged a long aluminum table up from his cellar one step at a time.

Zizi lived farther up the block where the string of fully attached three-family row houses broke off into a shorter stretch of semiattached brick homes. Eight-foot-high red-and-orange brick walls framed a small raised patio that buttressed the facade of each pair. They looked like tiny castles compared to the flat-faced aluminum-sided homes next to them. Tony broke into a full gallop at the first porch as Alex trailed behind.

★

Dee finished washing the saucepot and placed it upside down in the drying rack. She wiped down the kitchen table, tossed the rag into the sink, and reached for the pack of Pall Malls, lighter, and ashtray resting on the stove between the two rows of burners. The house was empty, and she could enjoy another cigarette. Her husband and sons complained incessantly about her smoking, Paulie especially, faking a violent coughing fit even when she exhaled out an open window. Dee lit one and took a deep drag. A trail of smoke followed her path from the kitchen, through the entire apartment, and into her bedroom. At the front window overlooking the gate and sidewalk, she sat down on the rocking chair that had once been her mother's and set the ashtray, cigarettes, and lighter inside the sill. The slight breeze, which had greeted her when she opened the bedroom window an hour earlier, had vanished and was unlikely to return. The weatherman on 1010 WINS predicted that the temperature would hit ninety by noon. She took another drag.

Usually, this was Dee's favorite time of the day—Paulie off to work, her children in school. That certainly had not been the case recently, with her husband on strike and the kids out for the summer. She shuddered remembering the CWA strike of '71. Those had been the most horrible nine months of her life—her husband home every day, pacing nervously. She hadn't been able to enjoy a solitary cigarette. This strike was just a few weeks old, and she was already overcome with that same sense of dread every morning.

"Girlfriend." Dee grunted the word, exhaling a whirlwind of white smoke. She would have words with the monsignor next Sunday. This is what went on in that school? Fourteen years old . . . *Girlfriend . . .*

Another series of loud bangs erupted. She flinched and then shook her head. As much as Dee dreaded the Fourth, she dreaded the day after even more. That's when she'd flip through the paper and read about how many boys had blown their fingers off playing with fireworks. That wasn't happening to her kids. *I watch my kids,* she repeated to herself.

Across the avenue, the B train rumbled over the El on its approach to the station. She watched the train cars, each defaced with spray paint, pull into the station, heard the brakes screech as they lurched to a stop. For years she'd ridden that same line to work every morning, after she and her mother had moved to Brooklyn from their tenement on the Lower East Side. Trains were pristine then, with seat cushions and gentlemen in hats who gave up their seats for a woman.

Dee sighed as her thoughts went back to those years, back when she still dyed her hair red and stylishly wore it up in a beehive. She hadn't had a showy job, just another girl in the typing pool at Metropolitan Life. Every day after work, she came home with a smile on her face for her mother, her best friend. She was happy. Then her mother died, cancer. Not long after, she met Paulie. She wished she could say there were fireworks, but that's not what happened. He was just a guy, and she was just a gal, both already in their thirties. The guy tired of living with his widowed sister, his two older married brothers long out of the house; the gal still wearing black from the loss of her mother months earlier, in possession of a half-empty rent-controlled apartment. Fifteen years of marriage, and what had her life become? Union strikes, teenage girlfriends, children with missing fingers. She lit a new cigarette with the smoldering tip of her last and then crushed the stub into the ashtray.

CHAPTER 4

Of course Paulie couldn't find a spot to park. With block parties scheduled on every other block, half the streets were completely empty and the other half lined end to end with double-parked cars. Next to being stuck in traffic on the BQE, this was his worst nightmare.

His search unfolded in an expanding concentric loop around the surrounding blocks that weren't barricaded off for the day. Even the metered spots on the avenue were all taken, since payment was suspended for the holiday. He cursed through gritted teeth as he hit the brake at every vacant gap only to find a hydrant or driveway. At one such stop, he lingered a moment to reach across the front seat and roll down the passenger window to get a cross breeze. With no air conditioner, his car felt like the inside of a blast furnace. The station wagon behind him honked, and he cursed and stomped on the gas pedal. His car lurched forward as he was thrust back into his seat.

He should have defied his wife and insisted they accept his brother Vic's invitation to spend the Fourth on the Island along with the rest of his family.

"Come out for the whole weekend, I got plenty of room," Vic had urged during their phone conversation last week. Paulie, averse to rush hour and normal holiday traffic, shuddered at what he imagined would be hours of bumper-to-bumper Bicentennial traffic on the BQE. "So, beat the traffic," Vic had replied. "Come Saturday and stay a few days. I got five bedrooms now." This was a fact his brother seemed to interject into every conversation since he'd bought and moved into a new home. Paulie and Dee's apartment totaled five rooms—if you counted the bathroom. Paulie said he'd let Vic know after speaking to the wife, but unsurprisingly, Dee quickly put the kibosh on the idea. "We have our own beds," she'd said.

"You're a bum," Vic, only half in jest, told Paulie after he'd declined the invite. The Bicentennial was a big deal. Everyone was supposed to not just celebrate but celebrate big—and Italians celebrated with family. Frank even called to chastise him. He offered to squeeze everyone into the new powder blue Cadillac he'd bought for himself as a retirement gift. Frank had a clear head, Paulie thought. His brother was set for life, still only in his late fifties; he'd put in his thirty years on the force. Paulie had worked his whole life, too, since he was a child running alongside his father's fruit cart. He had sixteen years with the phone company, and where had that gotten him? Where was his Cadillac? Paulie came to the end of another block; still no spot for him. He sped across the empty avenue, continuing his search.

"Aaaaaaaaah" was the dismissive sound Frank had made over the phone when Paulie confided that his wife didn't want to go to Long Island.

"You know how she is," Paulie confessed. No one ever told Frank what do. Paulie remembered once, when Tony was little, Tony had asked his uncle Frank if he feared getting shot. Frank, in full uniform, tapped his baton against his badge and told his nephew, "Bullets are scared of me." After thirty years on the force, Frank didn't have a scratch on him.

Paulie slowed to a crawl on the next block—driveway, driveway, hydrant, driveway. *Strike better end today,* Paulie thought, the strands of his fragile optimism beginning to fray. It really felt like the horns were on him lately. *Yankee Doodle, my ass.* He spun his head from side to side, searching. He looked forward to the days he was assigned picket duty: better to bake under the sun, walking in circles outside the chain-link fence of his plant's loading dock, than be at home. God forbid he sit down on the couch for more than a minute; Dee would scowl at him like he was a railroad car hobo. If he went for a walk outside, she'd complain that he was going to OTB to lose more money. He'd been working since he was six years old, and she was going to tell him he couldn't place a two-dollar bet if he wanted to? She made him feel like he'd been out of work for a year, like he'd never worked a day in his life.

His oldest son wasn't even around anymore to act as a buffer. Paulie couldn't remember the last time they'd sat and watched a ball game together. Even with school out for the summer, Tony was either off playing baseball or working at the deli, not that Paulie spited the boy for having a job to go to; he wished he did. As for Alex, all his youngest ever wanted to do was watch cartoons and read comic books. And now Tony was messing around with girls? Jesus Christ!

Paulie slowly drove up the next block—again, driveway, driveway, hydrant, driveway. The station wagon still trailed directly behind him and honked again. Paulie's gaze shot to the rearview mirror. Seeing a female driver behind the wheel, he began barking curses, spittle splattering across the inside windshield. He floored the gas pedal and lurched forward, only to immediately jam on the brakes again. The station wagon almost slammed into him. Paulie floored it again, still barking curses out the open window. This time the station wagon remained still, not rolling forward until Paulie's car had reached the end of the block and turned right, the barrage of obscenities trailing off into the distance.

CHAPTER 5

Upon arriving at Zizi's stoop, Tony leaped up the rounded concrete steps, Alex trailing behind him. At the top of the landing, Tony leaned his shoulder against the front door. Unlocked as usual, the door swung open. Tony and Alex stepped inside the hallway, dark as a cave except for a small pale beam of light stretching down from the frosted skylight. The hallway smelled of antiseptic cleaner with a twist of citrus. Alex, unsure whether he enjoyed the scent or not, sniffed twice, then scrunched his nose—no, he didn't like it. Zizi's door waited at the end of the hall.

Zizi wasn't actually the boys' or even Paulie's aunt but rather a distant cousin who had ascended to the title of aunt simply by refusing to die. Somewhere between eighty and one hundred, though no one was certain of her exact age. She had grown less and less chatty over the last decade, and when she did speak, she did so only in her native dialect, which no one else completely understood. Mostly Zizi just sat in her apartment, still draped in mourning black for her husband, twenty years deceased this past April.

As they walked past the stairway, Alex gave a quick glance upstairs where Aunt Alice, his father's sister, lived with her son, Richie.

"Did they go to Uncle Vic's?" Alex asked Tony.

"I guess so," Tony shrugged. "Probably hitched a ride with Uncle Frank."

Richie was, by far, the brothers' favorite cousin. Though almost twenty, Richie was the closest in age to the brothers and never treated them like little kids, even when, like with Alex, they actually were. Despite living on the same block, the brothers hadn't seen much of their cousin since he'd graduated from New Utrecht High School. Richie had taken a job at some fancy restaurant in the city, so he slept by day and waited tables by night.

His hands still full, Tony knocked on Zizi's door by kicking it twice and then glared down at Alex, who took a moment to realize his brother wanted him to turn the doorknob. Alex spun the knob, and as the door cracked open easily, Tony barreled past him. Alex quickly followed.

"*Come stai?*" Tony shouted at the back of Zizi's head.

Zizi sat silently in the lone burgundy-cushioned armchair, draped in blankets, only the tightly wrapped strands of her silver bun visible. The small television resting on a bronze caster-wheel stand opposite her was on, but she didn't seem to be watching it. Tony came around to face her, smiled wide, and bent down to kiss her on the cheek.

Tony motioned for his brother to come over and do the same, but Alex hesitated. Very old people freaked him out—he thought they all looked like shriveled, dug-up corpses from a Dracula movie. Tony flashed his brother a look, and Alex reluctantly approached. Cautiously, he pecked her on her cheek. It felt like kissing a cactus. Zizi's tiny black eyes, sunk deep within her wrinkled face, darted between the two boys. She finally nodded in recognition and smoothed out the hem of the black mourning gown forever draped over her small frame.

Once, Tony had asked his father, "Who died?"

"Everyone in Italy," Paulie had replied. "Just to get away from her."

Tony lifted the Tupperware in display for Zizi, like a priest raising a chalice, then quickly delivered it into the adjoining kitchen. Alex smiled nervously at Zizi. Zizi scowled back. She always smiled at Tony, but for some unknown reason, scowled at him. After a long, silent moment, without moving her head, she glanced down at the narrow glass coffee table. Resting on a lace runner was a small china plate containing three Stella D'oro anisette cookies. Like Frankenstein's monster brought to life, she flicked one finger in their direction while eyeing Alex. Cautiously, he reached for a cookie.

"Pssssssssst," Tony hissed from the front door. Alex looked up. Tony whispered something. A confused Alex shrugged. Tony whispered again, motioning toward the door. Alex looked back blankly, then glanced over at Zizi, who stared at him suspiciously.

Tony shook his head and darted over to his brother and leaned down to whisper in his ear. "I gotta go do something. . . . I'll be right back. . . . Wait here." Tony then sprang upright and turned to Zizi. "I'll be right back," he said, his hands pointing along in pantomime. "Alex is going to stay here and watch TV with you." Zizi squinted one eye. No one was quite sure exactly how much English she understood.

"Where are you going?" Alex asked, concerned.

"Don't worry about it. I'll be right back. Just watch TV." The door slammed shut behind him. Zizi looked over at Alex like he was a turd that had just fallen out of a donkey's ass. She spoke to him in Italian. Alex just stared back blankly. His parents managed fragments of Italian when they had to but never spoke it at home. Tony, when younger, had asked his mother to teach him the language, but she had snapped back, "We were born in this country. Speak English."

Alex smiled nervously back at Zizi. He proclaimed, "Happy

Fourth of July!" hoping to maybe reset their summit on a celebratory note. He smiled even wider and pointed to the buttons on his T-shirt. Her face soured further. The television was tuned to WPIX, the local NY channel. A Navy fleet filled the Hudson while "You're a Grand Old Flag" played in the background.

"No mi interessa di questo," Zizi said, gesturing toward the screen and then scratching the hairs on her chin.

"Tony will be right back," Alex reassured her. He took another bite of his biscuit. Something strange sparked in Zizi's eyes. She extended a bony finger toward the front door and said, *"Lui sta per imparare ad affilare la sua matita."* Alex furrowed his brow. She arched one eyebrow and raised the extended finger, jabbing it up toward the ceiling, nodding in a knowing manner. Alex chewed slowly, eyes straining, trying to decipher the pantomime. Zizi squinted back at the boy, looking for some spark of comprehension. She shook her head and raised the opposite hand, looping thumb and index finger together at the tips to form a ring and proceeded to repeatedly thrust the extended skeletal finger in and out of the small hole with an alarming fervor. The strange spark in her eyes returned, and her lips spread into a wide, toothless grin. Alex almost choked on his cookie. He coughed violently, spraying crumbs over the pristine lace.

"Che schifo!"

"I'll clean it up. I'll clean it up," Alex blurted, flustered, and rushed into the adjoining kitchen. He scanned the room and spotted the paper towel dispenser resting on the black Formica counter. He ran over, tore off a sheet, and sprinted back inside. He quickly swept the crumbs into the towel, scurried back to the kitchen, and dropped it into the trash.

Alex took a deep breath and exhaled. Maybe he was better off waiting outside on the stoop for his brother to return. He scanned the kitchen, regarding the gold-and-silver geometric pattern of the wall-paper. Three-dimensional cubes crisscrossed the walls, and Alex's head swayed in diagonals, trying to follow their path. His kitchen was painted a boring light yellow. He paused, noticing what looked like a small, narrow thermometer jutting out from the wall beside the light switch. He took a closer look. Inside the metal box, a thin red needle bisected the seventy-degree mark. *Hmmmmmm, that's all wrong,* he thought. He was sure that he'd heard the weatherman on the radio, not an hour before, proclaim the temperature was already ninety degrees. Wanting to atone for the small mess he'd made with the cookie, Alex took it upon himself to remedy the perceived error. He stood on his toes and, spotting a tiny plastic lever, slid the lever to the right until the red needle split the ninety-degree hash. Satisfied, he grinned proudly and returned to the sofa. As he sat, the plastic sealed cushion exhaled a death rattle of trapped air. He turned to Zizi and said, "I fixed your thermometer." Zizi shrugged and turned back to stare at the television.

★

Tony darted out of Zizi's apartment and closed the door behind him. He felt a pang of guilt leaving his little brother behind, but he quickly brushed it aside. The way his parents had acted left him little choice. Tony was a good kid. He knew he was—he'd been told so many times over, by teachers, priests, coaches, and neighbors. He'd been a good kid for fourteen years now—a career straight-A student, an all-star infielder since Little League. And, for the past year, a steady wage earner at Prima Delicatessen, working shifts after school and on weekends. Come the fall, he'd be attending Xaverian, one of the best Catholic high schools in Brooklyn, on a half scholarship. Sure, there'd been resistance as soon as Tony mentioned Xaverian to his parents; Dee was nervous about her son riding a city bus twice daily, and Paulie felt stomach pangs the moment he discovered how much the tuition cost. Both parents preferred Tony to attend New Utrecht, the free public high school just a few blocks away that had also gained recent national notoriety for appearing in the opening credits of *Welcome Back, Kotter.*

"They have the honors program there. Why do you want to ride the bus every morning?" Dee said.

"You know who graduated from there besides Mr. Kotter?" Paulie teased. "Buddy Hackett!"

"I can't come and get you if you're sick. I don't drive," Dee reminded him.

"Why would you have to come and get me?" Tony replied.

"What about the time you made in your pants?"

"I was in first grade!" Tony exclaimed.

A letter arriving in May stating that Tony had been awarded a half scholarship had mercifully ended the debate. Why was everything so difficult with his parents? He wished his parents were like Maria's. Maria had the same freedoms as her older sisters, both already in high school. At least that's what Maria told Tony. He had only met her parents once.

By the end of the school year, Tony and Maria's relationship was almost four weeks old, which, for elementary school, equated to two adult years. Their courtship had blossomed that spring, brokered mainly through a chain of whispering and giggling intermediaries, as was protocol. Maria had just broken up with another classmate, Benny Lombardi. Benny, a real prick, was the youngest of the three Lombardi brothers, all pricks, who also lived on Maria's block. Tony and Benny were already long-standing rivals when it came to academics and athletics. Usually, Tony was able to edge Benny out, barely, on both test scores and in the schoolyard. However, for the better part of the year, Benny was winning when it came to romance. Tony still didn't understand what Maria ever saw in him. Whatever the attraction, when word got out that Benny had cheated on Maria over Easter vacation with some public school girl, the romance had ended in a violent screaming match that echoed through the schoolyard. Benny barely evaded a wild right hook from Maria before the nuns broke things up.

Soon after the breakup, Tony had walked Maria home every day after school, first in a small group, then, after a few weeks, splintering off to take a slight detour together. The smitten young couple would pause occasionally to duck inside a secluded alley or behind a wide tree to make out. By the second week of their romance, an emboldened Tony took to sliding his hand up Maria's blouse. After parting ways with Maria at her corner, he spent the short walk to the deli for his afternoon shift trying best to conceal his erection from passersby.

On the final day of school, Tony, as usual, had walked Maria home. Along with her family, she was leaving for a ten-day vacation in the Bahamas and wouldn't return until the third of July. The lovebirds lamented their imminent separation, often pausing to embrace as if the other were off to gallows. Upon reaching Maria's corner, they hugged, and Tony leaned in for a final smooch. Maria drew her head back, pouted, and said, "I'm going to miss your birthday."

"That's okay. I'll be fourteen all year," Tony said.

Maria thought for a moment, then smiled and said, "Walk me to my gate." Tony had some time to kill before heading to work and was beyond thrilled to prolong their time together. After strolling down her block, hand in hand, they arrived at her home to find Maria's parents standing inside their front gate, chatting with neighbors. Tony was stunned at the casualness with which Maria introduced him as her boyfriend. Her father, a brawny, square-jawed man, spared Tony a nod while continuing a conversation with his next-door neighbor over the adjoining gate.

"Nice to meet you, Mrs. Tarantella," Tony said, turning politely to Maria's mom.

"JoAnne," she insisted. She wore tight pants and a knit tank and looked more like someone's older sister than a mother. Both of Maria's parents looked at least a decade younger than his own. JoAnne, like her daughter, was big in the chest, and Tony tried desperately not to stare. JoAnne gently placed her hand on Tony's shoulder and asked if he was hungry. Tony, thrown off by her touch, found himself tongue tied. He shook his head no.

"We're going inside," Maria said, grabbing Tony's hand and leading him through the front door. Tony followed and half turned his head, expecting either or both of her parents to shout some admonishment that would stop them in their tracks, but all he heard was the front door closing behind him as he stepped inside. Maria led him by the hand, downstairs into her parents' finished basement. She assured him that they were alone in the house except for her older sister, upstairs gabbing away on the kitchen phone. They began to kiss and soon groped each other feverishly until Tony, sadly, realized he'd be late for work, even if he ran. Still, he lingered a little longer, one more minute, maybe. Suddenly, Tony felt Maria's fingers trace over the outline of his erection against his gray school slacks. He flinched, and Maria laughed. She leaned up to whisper in his ear, "You'll have to wait for your birthday present until I get back." All Tony could think to reply was, "Okay." He had been counting the seconds until their reunion ever since.

Now, making his way down Zizi's hallway, his anger at his parents rose with each step. He hadn't done anything wrong. What the hell was wrong with having a girlfriend?

Suddenly, he heard voices coming from upstairs. He glanced up the stairwell through the array of rectangular spindles and spied a pair of bare female legs, legs that definitely did not belong to his Aunt Alice. At first it sounded like two people arguing, but then he heard the woman laugh. Tony crouched farther down, hoping for an angle that would reveal how high up the bare flesh extended. As he shifted his weight, the floor beneath creaked loudly.

"Someone's downstairs," the woman said.

Tony froze, plastered against the wall. He closed his eyes as if this would magically render him invisible. Then, from upstairs, another voice: "Tony?" Tony looked up in the narrow space between the wall and banister and found his cousin Richie smiling down at him.

"Hey, Richie," Tony said as casually as he could, still plastered to the wall. "Happy Fourth?"

"What are you doing down there? Come upstairs," Richie shouted down.

"Tony who?" the woman asked.

"Tony . . . my cousin . . . from down the block," Richie said, pausing briefly between each descriptor. Tony eyed the front door. "Get up here," Richie repeated. Reluctantly, Tony climbed the stairs.

At the top of the landing, Richie greeted him with an embrace, and they exchanged brushing pecks on the cheek. Stepping back, Tony realized Richie was also bare legged, standing there in a pair of leopard bikini briefs and a completely unbuttoned denim shirt. The bare-legged woman was nowhere to be seen.

"You look good," Richie said, nonchalantly scratching his chest hair. His deep tan was already in midsummer form. He ran a hand through his thick head of dark feathered hair, slightly and uncharacteristically mussed. Richie, once lean and slender like Tony, had fleshed out a bit since working at the restaurant. He was of average height, like all the men in their family, so just a little extra weight on his frame made him looked husky, not that it appeared to be hurting his love life. Slender or beefy, Richie always had a natural swagger, one that Tony had always aspired to.

"You look better," Tony told his cousin. "I thought you'd be on the Island."

"Me? C'mon, all the action's in Brooklyn on the Fourth. What am I gonna do out there—sit and watch the grass grow?" They both chuckled. "Plus," Richie added, "with my mother out of the house . . ." Richie grinned and made a tilting motion with his head toward the open doorway to his apartment. "Why are we talking in the hallway like a couple of Puerto Ricans? C'mon, come inside. Hang out." Tony looked at the door, then back down the stairs as he shifted his weight from leg to leg. "You got somewhere you gotta be?" Richie chided, seeing his cousin's reluctance. "C'mon. Maybe she likes you too," Richie added a wink. Tony wasn't sure if his cousin was joking or not. Richie curled his arm around Tony's neck and led him inside. "How come you're not on the Island? Your pop's Olds leaking transmission fluid again?"

"Honestly, no clue," Tony replied. Inside, the apartment reeked of pot and cigarette smoke. Tony coughed repeatedly.

"Yeah, I gotta air this place out," Richie said, unhooking himself from Tony. He took a few steps and retrieved a pack of Marlboros from the end table between two paisley sofas perpendicular to one another. He tapped out a cigarette, lit it, took a drag, and gave his younger cousin a look up and down. "So, what you been up to?"

Tony shrugged. "School, baseball, work, y'know," he said. Tony glanced around the apartment as casually as he could. At the end of the hall, he spotted his cousin's bedroom door slightly ajar. A flash of blond hair and exposed flesh whizzed past the opening. Tony craned his neck to get a better look.

"Yeah? Where you working?" Richie asked. Then he noticed his cousin's neck, bent almost completely sideways, and began to laugh. "You're gonna pull a muscle like that," Richie said and slapped Tony's shoulder. He started walking back toward his bedroom. "C'mon, don't be shy."

Tony remained still; his mouth went dry. Waving Tony over, Richie poked his head into the room and spoke to whoever was inside. "What are you getting dressed for? My cousin's gonna be a doctor." He turned back to Tony and said, "Right? You've been studying the human body."

"Uh-huh," she said dismissively. Richie grabbed Tony's arm and pulled him into the room. Tony blushed and lowered his head to stare down into the blue shag rug. He noticed a set of bongos sitting beside the bed, half-obscured by the twist of purple silk sheets dangling off the mattress. Richie gently slapped Tony on the back of his head, and Tony looked up. The woman sat at the foot of the bed, back to him, naked to the waist. Long frizzy hair fanned out over her slender frame. Tony opened his mouth but didn't say a word. He watched her fold over. She quickly snapped back upright and pulled an orange halter top over her head.

"Tony, meet Denise," Richie said.

"What's up?" Denise said without looking back.

"This is my cousin, Tony," Richie said proudly. "He's a brain and an all-star baseball player, right? Gonna be the first shortstop to do brain surgery." Tony had no idea where Richie was getting this doctor stuff. He couldn't even stand the sight of blood. His cousin had the gift of gab, though Tony had also heard Richie referred to as a bull-shit artist. He wasn't quite sure yet what, if any, was the difference between the two.

"Uh-huh," Denise repeated as she slid on her sandals, stood up, and walked right past them. "I gotta get home."

Tony took this cue to finally lift his gaze. Two things quickly struck him: Denise's face looked much older than her bare legs and back. She wasn't *old* old, but she was older than Richie. She also looked familiar. He couldn't place her, but he was sure he'd seen her before.

"Where you going? Three makes it a party," Richie joked.

"You two enjoy your party," she replied.

"I gotta go too," Tony said and followed Denise through the apartment and into the living room.

"Where you gotta go?" Richie called from behind. Tony paused and turned.

"I need to go see my girlfriend, quick," Tony said. "Her parents invited me over to their block party, but my parents won't—" He broke off, suddenly self-conscious, realizing Denise was now staring straight back at him.

"You got a girlfriend, kid?" she said. Not waiting for a response, she added, "Treat her right. Don't be a creep like your cousin." She walked over to the far living room window, which led out to the fire escape, and slid it open.

"Why is she going out that way?" Tony whispered the question.

"It's the same way she came in," Richie said. He then turned to-ward Denise, held out both arms, and exclaimed, "How am I a creep?" She ignored Richie and sat down on the sill, hands at her sides. Tony noticed the diamond wedding ring she wore on her left hand. She raised both legs in unison, bent at the knees, twisted herself around, and slid out the window with ease. Richie turned to Tony and asked, "Where does your girlfriend live?"

"Up the block from the laundromat," Tony said.

Richie thought for a second, then said, "Follow Denise. She knows a shortcut."

"What?"

"Listen to your cousin. Go." Richie slapped Tony on the back again, urging him out the window. As Tony climbed onto the fire escape, Richie whispered into his ear, "Always remember, coz—older women. Older women." Tony nodded mechanically and followed Denise onto the steel grating of the fire escape and then carefully out through a small opening onto its narrow ladder. After descending several rungs, Denise leaped down onto the concrete path between the cellar and a patch of tomato plants. Tony followed.

CHAPTER 6

Finally, Paulie found a parking spot three avenues from his home. On the bright side, the spot was directly across from the OTB. Maybe his luck was changing for the better. He climbed out of his car and locked it. He hurried across the street and, with his right hand, patted his back pocket to make sure it still held the folded newspaper racing page. He squeezed between two parked cars, a copper Ford Pinto and a dented station wagon, and hopped up onto the sidewalk. As usual, clusters of men filled the sidewalk directly in front of the OTB. As he navigated through the crowd, one conversation caught his attention. He turned toward two men leaning against a powder blue Cadillac, parked in front of a hydrant. The two men, clad in short-sleeve knit shirts and slacks, both nodded rhythmically, arms folded in front of them, listening intently to the shorter, potbellied man that addressed them. The man paused in his address, took a breath, removed his white linen cap for a moment to wipe the sweat from his brow with his forearm, then continued his passionate address.

"The five in the second. The five, I'm tellin' ya," he asserted. Both colleagues shook their heads, dubious that the five horse, a thirty-to-one shot named Bossy Aussie, had a chance. Paulie, usually one to mind his own business, reflexively slowed his pace and tilted his head in their direction upon hearing the tip. The man in the cap continued. "Listen to me. Finn told Big Dom that the five can't lose." That stopped Paulie in his tracks. Everyone in the neighborhood knew Big Dom. Giving Big Dom bad information—or worse, losing Big Dom money—was detrimental to one's health.

"I don't know," persisted one of the men leaning on the Caddy. "The two horse is a big favorite, lotta speed."

"*Don't worry* about the two horse," assured the shorter man, which ended the debate. Paulie made a mental note but unfortunately eavesdropped too long. Some sixth sense was already triggered among the other men, and in sync, all three turned and shot Paulie a dirty look. Paulie flinched and hurried inside the OTB, pulling the door closed behind him.

Recreational bettors and degenerate gamblers alike crowded the narrow single-room establishment. Overhead, a dense cloud of cigar and cigarette smoke obscured the entire ceiling. Dee frequently pointed out the hypocrisy to her husband that he could "Stand in OTB all day like it's a rose garden, but my cigarette bothers you." Paulie began to burrow through the masses, trying to make his way to the betting windows at the far end.

His progress came to an abrupt stop. Paulie found himself wedged inside an even thicker cluster of men in polyester pants and short-sleeve button-down shirts, all staring up at the scratch sheet, posted inside a locked glass case like it was a copy of the Declaration of Independence. Desperate eyes scanned the tiny print, making sure their "locks" and "can't miss" horses would still run their respective races. As Paulie craned his neck to peek over the fedora-topped head hovering in front of him, he felt a tap on the shoulder. He spun around and looked up. It was Barney Short, ironically named, as he stood six foot three. Five days a week Barney and Paulie carpooled to the New York Telephone factory in College Point, Queens. Barney was responsible for getting Paulie the job with NY Tel after working there for two years himself.

"You got any winners for me, Paulie?" Barney smiled; dimples flashed on each pink, clean-shaven cheek. He extended his hand to Paulie. "Happy Fourth." With his height and crew cut, Barney looked like he should be pacing the sidelines of a high school athletic field with a whistle around his neck. Instead, he, like Paulie, had spent the majority of the last two decades soldering multicolored wires into steel plates for Ma Bell.

"I hope, Barney. I hope," Paulie said. "Problems, Barney. All I got is problems."

"What happened?" Barney inquired. Paulie took in a long, dramatic breath.

"The older one tells us this morning he has a girlfriend," Paulie reported.

Barney's eyebrows pulled together, and he shrugged his wide shoulders. "So? What is he, fifteen, sixteen now?"

"Fourteen."

"Eh, that's the age. You forget what fourteen was like?" Barney chided. "Coulda been worse. He coulda told you he had a boyfriend instead."

Paulie considered the comment for a moment, but it was too much to process.

"Well, I got two tidbits of news that I bet will cheer you up," Barney said with a smile.

"They signed?" Paulie asked, his eyes flashing with joy.

"Well," Barney hesitated, "let me give my other news first."

"Jesus Christ." Paulie raised his voice. "Is the strike over?"

"Yeesh, you gotta relax, Paulie. You're gonna give yourself a heart attack." Paulie's anxious expression remained unchanged, so Barney continued. "So, I ran into Robby Scantro at Korvettes last night. We were both with the wives. You know the women and all these Bicentennial sales. So anyways, he pulls me aside and tells me he ran into Billy O'Day, who told him he saw Mickey Connelly pulling into his driveway yesterday afternoon. . . ." Connelly was their shop's union representative on the negotiation team. Hearing Connelly's name, Paulie leaned in closer.

"Anyways," Barney continued, "Billy told Robby that Mickey had told him that he'd only be back from negotiations for the Fourth if there was an agreement." A huge smile stretched across Paulie's face at hearing this.

"You really think it's over, Barn?"

Barney bit his lip and nodded. "Gotta say, it looks good. It's like everyone thought: the bigwigs are saving the big announcement for today." Paulie looked like a man who'd just received his death row reprieve. Barney continued. "Best part is we'll get a check next week for back pay, just like last strike. Free money."

Speaking of cash, Paulie reached around and patted his back pocket again to feel for the envelope filled with Tony's first tuition installment. Wouldn't be surprised if there was a pickpocket in this crowd. Finding it there, Paulie let the cool feeling of relief sink in.

"Jeez, I almost forgot my other news," Barney blurted out. "Guess who I just saw on the corner walking back to his car?"

Paulie shrugged.

"Johnny Truz. I hadn't seen him in years."

"No kidding," Paulie replied, his smile turning uneasy. Johnny Truz, short for Truzino, had been the best man at Paulie's wedding—best friends since they were children. It had now been almost ten years since they'd last spoken.

"Looks like a million bucks, that guy. Can't remember the last time I saw him in the neighborhood," Barney added.

"What's he down doing here?" Paulie asked. As far as he knew, Johnny still lived in a five-bedroom colonial out in Roslyn, just off the North Shore.

"The second wife's sister's house, I think. Something like that," Barney said and chuckled. "Didn't seem too excited about it. Said he told them he was going out for a pack of cigarettes and came right here. You just missed him."

Paulie pressed his lips together, his head nodding slightly.

"First thing he did was ask about you," Barney said and pointed to Paulie. "'You still work with Paulie?' he asked me. 'When we're not on strike,' I told him." Barney chuckled again. "Anyways, he said he might swing by your block later and surprise you. So I go, 'How do you know he's home today?' And he says, 'That *wooden Indian*, I bet you a million dollars he's standing in that gate like he's holding cigars.'" Then Barney stiffened to reenact Johnny's imitation of a wooden Indian.

Paulie managed a small grin, mostly from nostalgia at the nickname Johnny had christened him with long ago, one he hadn't heard in years. As the grin faded, Barney went on.

"Anyways, throw in a few extra exactas today, ya cheapskate," Barney kidded with a big smile and a pat on Paulie's shoulder. "You got free money coming your way. Actually, why don't you and Dee come by later for some coffee and cake? We'll celebrate," Barney offered.

"Maybe," Paulie said. "Maybe."

"I gotta get back." Barney reached out to shake Paulie's hand goodbye. "Relax, will ya. It's done." Before turning to leave, he cajoled Paulie. "Enjoy yourself, for Chrissakes. It's the Bicentennial."

As Paulie resumed nudging his way toward the betting window, the brown steel door in the corner marked Employees Only swung open. A wrinkled old woman hobbled out. The crowd pushed back to make a path as she slowly made her way to the enclosed glass case on the wall and then sorted through a ring of keys. She opened the lock on the case's sliding glass panels and then fished out a black felt marker and a small spiral pad from her pocket. She lifted the pad, squinted, reached up, and began scratching thick black streaks over the horses no longer running that day. When she was done, she closed the case, locked it, and ambled back the way she had come. The crowd pressed forward.

Paulie scanned the posting. There, in the second race—the two horse had scratched. *Don't worry about the two horse.* Paulie replayed the short man's words in his head. Paulie scanned down the entries to the five horse—Bossy Aussie, still a thirty-to-one shot. Paulie reached behind and felt for the envelope of cash. He considered the moment: the Bicentennial, the tip outside, the scratch—hell, even Johnny Truz back in town. Was it all a sign? Paulie scratched the stubble at his chin. What was it Barney had said . . . ? Take a chance?

CHAPTER 7

Alex tried to sit still inside Zizi's apartment, but it was becoming uncomfortable—and not just from Zizi's dirty looks. It had grown terribly warm since Tony left. The backs of Alex's thighs, slick with sweat, now stuck to the plastic sofa covers. Each time he pried one leg loose, the parting of flesh and plastic made a slurping suction noise, eliciting another dirty look from Zizi. She seemed to have just nodded off, though Alex remained cautious in his movements.

On television, a marching band hammered out the final notes of "America the Beautiful" in front of a bandstand draped in stars and stripes. When the music stopped, an older man with white hair wearing a dark suit stepped to the podium and began to speak. Alex recognized Mayor Beame from seeing him on the nightly news as well as the front page of his father's newspapers. The television volume was too low for Alex to hear what he was saying. Mayor Beame made a grand gesture with his right hand, and another man seated in the first row of the grandstand rose gracefully and strolled to the podium. He was a tall older man with a long distinguished face and thick gray hair, impeccably combed. Alex regarded him closely. The man carried himself with the air of a statesman, maybe even royalty.

He said a few words, and the people seated behind him stood and cheered. Zizi suddenly stirred in her chair, opened one eye, and mumbled, *"Scommetto che ha i testicoli come un toro. Come ha fatto mio marito. Dio l'abbia in gloria, pace all'anima sua."* Her crooked smile returned for a moment, then vanished just as quickly.

"Isn't that Mr. Coffee?" he asked, but Zizi had again dozed off. Alex fanned himself with one hand. It was getting really, really hot in here. He spotted a small oscillating fan on a three-shelf stand alongside the back wall. Slowly, he pried himself loose from the sofa and went to turn it on. He pressed the first of the three blue buttons at the fan's base, and the blades began to whirl. He turned to go back to his seat just as he spotted something dart past the backyard windows. It looked like his brother.

★

Tony followed Denise through a maze of tomato plants and fig trees, squeezing between small gaps in the chain-link fences and wrought iron gates that separated one adjoining backyard from the next. He tried to shake the fear that his mother was likely at this very moment marching up the block, wondering why her sons were taking so long to return from what should have been a quick and simple errand. Tony worried that Alex, who spooked easily, might have bolted in tears from Zizi's and fled home. Despite these concerns, Tony couldn't take his eyes off Denise's ass, the curve of alternating cheeks slipping below the bottom of her tight shorts each time she took a wide or high step. Thoughts of Maria immediately followed and, with them, threats of a returned erection.

Well, there was nothing he could do to alleviate any of these concerns now. He had to see Maria immediately, not for the sordid rendezvous he'd fantasized. Instead, he wanted to break the bad news in person. Explain his circumstances, plead his case. He knew full well that Maria had a reputation for being . . . volatile. Maybe a phone call would be easier, safer. But with Maria's two older sisters, the phone was always busy. Plus, he wanted to see her. Even if the news he brought with him would be disappointing, even if she got mad at him. He had to see her.

After hopping several fences, they reached the backyard of Dr. Malachi, the chiropractor. His office occupied the ground floor of a two-story brick cube, while he lived upstairs with his wife and teenage son. The paved backyard was empty, no sign of the black Lincoln Continental he kept impeccably polished.

A tall chain-link fence divided the lot from the back alley of the apartment building on the opposite side. Denise scurried to the fence's farthest corner, where the concrete rose in tiered ledges to a high flat wall. In three quick leaps, she vaulted from the highest ledge to the top of the fence. She paused midstep, one leg bent, her foot planted atop the steel frame. She glanced down at Tony, who followed closely behind.

"You checking out my ass, kid?" she said. Tony froze, suspended in a Spider-Man pose across the fence. Without waiting for an answer, she vaulted over the fence and dropped down onto the closed lid of the garbage dumpster below.

"Watch what you're doing," she scolded through the fence as she leaped down to the pavement. "Last thing I need is a dead kid on my head," she mumbled, mostly to herself.

Tony scaled up and over the fence. Like Denise, he dropped down to the dumpster and then onto the concrete, landing directly in front of her. Denise lowered her gaze for a second, then raised it back up to look him in the eyes. "See ya, kid," she said, then spun around and scurried through a narrow alley that separated the apartment build-ing from its twin beside it. Once at the sidewalk, Denise's pace slowed as she crossed the street, veering up the block toward the schoolyard of PS 68. The three-story cement fortress ran the entire length of the avenue. At each end, single-story annexes extended, walling off a portion of the schoolyard. Parallel chain-link fences sealed off the remainder of the schoolyard from the pedestrian sidewalks. Denise crossed the street; one last shortcut remained.

Tony, at least, was back on familiar ground. He'd attended kin-dergarten here before his mother had insisted on Catholic elemen-tary school. The only person less happy about the switch than Tony was his father. Why pay for Catholic elementary school tuition when there was a free public school practically around the block from their apartment? His mother had been insistent. She wanted her son under the watchful eyes of priests and nuns. She knew the sort of kids on the block that went to public school. These were the kids that ran wild, unwatched by their own mothers. These were the kids that grew up into the teenagers who "gypsied" around the neighborhood, smoking, drinking, doing God knew what.

Instead of continuing up the sidewalk toward the open gateway, Denise abruptly crouched down and slid through a clipped-open sec-tion of fence that ran up from the sidewalk like a scar. She popped upright and squinted as the glare reflected off the expanse of sun-bleached concrete that stretched across the schoolyard. She must've heard the rattle behind her and spun around to find Tony still trail-ing her. He slid effortlessly through the same slit and sprang up only to be met by the twin daggers of Denise's glare. Not a lip reader by practice, Tony was still easily able to translate the "What the fuck" contortions of her mouth. He raised both hands, palms up, unsure what she was upset about. He followed her lead and silently mouthed back, "My girlfriend lives across the street." Denise's face flushed in anger; the features of her face pinching closer together as the dirty look she flashed intensified. As she shooed him off with a violent flick, Tony saw something descending from above, arcing just over Denise's head, smoke trailing behind.

"Watch out!" Tony yelled.

Denise jumped and backpedaled just as an M-80 exploded in a deafening burst, a cloud of gray smoke billowing in the exact spot she would have been standing in if not for Tony's shout. She threw her hands up around her ears, her legs tangled, and she tripped backward. Instead of crashing into the ground, Tony caught her, left hand under her left armpit, his right momentarily cupping her right breast before it slid beneath her other arm. He quickly lifted her upright. She wrenched herself away and spun to face him. Tony raised both hands in a gesture of surrender. His expression—*Hey, I was just trying to catch you.* Despite the ringing in their ears, both heard hysterical laughter coming from the annex's roof.

"Motherfuckers," Denise shouted. Tony spotted three shapes that he immediately recognized—the Lombardi brothers. Vito, the oldest and largest, was the easiest to make out, trailing his younger brothers. The dark strands of his bowl cut barely covered his prominent brow as he lunged forward with a simian gait. Just ahead of Vito was Marco, the mean-spirited middle brother. Benny at least was a smart and athletic dick. Marco was just a dick. And though Tony only caught a quick glimpse of his face, he was sure that was Benny, Maria's ex, leading the way. One by one, the three veered away from the edge of the roof and vanished from sight.

Tony wondered which brother had thrown the M-80 and, more importantly, whether he was the intended target. Having once been Benny's Little League teammate, Tony knew that Benny could put the M-80 between his eyes if he wanted. His rival's pitching career had spanned all of six games: twenty innings pitched, seventeen strikeouts, five hits allowed, and fourteen walks—all from hit batters. If Benny gave up a hit, he threw at the next three batters, seldom missing.

Denise grumbled something to Tony that might have been a thank-you. She turned and walked away, adding, over her shoulder, "You can stop following me now!"

"My girlfriend lives on that block," an irritated Tony shouted back. He pointed across the schoolyard at the opposing string of houses. Denise stopped and turned, pivoting on one foot.

"What's your girlfriend's name?"

"Maria."

"Maria what?"

"Maria Tarantella."

"Oh, fuck me!" Denise said. Tony's eyes widened.

★

Dee stepped out of the house into the front gate. *Disgusting,* she thought. *Another hot, disgusting day.* At least Mr. George, the landlord, hadn't planted himself on the bench yet. Not that Mr. George took up that much space—his emaciated frame swam in the huge faded blue parka he wore regardless of the season. She hated watching the way he slowly shuffled across the gate, the soles of his worn black loafers scraping against the concrete. Yet, miraculously, on the first of every month, he could dance up the flight of stairs like Jimmy Cagney to collect his rent.

She traded her usual seat for a spot on the bench closest to the sidewalk. She stood in the narrow space between the bench's edge and the black iron ribbons of the front gate to gaze up the block. Dee wondered what was taking her sons so long. She furrowed her brows, thinking something was not right.

Bam! The loud echo of another nearby blast made her jump. She lit a cigarette to calm her nerves. She tried to remember if the Fourth was always like this. She didn't think so. Ever since she had children, everything seemed louder. *Bam!* Another explosion, this time closer. She took another drag.

Dee heard a familiar rattle. She turned and saw Mr. Song rolling up the steel security gates of the corner fruit and vegetable. A national holiday, and here were Mr. Song and his wife, the always-smiling Mrs. Song, Dory, at work, always working, always hustling. Dee snorted. Dory wasn't really Mrs. Song's first name. Mrs. Song had tried to pronounce her real name for Dee seven years ago when the Songs had first purchased the store from Paulie's brother Vic. Paulie's father was the inaugural proprietor of the store, after having spent years peddling produce from a horse-drawn wagon. Frank had already joined the force by the time his father passed away, so the store went to Vic. Vic made a killing for almost fifteen years before selling it and moving out to the Island. He opened a new store twice the size of his old one and, of course, upgraded from a two-bedroom apartment to his five-bedroom colonial with a fenced-in backyard and above-ground pool—show-off that he was.

After purchasing the store and a whirlwind weekend remodel, the Songs had reopened on a crisp fall Monday morning. Dee was sure to poke her head inside. She'd perused the aisles, suspicious of the raised prices. After filling her wire basket with three pears and a bunch of green bananas, Dee strolled to the front counter and introduced herself. "I'm Vic's sister-in-law. Vic, y'know? The last owner."

"Hello, Mrs. Vic." Mrs. Song replied with a bright smile.

"No," Dee shook her head, annoyed. "I'm not Mrs. Vic. I'm Dolores. Dee." Dee tapped herself on the chest with her index finger.

"Ah. I am Do-hee." Mrs. Song smiled wider and pointed to her own chest. She said her name so quickly that Dee thought she'd also said *Dee*, which further annoyed her.

"Your name is Dee too?" Dee had asked in a defeated voice. *Figures,* she thought to herself. Vic had given her husband first crack at buying the store. It wasn't even a discussion. She knew her husband wasn't like his brother; he was no hustler. Same story when they had an opportunity to buy the house up the block right across the street from Zizi. Paulie wasn't one of these men who knew how to keep up a house. And they wanted $22,000 for it? Forget it. They'd be broke and probably homeless if they had bought either.

"Do-hee," Mrs. Song repeated, and slowly tried to stress the two syllables.

"Dee?"

"Do-hee."

"Doreen?"

"Do-hee."

During the negotiation, Dee's neighbor's, Angelina Pucci, had waited impatiently behind her in line to pay for the cluster of red grapes she cupped in her palms. Eventually Dee and Do-hee settled on the name Dory, which made Dee happy, and truly, Mrs. Song couldn't care less—as long as Dee and everyone else paid cash, no checks.

Now, Dee heard a small voice calling to her. She turned and spotted Alex's two little friends, Vito and Tommy, pedaling their bikes down the middle of the deserted street. Vito, olive skinned and wiry, arrived first, screeching to a stop just before the steel curb. Tommy, the chubby one, labored behind. His bike still sported a set of training wheels whose aluminum brackets had begun to buckle under the boy's weight. The bike wobbled from one side to the other with each arduous revolution.

"Where's Alex?" Vito blurted. Dee glared down at him and thought, *Their mothers tossed them out into the street already.*

"He'll be back right back. He had to do something," Dee said.

"Do what?" Vito asked. Dee sneered back. *Little wise ass. Sneaky too.* Dee never cared much for Vito, but her disdain had doubled since she caught him trying to steal one of her cigarettes from the pack. Before Dee could tell the boy to mind his own business, Alex's other friend, Tommy, finally arrived, his bike coming to an abrupt and awkward stop besides Vito's.

"Good morning, Mrs. A. Happy Fourth of July!" Tommy said and smiled wide.

"Happy Fourth, Tommy," Dee replied. At least this one had manners. The other one—a born troublemaker.

"You making your baked ziti today?" Tommy asked.

Before Dee could answer, Vito chimed in, "Tommy's so fat he gave his bike two flat tires."

"Watch your mouth," Dee snapped at Vito.

"So, where's Alex?" Vito asked again. Yes, where was Alex? And Tony?

CHAPTER 8

Tony tried in vain to remain a few paces behind Denise as they finally crossed the schoolyard, but he was in too much of a rush and kept catching up. Denise stopped, held her hand out like a crossing guard and told Tony, "Wait. Just wait. Let me go first."

Tony crossed his arms and watched her walk away, but each step she took felt like hours. For all he knew, his mother was about to come storming into the schoolyard, looking for him. Just like she always "popped up" at the deli just before closing time. "I forgot we needed milk," she'd tell her son; sometimes it was cold cuts, or some soft rolls for sandwiches. But Tony knew she was making sure he came right home. He knew that she didn't want him hanging out with the kids she deemed "losers" that congregated on the street corner outside the deli. Most of whom were kids he'd grown up and played with all his life, like his best friend, Sally.

It now occurred to Tony that his mother probably didn't want him talking to the neighborhood girls that congregated on the corner with the so-called losers either. School, baseball, work, home—that was his life, under the watchful eye of nuns, his coach, his boss, and always his mother. The more he thought about it, always someone watching him, like he was some kind of convict, the more his neck and face flushed. Or maybe it was effin' Benny and his brothers or remembering how his parents had treated him earlier. Regardless, the air tasted hotter with each breath, was more difficult to breathe. He watched Denise crouch down, climb through another gash in the fence. He couldn't wait anymore. He had to move, to run. Tony launched himself at full speed. Hearing the chain links rattle behind her, Denise spun around just as Tony emerged from the slit.

"I told you to wait," she barked at him.

"I waited. You're slow," Tony said as he flew past. He'd pushed her out of the way of the M-80. He didn't owe her. If anything, she owed him. Tony rushed across the street and up onto the sidewalk. He hadn't taken two steps when a shirtless potbellied man strolled out from behind the recessed garage between two brick homes. The garden hose he held in one hand blasted a jet of water across the sidewalk, directly in front of Tony's next step. Tony stopped short and danced back from the splashing stream. He shot the guy a dirty look and, instead of hopping up onto the sidewalk, walked parallel in the street past him. The man stared back, one hand resting on the highest point of his belly, the other gripping the nozzle. Tony shook his head. His block had a few sidewalk waterers too. Crackpots. He jumped back onto the sidewalk and quickened his pace.

It was weird. He was only a few blocks from his own street, but sometimes other blocks felt like they were miles away, in foreign territory. Most of the homes here were completely different from the ones on his block. No row houses or brick porches in sight. Instead, Maria's block was filled with semiattached two-family homes, newer, with mostly brown-brick faces and random vertical peach bricks interspersed in a geometrical pattern. Some had attached driveways, like the one from where Mr. Hose had popped out. The front gates were also different. They resembled miniature front yards, framed out with majestic brick columns and sculpted flowerpots or ornate wrought iron fences. The sole eyesore on this block was the apartment building on the opposite corner of New Utrecht Avenue, where the Lombardi brothers lived. The wide, five-story giant was lined end to end with faded gray bricks, its bleak pattern broken only by rows of narrow windows and a bolted fire escape. It looked like someone had built a prison in the wrong spot.

Tony felt suddenly exposed. He took a cautionary glance over his shoulder, then quickly scanned the rooftops. After the M-80 incident, snipers weren't out of the realm of possibility.

Finally at Maria's house, Tony galloped up the concrete walkway to her front steps. The cement was gray and smooth, like icing on a cake, not cracked and littered with sand and pebbles like his front sidewalk. To his left was a short black fence that framed a rectangle of grass, modest save for the tiered stone fountain in its center. A sculpted cupid sprang from the fountain, his neck and head craned, lips puckered, ready to spit out a stream of water that never emerged. Then, from the corner of his eye, Tony caught a final glimpse of Denise crossing the street just a few houses down from where he stood. He watched her step up onto the sidewalk, then tug down the edge of her shorts. She shook out her frizzled mane, turned into a driveway, and vanished from view. *Guess I know someone else who lives on this block,* Tony thought. He took in a deep breath, climbed the steps, and rang the doorbell. Anxiously, Tony bounced on his heels and counted the milliseconds, waiting for someone to answer.

★

Paulie hurried home, one hand cradling his belly. He'd bet the tuition money. All of it. The decision had almost instantly sent his bowels into a full spasm. He bet Bossy Aussie heavy to win. He wheeled Bossy Aussie in exactas with the rest of the field. He bet Bossy Aussie in the early double. He bet it all.

Another spasm struck, stopping Paulie in his tracks. He clenched every muscle he could clench until the spasm passed. Too close. He desperately needed a bathroom. Of course the one at the OTB was out of order. His cramps were so severe, he was tempted to abandon his parking spot to get home quicker. Instead, Paulie decided to brave it, possibly the second bad decision he'd made in the last ten minutes. He pressed on. He had to make it home.

★

Finally, Maria's front door swung open, and the top half of Maria's mother appeared, framed within the wire lattice-top screen of the still-shut storm door. Tony noticed her wide smile didn't match the surprised look in her eyes.

"Hi, Happy Fourth of July!" Tony returned her smile. "Is Maria home?"

"Happy Fourth," Maria's mom responded quizzically. "Tony . . . right?" She was wrapped in a cream-colored silk robe, loosely drawn together in one hand. A bit of blue lace frill peeked out from beneath it.

"I'm sorry, uh . . ." Tony forgot what he was going to say for a moment, struggling to maintain his gaze at eye level with Maria's mother.

"Excuse my appearance," she said, suddenly self-conscious, as she drew her robe shut and tied it at the waist. "Our flight was delayed yesterday. We got in late." She looked up to the sky for a moment then back to Tony. "It's a little early."

"I know, I know." Tony nodded apologetically. "I'm really sorry. Can I just *please* talk to Maria for like one minute?" He held up one index finger in emphasis, adding one last "Please?" He felt the heat of the sun burning the back of his neck.

Maria's mother pressed her lips together in a moment of contemplation, her reassuring smile returned.

"Let me see if she's up," she said. She withdrew from sight, closing the front door halfway. Tony exhaled in relief, but then flinched hearing the deep baritone of Maria's father's voice echo from inside, "Who the hell is ringing the bell . . . ? You said your family wasn't coming over until . . . !"

Tony grimaced. Stepping backward, he slowly descended to the landing, which seemed a safer place to wait. Nervously, he glanced around before finally hearing the muffled roll of footsteps from inside the house heading his way. The front door flew open, and he saw the freeze-frame of Maria standing at the threshold, smiling. She opened her mouth wide as if to let loose a scream, but instead bolted down the steps, dressed in just the tiny plain white terry cloth shorts and a tank top she'd slept in. Maria leaped up into Tony's arms, wrapping both legs tightly around his waist. He backpedaled a step, trying to maintain his balance, his arms reflexively wrapping around her. He closed his eyes as Maria's lips fell upon his, the bare skin of her legs against his arms sending a chill through him.

Tony watched as Maria's eyes popped open. She pulled her face back and smiled wide while still holding Tony's face between her hands.

"Hi," she said and kissed him again. Tony withdrew slightly.

"Your mother . . ." He started to protest, but Maria shook her head and laughed. "Please, she's caught my sisters doing it with their boyfriends like five times." Tony's eyes widened. She kissed him once more, and then unwrapped her legs and let her feet gently fall to the floor. "Happy birthday! Did you think I forgot?"

"No, no, of course not. Thank you," he said. Despite wishing to prolong the embrace as long as possible, Tony knew he was on the clock and had news, however bad, to share. He pulled back and looked her in the eyes.

"Soooooo," Tony started.

"What's wrong?"

"No, nothing. Nothing's wrong. I just gotta tell you something."

Maria's smile vanished, her expression a mix of shock and rage. "You're! Breaking! Up! With! Me!" she shouted and shoved him away.

"What?! No! No, no, no, no, no," Tony assured her, trying not to betray the blunt-force trauma he'd just suffered. *Why would she even think that?* "My parents are being . . . I don't even know what they're being." He shook his head, then blurted out, "They want the family together for the Bicentennial." They stared silently at each other for several moments before Tony saw something spark in her eyes.

"They don't want you to be with me?" she asked, a new, intense look in her eyes.

"Noooo. No, no, no," Tony lied. "They're just . . . old fashioned," he said, which, while just the tip of the iceberg, was technically true. He made an angry face and began jabbing his index finger out in panto-mime. "'It's a holiday. You must stay with your family.'" Tony pressed his lips together, hopeful. This was his best shot.

Maria shrugged her shoulders, smiled, and said, "So, I'll come to you." Tony opened his mouth to respond but at first wasn't sure what to say. He was ecstatic she wasn't mad, sure. But images soon flashed in his mind of Maria appearing at his front gate and his mother exploding in a fireball.

Despite some momentary trepidation, he was smart enough to smile wide and say, "That's a great idea." Her arms wrapped around him once more. He asked, "Are you sure that's okay with your parents?"

"Definitely." Maria nodded. "Probably won't be until after dinner. I won't mention it until my parents have a few glasses of wine in them." Tony was relieved and worried simultaneously. Why couldn't his parents be this reasonable? Normal. *My parents.* The immensity of that thought expanded and filled his head. He had to get back.

"I really have to go," Tony said. Maria pouted; they kissed and embraced again. Before releasing Tony, Maria whispered into his ear, "I haven't forgotten your gift." She whirled away, flew up the stairs, and vanished inside. Tony watched the door close and then broke into a mad dash back home.

★

Paulie rounded the corner. He was deceptively quick for his age and belly, but his legs moved only as fast as his clenched buttocks allowed. Across the avenue, he spotted Tony, like himself, sprinting toward home.

"Tony!" Paulie shouted.

Tony looked up and froze in his tracks. Paulie tried to traverse the intersection diagonally and was almost hit by a yellow Buick making a left turn. The car honked its horn, and Paulie cursed the driver as it sped away. He sprinted to the sidewalk to join his son.

"What the hell are you doing on the avenue?" Paulie asked. Tony opened his mouth, but no words emerged. Paulie, the impatience clear in his tone, repeated his question when the faint ringing of bells interrupted.

"I had to go to the deli, Pop," Tony replied matter-of-factly. He pointed across the street to the Prima Delicatessen, where he worked after school and on weekends, depending on his baseball practice and game schedule. Again, the bells rang as the deli's front door shut as a young man wearing an Uncle Sam tee and jean shorts exited while forcefully packing his newly purchased Marlboros into his open palm. He tore the cellophane from the pack and dropped the refuse onto the sidewalk as he walked away.

Paulie stared into his son's poker face. Did his kid really think he was this stupid? Maybe he hadn't been an A student (or a high school graduate, for that matter), but he wasn't a moron. He'd grown up on the streets of Brooklyn, served his time in the army. Maybe the only action he ever saw was the inside of a mess hall, but he certainly knew what a kid chasing a broad looked like.

Before he could challenge his son, Paulie's bowels spasmed once more, and one hand flew to his stomach. Nearly getting run down had thrown his intestines into new levels of distress. He looked across the street at the deli, its windows a messy cluster of multicolored scalloped posters, like blotches on an artist's palette, advertising the price of Boar's Head cold cuts, milk, cigarettes, and Entenmann's cake. Paulie could deal with his son later. Now, he needed a toilet. He grabbed his son by the arm and said, "C'mon, let's go buy your milk."

CHAPTER 9

Alex quietly exited Zizi's apartment and slowly made his way through the dim hallway, its coolness a welcome relief. He paused for a moment, uncertain. Alex usually did what he was told, whether it was his parents, teachers, or brother giving the orders. Tony had said to wait in Zizi's, and he had waited. Even after he was pretty sure he'd seen Tony whiz past the backyard window, he waited. But it got so hot in there, even after he'd turned the fan on. Zizi, asleep for some minutes, had stirred momentarily, then mumbled in Italian before she dozed off again. Several more minutes dragged. Thirsty but reluctant to wake Zizi to ask for a glass of water or take the liberty of helping himself to one, Alex fled the hotbox.

Passing the stairway to the second floor, Alex briefly considered sitting on the steps to wait for Tony, but the hall still smelled funny, so he ventured outside.

Alex swung open the front door. Blinded by the brightness of the day, he squinted and shielded his eyes with one hand. His eyes adjusted to the glare of the rising sun as he stepped out onto the cement porch. Despite the intense illumination, he felt compelled to slowly peek past the edge of his hand, to gaze directly up at the glowing white ball hovering high above the homes lining the opposite side of the street.

"Don't stare at the sun—you'll go blind." He heard his mother's scolding. For a fleeting second, he thought he'd imagined it, a heat-induced mirage. A glance down at the sidewalk quickly confirmed otherwise. He saw his mother approaching. She didn't look happy.

She stopped her march just a few feet shy of the porch's bottom step.

"Get down here," she commanded as she arrived, pointing down at the sidewalk to the spot she willed her youngest. Alex held the handrail as he descended. "You're all flushed," she said.

"It was really hot inside," Alex responded. His mother patted his small forehead again. She shook her head and then turned her gaze upon Zizi's front door.

"Where's your brother?" she demanded. Alex opened his mouth and began to point toward the backyard when they both heard shouting coming from up the block. It was Tony's voice.

"Right here. I'm right here," Tony shouted, racing down the block, brown paper bag clasped in one hand, the shape of his father trailing behind him. Keeping his stride, Tony jogged past his mother and up the porch steps. "She asked me to go buy her milk," Tony said and shrugged both shoulders.

Alex's brow furrowed. Dee's expression skeptical, she began, "Didn't I tell you . . ."

The inquisition was interrupted by his father's arrival. "She asked him to go buy milk; whaddaya want him to do?" his father said. He was breathing heavy, like he had just run a marathon.

Alex watched his mother transfer her angry glare from her children to her husband. Confused, Alex wondered, *Why didn't he take me with him?* He looked up at his brother. Tony looked relieved, almost as if he were trying to suppress a smile. Alex glanced back at his mother, whose face had begun to twist into a reply just as the front door swung open loudly. It was Cousin Richie. He emitted a great roar of a yawn, like a bear emerging from its cave after a long hibernation. Unlike most bears, Richie wore an unbuttoned shirt and spotted briefs, a lit cigarette dangling from one hand.

"Happy Fourth," Richie proclaimed, gesturing with his arms like he was inviting a room to dance.

"Go put some pants on," Alex's mother said, averting her eyes. "Like a gigolo he walks around," she muttered to herself. His father and Tony tried not to chuckle.

"Happy Fourth, Richie," his father shouted back to his nephew. "You staying out of trouble?"

Richie swiveled his hips and said, "What do you think?"

"I gotta bring Zizi her milk," Tony interjected, seemingly still in a hurry. Before he could reach for the door, Richie stepped in front of him.

"Milk? I'll bring it in," Richie said. "I just came out for some fresh air." He sucked in several deep breaths through his nostrils. Richie then flicked his cigarette over everyone's heads out into the street and snatched the brown bag from Tony. "See ya later, alligators," he said as he spun around and disappeared back inside.

"Back home, the two of you," their mother barked. Alex opened his mouth, eager to share his side of the story, but Tony flew down the stairs, scooped him up over his shoulders, and began carrying him down the block. Alex giggled with glee at the attention, all his questions gone in an instant.

"Be careful," his mother shouted. "You could crack his skull."

"Let 'em go," his father said. "They're boys."

Dee shook her head. She shadowed her sons down the block as she lit another cigarette.

Paulie watched them walk away for a few seconds. When he felt they were far enough away, he sat on the porch's bottom step and took out his wallet. He removed the OTB tickets and cradled them secretively like a poker hand. Another spasm echoed from within his bowels.

★

As Richie strolled toward Zizi's apartment, he paused. He did feel a bit peckish, as he often did after some fun. He looked down at the bag, shrugged, then turned and headed up the stairs. He hoped his mother had stocked the pantry with Chips Ahoy! or Oreos. A little milk and cookies, maybe a quick nap, and then the fun would start.

JULY 4, 1976

AFTERNOON

CHAPTER 10

Half past one p.m., the sun blazed white overhead, but the kids, running wild on the block, pedaling their bikes up and down the street, didn't care. No rules today: run in the street, don't look both ways, tag you're it, go deep, stay short, swing for the fences, watch out, look at me, all while "Boogie Fever" blasted from the DJ's twin thirty-inch speakers. The youngest girls played hopscotch and Chinese jump rope while the youngest boys flicked red, white, and blue bottle caps across skully boards sketched in thick chalk lines. Everyone was moving, drifting from sidewalk to street, Tony included, flowing from one gate, one conversation, to the next: *Happy Fourth, Yankees are back, fuck Ford, disco sucks, U-S-A!* Tony paused for a moment, spun the gold chain around his neck, glanced left, right, scanning the block. Maria was coming. *I have a special birthday present for you.* Her words still buzzed inside his head. Tony wished he had a better idea of when she'd arrive. That, of course, posed an even greater question—when she came, where could they go to be alone? How to escape his mother's watchful eye? He needed a plan but had none.

As Tony weaved around passersby in the street, Vito, Alex's little friend, almost crashed his bike into him, swerving at the last second.

Tony, more curious than annoyed, turned to watch the convoy of riders trailing Vito. Little kids, sprung from their cages, out the door, out of their gates and into the streets—*Freedom!* Not Tony: he still felt trapped. The street, barricaded at both ends, was a bigger cage.

Tony drifted over toward the older kids, the ones that at least got to act older. They drifted languidly through the street and sidewalks. They clustered together in front of one gate or stoop, then briefly dispersed, then reconvened suddenly in another spot. Most he knew and nodded to; some nodded back, some didn't. Today it was the couples that caught his eye. There went Frankie Wheels, who owned a mint black Trans Am that he sped through the neighborhood, radio blasting and windows down, be it summer or winter. He had his arm, like an orangutan's, curled long around his high school girlfriend, his hand dangling down over her shoulder, fingers resting just against her bare upper chest, just shy just of her burnt orange stretch tube top. Across the street, "Rocker" Ralph strutted, draped in a loose black Rolling Stones T-shirt, attached at the hip to his fair-skinned rocker girlfriend. She had jet-black hair and crooked bangs; their arms, as always, hooked around each other's waists. They pressed close together, not a glimmer of sunlight visible between them. Girlfriends. Finally, he had one too.

Tony looked around. The block was packed, people everywhere now—especially the girls. Many huddled around the DJ, stationed midblock. He was a short, thin middle-aged man sporting Elvis sunglasses that covered half his face. He bopped, hovering over twin turntables set on a six-foot wooden table that extended diagonally from the curb, music blasting from two immense speakers set like monoliths at either end. One pointed up the block, the other down. Tony barely heard the music, too busy noticing all the new female faces in the crowd. He studied their feather cuts, cutoff shirts, bare bellies, short shorts, and long bare legs on parade. Two girls standing together, arm in arm, caught his eye, despite not looking familiar. Both wore hot pants: one sparkled red, the other blue. Up top they both squeezed into their respective white tank tops, tits not huge, but not flat chested either; nope, not at all. Tony watched them dance halfheartedly—the music was loud, thumping, but it was still early. Blue Hot Pants pointed to the DJ; he had more hair on his exposed chest than his head. The DJ smiled and pointed back. The girls laughed, spun around, and danced away. Tony watched them fade into the crowd and immediately wished they'd reappear.

Maria was coming, he quickly reminded himself. Last thing he needed was to have her catch him staring at two other girls. Maria could be jealous. She'd refused to talk to him for two whole days during the last week of school after catching him talking to an overdeveloped seventh grader one morning. A stack of books had tumbled from the girl's hands as they changed classes. Tony had stopped to help. The brief conversation that followed:

"Thank you. I'm such a klutz."

"No problem."

Then Maria had appeared suddenly beside him. She had a look her eyes; Tony found it simultaneously frightening and thrilling.

Now, Tony took a quick glance down the block. Through the dense crowd, he could still discern the shape of his mother, standing in their gate, feel her staring back at him. A hard slap across his back startled him. He spun, looked up, and smiled. It was Sal Randazzo, Sally, Tony's best friend, who lived at the other end of the block. Sally was still his twitchy self, as always, long arms and legs always in motion, snapping back and forth as if each of his limbs possessed an extra set of joints. Sally tapped Tony up and down the sides of his torso, his greeting akin to a cop's pat down.

"How's it going? Good? Good. You look good. How's your parents? Good? Good." Sally went to public school, so for years their friendship had always been tied to the block, playing together and hanging out after school and on weekends. But between work and baseball, they'd hardly seen each other this past year. Sally made a point of visiting Tony at the deli whenever possible, but if Mr. Prima was there, he was quickly chased away. "Thissa place a'business!" Mr. Prima yelled. "No a hangout."

Tony managed now to sneak in one "Good" in response. He reached up to give Sally's peach fuzz a rub. "Your mom still makes you get a crew cut, huh?"

"Love it," Sally said as he rubbed his newly sheared scalp like he was polishing an apple. "Nice and clean. Hey, what're you doing now?"

"Nothing." Tony shrugged.

"Nothin'? Good, good. We're gonna play some stickball."

"Who?" Tony asked.

"Who? Me, you. Everyone. C'mon."

"I don't know." Tony shrugged.

"What's wrong? Can't hit a ball with a skinny broomstick anymore? You need to go get one of those big aluminum clubs. Go home and put on your pretty uniform, and we'll all whistle at you," Sally teased, tapping him repeatedly on the shoulders.

"Knock it off, I'll play," Tony said. "Ball-breaker."

Sally grinned. "Good, good." He stuck his two index fingers into the opposite sides of his mouth and let loose with an ear-piercing whistle. Dogs five blocks away howled. Then, one by one, familiar faces began to appear.

CHAPTER 11

Paulie sat on one end of the bench, fidgeting with the antenna and knobs of a portable AM/FM radio. Loud static buzzed from the speaker, interspersed with occasional belches of local news. Dee stood sentry at the opposite end of the bench, one hand resting on the upper iron bar of the front gate. She scanned the street for a reassuring glimpse of both boys, then lit another cigarette. She exhaled a puff of smoke toward the sidewalk, but a few white curls drifted back over her shoulder and settled just above Paulie's head. He began coughing violently.

"Do you have to smoke right next to me?" he complained, adding a few hacks for good measure.

"I'm blowing it away from you," Dee barked. Paulie kept coughing, despite dismissing the faint traces of smoke with one swipe of his arm. "You're worse than a woman," his wife sneered, then stomped out of the gate with her cigarette. Paulie stopped coughing.

He set the radio down beside him and bent the antenna at a steep angle. The static was replaced by the sound of the weekend sports anchor rattling off the scores of the early baseball games. The volume was very low, but he was afraid to touch a knob and disturb the clear reception. He lowered his head closer to the speaker.

The racing results always came last during the sports report. Hopefully a harbinger of the larger victory to come, Paulie's hunch in the first race, Lady Liberty, had already won. Usually, he'd kick himself for not betting on it straight to win, but not today. Today Paulie was riding the stars-and-stripes express all the way to the top. When Bossy Aussie won—not *if*, mind you, *when* he won—Paulie would hit the double, he'd hit the exacta, he'd win big for the straight bet. Paulie tried to do the quick math in his head. Tony's tuition, rent for the rest of the year, all paid with plenty left for Christmas presents. *"I'm a Yankee Doodle Dandy."* The music was back. He leaned even closer, his ear almost pressed against the speaker.

"Paulie!" Someone called. Startled, Paulie turned to find Mario, his neighbor, looming over him from inside the adjoining front gate. Despite spending six days a week with his head buried in transmission and brake jobs, Mario always looked sharp, like a maître d' at the fanciest restaurant; tall and fit for his age, his salt-and-pepper hair always trimmed impeccably. His bronze tan glowed in contrast to the crisp white of the short-sleeve linen button-down that hung perfectly, its top two buttons unfastened, a gold crucifix nested in a thick cluster of chest hair.

"Mario." Paulie acknowledged his neighbor with a quick nod.

"You know where I hadda park my car? Not one but two avenues down," Mario said, holding up two fingers on his right hand.

"No kidding," Paulie replied, trying to keep his attention tuned to the voice on the radio. He looked away and rolled his eyes.

"Took me maybe twenty, twenty-five minutes to find a spot," Mario said, and then folded his arms across his chest.

"You forgot what it's like, huh?" Paulie shrugged. Prior to Mario's extensive home renovation last year, he had been subject to the same low-supply, high-demand parking issues as most everyone else on the block. However, Mario was a man of vision. His home now boasted a handsome stone facade, something that looked like it belonged on a European castle. He had even replaced the wobbly chain-link fence that separated the two front gates with an impeccably laid wall of mortar and stone. Mario's crowning achievement, though, was obtaining the zoning approval to convert his front sidewalk into a pull-in driveway. Sure, some of the newer homes at the opposite end up the block had been built above sunken driveways, but this was something previously unseen, something considered impossible. Paulie, and most men on the block, gazed at the finished product with a mix of jealously and disbelief, as if they'd just witnessed water turned into wine.

"I don't miss alternate side," Mario muttered, more to himself than in response. He turned to Paulie and said, "I told you. You ever need a spot, you park in front of my house." He gestured with two outstretched arms, like he was parting the Red Sea.

"Mmmm-hhhmm," Paulie acknowledged, his focus keen on the broadcast. Not that he'd ever give Mario the satisfaction of accepting the charity. There was nothing Mario would enjoy more than buzzing Paulie's doorbell to tell him to move the Olds so he could pull out his brand-new Lincoln Continental. Then from the radio, Paulie heard, *"And at the second race at Belmont . . ."*

"So, what happened?" Mario interrupted. "I thought we were going to barbecue . . . ?"

Paulie shushed him violently, flailing overhead with an open hand. Mario held up both hands and took a half step back. Paulie folded almost completely in half to listen closely.

"The winner, Okey Dokey paid $6.85 . . ."

The color drained from Paulie's face.

"Running second, Quick Strike, paid $3.10 for place . . ."

Paulie felt his bowels begin to knot inside him. What happened to Bossy Aussie?

The report continued. *"The early double paying $32.56 and the exacta $14.10."*

"Fuck, fuck, fuck, fuck," Paulie cursed. He clenched a fist, wanting nothing more than to smash the radio into pieces. Instead, he hammered away against the top of his leg, just above the knee.

"Paulie? Whatsa matter?" Mario inquired, concerned.

Paulie dismissively flailed one hand. He froze for a second. Bossy Aussie must have been a late scratch. No way that tip could have been wrong. Couldn't be. Not today. The horse scratched, and his bets would be refunded. Had to be. Before he could take further solace in his hypothesis, the reporter added, *"In tragic news, the five horse, Bossy Aussie, broke his leg rounding the far turn and had to be put down."*

"Fuck!" he cried out again. He'd lost it all. If he hadn't overheard that tip, if he hadn't listened to frigging Barney, he'd have hit his own double. "Fuck!" he exclaimed again. People nearby turned their heads, glared in disapproval. One mother shielded her toddler's ears with both her hands. "Fuck!" once more, less in response to the loss but instead for the scene Paulie visualized the minute his wife found out. Sweet Jesus, he couldn't let Dee find out.

"Ahem." Mario cleared his throat to get Paulie's attention and then gestured out toward the sidewalk and street. His own two daughters were inside helping their mother in the kitchen, but there were still plenty of children nearby, close enough to hear Paulie curse. Paulie pressed his lips together. His face flushed both in embarrassment and increasing rage.

Mario studied Paulie. He pressed his lips together and then said, "See, thatsa why I no gamble. I no like to lose." Mario then raised his right hand and slid his fingers into the dark curls of his chest. "I put my money in my business," he said, then gesturing to his left, "or my house." Mario glanced back over his shoulder and admired his handsome facade.

Paulie's head vibrated like it was about to explode. He stood up; he needed to go for a walk, something. Just as he reached to turn off the radio, he heard, *"In business news, talks broke down late last night between New York Telephone and the Communication Workers of America, signaling . . ."*

★

Dee motioned to flick the stub of her cigarette into the street, but kids kept running past. She happily took the opportunity to excuse herself for a moment from a conversation with Vivian Chipparetti, Chippy's mother. She walked to the curb, dropped her cigarette into the street, and crushed the stub with the sole of her flats.

Despite Dee momentarily stepping away, Vivian continued to rant about the police department's continued harassment of her son. Almost sixty years old, her gray hair up in curlers, as usual, she'd taken to draping her squat frame in paisley muumuus since losing her husband, Rocco, three years prior. After thirty years spent as an NYC firefighter, rushing in and out of burning buildings, the poor man had had a massive stroke and died two months into his retirement. Dee heard Vivian's continued ranting as she returned.

"And you can't even leave your door unlocked anymore, the crime, the dirt—but they got nothing better to do but ring my bell and bother my son. For what? Because he sells a few firecrackers? He never hurt nobody. That's why this city is going to hell, an old woman can't . . ."

Dee lit another cigarette and nodded absently. She didn't care much for listening to other people's problems—she had enough of her own, God knew. Still, Vivian's gate afforded the perfect vantage to keep an eye on both Alex and Tony. She wouldn't be human if her heart didn't go out somewhat to the poor woman blabbering on and on beside her—her husband dead; her oldest son living on the other side of the country, married to some Jewish girl; her own grandchildren never baptized. And her youngest son, Chippy, was half a criminal. If Dee ever caught that bastard trying to sell that garbage to her sons, she'd break both his arms. Chippy, at the very least, had the decency to still live with his mother, though.

Dee's eyes followed Alex's path as he pedaled by. Despite the avenue being completely sealed off by wooden barricades, Dee couldn't help but hold her breath every time Alex approached the end of the street, exhaling in relief only after he safely steered a wide arc and started back up the block. Alex waved to his mother; Dee smiled and returned the gesture as Vivian droned on and on. Now, where had the big one wandered off to, she wondered.

CHAPTER 12

Over a dozen guys responded to Sally's call to arms: Joey G., Joey M., Big Guy, Little Petey, Fat Bobby, Mikey Dada, Tommy Bagels, Louie Legs, Tatulli. Tony couldn't remember the last time he'd hung out with these guys. None of them played league baseball; none of them went to Catholic school (he wasn't quite sure if half of them went to school at all). But on the block, no long catch-ups were required—just a "Hey, what's up," a nod of the head, a slap of the palms, and it was like old times.

Sides had been called, even-house side of the block against the odd side. Sally insisted on leading off the bottom of the inning.

"I'm feeling it today, I'm feeling it," Sally boasted.

Tony chuckled as Sally stepped up to the manhole cover, the block's historical proxy for home plate. Sally had the worst batting stance he'd ever seen. Even when trying to get set for a pitch, Sally's arms and legs still twitched and jerked independent of one another. When he swung, he looked like someone trying to kill a swarm of bees with a folding ruler. He struck out on three pitches.

"Tony, Tony, check it out," Tony heard Fat Bobby shouting, but his voice sounded muffled. His entire team had stationed themselves in front of the D'Angelo home. They all leaned against the front gate, cheering and shouting as Sally returned from his less-than-successful at bat, and Louie Legs took his turn up at the plate. All except Fat Bobby, who, Tony now noticed, had peeled off from the group and slipped inside the D'Angelos' front foyer. Tony laughed out loud. Fat Bobby, shirtless as always, stood behind the screen panel of the D'Angelos' front door, both arms outstretched and flexed. In truth, Fat Bobby's fat was limited almost exclusively to his belly, which curved out like a fishbowl from sternum to waist, the rest of his body thick but solid. With his boyish good looks and always perfectly coiffed hair, Fat Bobby was confident (a confidence stoked by his own doting mother) that, if not for his bulbous belly, he'd be a pinup in *Tiger Beat* magazine, the next Leif Garrett.

"Yo, check it out, Tony," Fat Bobby called again; everyone turned. "From the nipples up, I can't be beat." He'd found the perfect frame, the screen ending just above the belly. Tony's and his friends' laughter turned into hysterics as Mrs. D'Angelo suddenly appeared behind Fat Bobby. She chased him out the door, waving a wooden spoon threateningly above her head. By the time everyone had recovered, Louie Legs was on second, Little Petey on first after two consecutive singles. Tony was up.

Tony picked up the broom handle from the street and stepped up to bat. He stared out at Joey G., pitching from the chalk-scratched mound. Joey scratched his square chin, then bounced the Spaldeen once, twice, and then went into his windup. Tony's grip tightened around the bat, his arms and legs tense. Tony's swing sliced through the air like a whip—*smack!* The ball sailed well past two sewers—a home run. Tony began to round the bases. Why couldn't everything be this easy?

★

Dee scanned the crowds, anxious to reacquire sight of her oldest. She spotted Tony playing ball farther up the street. Dee wasn't thrilled about the crowd he was with—these were the good-for-nothing kids she'd done her best to separate him from. The kids in this neighborhood, like animals, thrown out onto the street by their parents, allowed to run wild with no supervision. Good-for-nothing kids grew up into good-for-nothing adults. Not her Tony. She'd made sure of that.

Dee didn't give a rat's ass about baseball, but she knew playing the game kept him off the block. Tony had just turned twelve when Dee took a brief respite from haggling with Joe the butcher over the price of his pork chops and chicken cutlets to instead begin pestering the man to ask his brother, Ray, to come watch Tony play for his church Little League team. Ray Massimo coached a team in the Gil Hodges League, one that his brother, Joe, sponsored—Massimo Meats stitched across the back of every jersey.

Dee didn't know a ball from a strike, but she knew her son was talented. She could tell that from the oohs and aahs she heard from the other parents whenever her son did something on the field. Tony had played on his church team since the third grade, but it wasn't a competitive league, not like Gil Hodges. There were no tryouts; everyone played every game, even the kids that stank. Practices were held right before games on Saturday morning, and the league only ran from the first Sunday after Easter until the end of the school year. Hodges would be a bigger time commitment, but it would be a productive use of the boy's time and keep Tony out of trouble. There would be no loitering on street corners for her son.

Tony had the brains to get a good job when he grew up. He could be someone's boss, a vice president or president of whatever. He was a good-looking boy; maybe he could read the news on television. If God wanted her son to be a big-time baseball player one day, she could live with that. Regardless, Dee would make sure her son didn't spend his days on street corners and alleyways; she'd make sure he didn't wind up stuffed into the back seat of a police car or possibly even worse.

She had pestered Joe the butcher for weeks, but still his brother never showed up at her son's games. Finally, Dee resorted to threatening to tell people she'd found a roach in the butcher's chopped meat. Sure enough, Joe's brother appeared the next Sunday morning at Tony's game. Ray stood alone, watching from behind the opposing dugout. He wore mirrored sunglasses and leaned into the chain-link fence that enclosed the field as he watched silently. Dee couldn't read his eyes, but she spied Ray nodding his head each time Tony swung the bat, blasting the pitch into the outfield. After the game, Ray approached and said he'd like Tony to play on his team (as if it was his idea).

"I don't drive. You'll have to pick him up and drive him home," she told Ray and walked away. And that's exactly what he did; Tony's performance on the field turned out to be more than worth the chauffeur service.

After another check on Alex as he cruised happily along, Dee turned her attention back to Tony. Unable to spot him initially, she took a few steps up the block until she caught sight of him stepping out from behind two larger boys. She hoped they weren't playing too rough. She could see Tony smiling, happy; he seemed to be enjoying himself. Good. She was happy her sons were happy playing where she could see them.

Just as Dee began to smile, she noticed two girls, teenagers, standing apart from the crowd, watching the boys play ball, watching her son. Even from a distance she could see half their asses hanging out of the shorts they wore. Then all the boys shuffled around as they switched. Tony emerged from the crowd, stickball bat in hand.

"Girlfriend." Dee spat out the word. Dee wasn't stupid. She'd noticed Tony over the last year, turning his head every time some little *buttana* walked by, or worse, the same girl turning to stare at her son. She'd realized that baseball wasn't going to be enough to keep Tony out of trouble. Unbeknownst to Tony, it was a string of heartfelt words whispered by his mother to Mrs. Prima, whom she sat behind at church every Sunday, that had arranged his employment at the deli.

Dee shook her head in disgust. What more could she do? Her gaze drifted directly across the street and fell upon the Piscottis' gate. Inside, Ralph Piscotti helped his aging mother, Rose, set the table. Ralph unfolded a red tablecloth, then flapped it in the air like a matador's cape, letting it float down and land, draped perfectly over the long folding table stationed in the middle of the gate. Now *that* was a good son, a good-looking boy, always polite and well kept, almost forty and he still lived at home with his parents. Dee watched Rose place a small vase filled with brightly colored flowers on the table. Ralph waited for his mother to turn away before properly centering the vase.

"Dee, Dee," Vivian shouted. She'd inched closer to tap Dee on the shoulder with two fingers to regain her attention. "They persecute my son, y'hear me? They persecute him."

Dee nodded her head in sympathy, not for Chippy's plight but instead for this poor woman beside her. This woman's husband, her sons—they'd broken her. *Not me,* she thought. *Not me.*

★

While his wife was watching the boys and getting her ear chewed off by Vivian, Paulie had raced upstairs to call Barney. Maybe the report was wrong. Maybe there had been a mistake. The phone rang eight times before someone finally picked up. Before Barney uttered the second syllable of "Hello," Paulie launched into a frantic, obscenity-laced ejaculation of questions and distress.

"Paulie, Paulie . . ." Barney repeated his name several more times before Paulie either ran out of breath or finally decided to let him speak. "Yeah, it all fell apart." Barney confirmed the worst.

"But what about Connelly? I thought . . ."

"Yeah. Well," Barney went on, "turns out his mother-in-law dropped dead. He'd been home for two days." A long silence followed. Barney finally broke it. "You still there, Paulie?"

"Yeah, I'm here," Paulie said. His voice was now empty, like a trailing echo.

"Well . . ." There was a long pause before Barney resumed. "That's not the worst of it." Paulie was sure his heart had stopped beating. He pressed the palm of his left hand against the kitchen wall to brace himself. "They started shooting people. Guys are already getting the calls. Motherfuckers can't even wait until after the holiday."

"What guys?!" Paulie yelled. "What's the date?" Layoffs would be subject to the terms of the prior contract, so, as always, seniority rules. Last in, first out.

"Ummm . . ." Barney was hesitant to answer.

"What's the fucking date, Barney?!"

"You missed the cutoff by a month. Sorry, Paulie."

Paulie hung up without another word. He stared down at the

linoleum floor, his breaths short and quick. After several minutes, he turned and left the apartment, plodding downstairs. Once outside, he sank back into the bench. *What now?*

CHAPTER 13

Today is awesome! Alex thought as he pedaled his Ross special limited edition Bicentennial bicycle. Alex did his best to keep pace with Vito and not leave Tommy too far behind. He smiled wide, overjoyed to be sailing smoothly over blacktop instead of the cracked, uneven sidewalk. The bright sun glinted off the steel handlebars as he weaved around pedestrians. Red, white, and blue tassels sprouted from the handlebar tops and whipped back as Alex pedaled faster. His grin stretched ear to ear. Forget being a big kid; he felt like a cowboy. He had no pistol sling, but he had his snaps. He dug out the small box from his pocket while steering carefully with one hand—hoping his mother wasn't watching.

Pop, he hit a manhole cover; *pop*, the base of a fire hydrant; *pop*, he hit Tommy by accident. "Sorry, Tommy," he shouted as he pedaled past him.

"Ride with both hands or else!" Alex heard his mother shout as he passed his own gate. Alex did what he was told.

"And don't go all the way up the block," she added.

Alex wasn't fazed by the imposed restriction—half a street was a million times better than riding on the crummy sidewalk. The crowd was too big by the DJ, anyway, unless you were Vito, who seemed to enjoy running into people. Alex spotted his brother playing stickball farther up the street. He thought for a moment about riding over, asking if he could play, too, but already knew what the answer would be. Alex didn't worry, though, like he might have on another day. Tony had already played two games of Wiffle ball with him that morning—right after they'd returned from Zizi's. He hadn't even needed to pester his older brother to play with him—*Tony had asked him*. He couldn't remember the last time that had happened.

Alex was all smiles. He attempted to whistle "Yankee Doodle Dandy" but blew out mostly spit. He glanced back and saw his mother looking away, likely for Tony. Emboldened, Alex decided to be just a little defiant and fire off one more snap from his mount. He quickly scanned for a target. Spotting the silver lamppost in front of the Orsini house—an inviting, if challenging, target—he veered his bike closer to the curb to his right. He wiggled a snap loose from the cluster still clutched inside his right hand. With the twisted paper pinched between two fingers, Alex raised his arm, aimed, and—*pop!* He looked at his hand, confused. He still held the snap. His back tire wobbled and sank. He had a flat.

★

"You hear that, Tony? You hear that?" Sally shouted in Tony's ear even though they were standing shoulder to shoulder. Tony wasn't really listening; instead, he was both lost in the memory of Maria's mostly bare legs wrapped around his waist and the pondering of how, when, and where he'd be able to replicate the moment today. Sally nudged him with his elbow.

"Yeah." Tony nodded absently. The impromptu stickball game had quickly petered out, Tony's second home run of the first inning put his side up by ten; the mercy rule was invoked, game over. Truthfully, the game wouldn't have held the crew's attention much longer, anyway, even had it been more competitive. It was too hot to run—there were beers to try to sneak, half-dressed girls wherever you turned, and, soon, things to blow up. Once the game ended, the entire crew drifted together from one sidewalk to its opposite and back again, slowly searching for the next amusement. They eventually wandered in front of Yosef Pryzbyski's gate and inserted themselves among a crowd already gathered.

"Listen, listen," Sally repeated, tapping Tony on the arm as he pointed inside the gate.

"I'm listening, I'm listening!" Tony snapped back, sharper than he'd intended. Sally pursed his lips and shrugged. Tony blinked several times and tried to focus his attention on Yosef Pryzbyski. The short but stocky middle-aged man seemed to be approaching the climax of the story he was reenacting for those huddled around, both inside and outside his gate.

"*Yo*-sef," Mrs. Pryzbyski shouted suddenly to her husband from their doorway. She carried a large steaming pot and looked like she could use a hand. But Yosef—or Joe P., or Polish Joe, depending on whom you asked and who was listening—shooed her off. He was just getting to the good part and couldn't stop now. She grumbled something and disappeared back inside.

Giovanni Verde, Yosef's next-door neighbor, gripped the cylindrical top rail of the iron fence that separated their gates and leaned eagerly forward, his upper body tipping into Polish waters. While there had never been any animosity between the two neighbors, they'd existed solely in a state of mutual benign indifference since

Yosef had purchased his home several months prior. It was just small courtesies and pleasant nods back and forth. The new neighbors were quiet and kept their gate tidy. But in this neighborhood, newcomers, especially non-Italians, stirred suspicion.

The neighbors' respectful but aloof relationship remained unchanged until the day the big Texan had roared into town and broke Bruno's neck. Bruno, Bruno Sammartino—the Living Legend. Beloved Bruno, the World Wide Wrestling Federation heavyweight champion, his neck snapped like a twig by that Texas lunatic, Stan Hansen. Hansen—huge, snarling, snorting, tobacco-chew-stained spit dripping from his mustache and chin—was more a modern-day Minotaur than a man. In the middle of Madison Square Garden late the night of April 26, a clothesline across the neck had cut Bruno, the mighty Sicilian, in two.

Both the *New York Post* and *Daily News* had reported the tragic injury the next day. Accompanying the story was a grainy black-and-white photo of a somber Bruno lying in a hospital bed, head and chin immobilized. The headline: "Is Bruno Finished?" Giovanni's own mother, a spry, toothless eighty-seven-year-old, had clipped out the photo and taped it to her bedroom mirror above the religious candle she lit nightly as she addressed her novenas. While Bruno convalesced, the fans demanded a vendetta. But who? Who would pick up the sword? Enter Ivan Putski—the Polish Hammer (both his nickname and signature move). Putski, the pride of Kraków, Poland—where, it just so happened, Yosef had also been born.

Yosef stomped across the gate, playfully chasing some little kids who had gathered. He mimicked Putski's signature finishing move, interlocking the fingers of both hands together, arms raised threateningly overhead. The children all screamed and leaped back.

Putski, acting as Bruno's surrogate, wrestled Hansen just a week ago at the Garden, the first card since Bruno's injury. Much to Mrs. P.'s chagrin, Yosef had insisted on taking her and his ten-year-old son (at $8.99 a ticket, no less) to the loud and smoky arena to witness what he felt was surely a pivotal moment in Polish American history. (Putski won the match by disqualification when Hansen, facing imminent defeat, struck Putski with a cowbell. The referee would have none of that.) The next day, Giovanni had overheard Yosef describing the match to Andy the postman. Since then, Yosef and Giovanni had become fast friends. Most nights, Yosef reenacted the match in his front gate to an audience of his wife, his children, and neighbor Giovanni, who insisted his wife and daughter also listen attentively. Today, Yosef must have felt like he was standing in the squared circle himself, performing in front of a packed Garden crowd.

"Polish power!" Yosef shouted, snapping his raised arms down like a mousetrap.

Giovanni shook his raised fist in solidarity, also shouted, "Polish power!"

Yosef, seeing some new faces gathered around, decided to restart his reenactment of the match from the beginning.

Tony felt his crew stir and begin to drift away. He followed them, walking beside Sally, who nudged him again in the side with his pointy elbow.

"What's wrong? You got a puss on your face," Sally said.

"Nothin'," Tony replied.

"C'mon. Don't try to bullshit a bullshit artist," Sally said.

Tony slowed his pace, letting the rest of the pack pull away. He sighed and quickly tried to sum up his plight. Sally nodded slightly the entire time, maintaining a pensive expression. Then a smirk stretched across his face. Sally reached over and pinched Tony's cheek, like a grandmother would, and began dancing around his friend, chanting, "Tony's got a girlfriend, Tony's got a girlfriend."

Tony shook his head, more defeated than annoyed.

Seeing Tony despondent, Sally stopped and slapped his friend across the back. "C'mon, I'm just breaking your balls. We'll figure something out. I got your back."

Tony turned and watched Sally tap his index finger against his temple. He struggled to remember a time when Sally had been a solution to a problem instead of its cause.

They continued their stroll, behind the other boys. After a few paces, Sally leaned his head closer to Tony and said in a hushed voice, "Things don't work out, Fat Bobby's sister will give you a hand job for five bucks."

★

Paulie was startled by the sound of a loud sizzle and hiss behind him. He turned and saw that Mario had just plopped down a thick tenderloin steak onto his grill. Paulie resisted the urge to turn his head. Instead, he pivoted slightly, still seated on the bench and, from out of the corner of his eyes, observed Mario's reflection framed inside one of Mr. George's front windows.

Paulie watched Mario as he reached down into an unfurled cluster of brown butcher paper and extracted a long string of hot dogs. Carefully, Mario lowered each link onto the grill like it was a tiny marionette being laid gently to sleep. A burst of orange flame then exploded from the drippings, and Paulie salivated just a tiny bit at the first whiff of grilled meat. Alex, sitting beside him, rose from the bench and rushed over to just opposite Mario on their side of the shared gate.

"Alex, you hungry? I make you a hot dog," Mario offered.

A smile stretched across Alex's face, but before he could reply, his mother interrupted.

"No. Thank you. We got food in the oven," Dee told Mario, then glanced up toward her apartment—the ziti was cooking in the oven and would soon be ready. Then, to Alex, "Alex, come sit here."

Mario repeated his offer. Paulie had already risen to fetch Alex, whose gaze remained locked on the swirls of white smoke rising from their neighbor's grill.

"Thanks. But we're gonna eat soon," Paulie said.

"I got a-plenty." Mario shrugged. Paulie muttered to himself as he planted his son down into the wooden fold of the bench between himself and his wife, who had also now taken a seat.

The family sat together on the bench in silence for several minutes, basking in the smoky aroma. Abruptly, Alex jumped up and shouted, "Toyman!"

Crap, not this guy, Paulie thought. The Toyman, as he was affectionately known by the neighborhood children, was a squat bald man, who appeared most frequently at block parties but was also a relative fixture during most summer weekends. Paulie turned and saw the Toyman round the corner pushing his homemade cart, which was the bottom half of a giant cardboard appliance box affixed to a wooden dolly. The cardboard container overflowed with inflated plastic toys, pinwheels, Hula-Hoops, flags, coloring books, bottles of bubbles, toy hats and masks, cellophane bags of little green faceless soldiers, whistles, and cap guns—a traveling five-and-dime store.

"Can I buy something?!" Alex begged. Paulie flinched.

"You have enough toys to play with. Sit and read your comic book." Dee gestured to the oversize treasury edition *Captain America's Bicentennial Battles*, holding the place where Alex had sat.

"I just read it twice. Pleeeeeassse, I'll use my allowance."

"Don't waste your money on garbage," Paulie told his son.

"But it's my money." Alex raised his voice, stomped one foot, and crossed his arms. Paulie felt his neck flush. If he'd ever spoken to his old man that way, his behind would still be sore from the spanking. As Paulie took a step toward his son, he noticed Mario glancing up from his grill, eyebrows raised, listening to the whole exchange.

Paulie mumbled something under his breath. He grabbed his son by the arm.

"C'mon, then," he barked as he rushed his son out of the gate and into the street.

The Toyman slowed and edged his cart to a spot alongside the curb. His immense stomach, thinly veiled beneath the strained fabric of a white undershirt, hung down well over his thighs. It looked as if he had no knees when he walked, just two stumps hobbling forward. A young girl, no more than five, blond pigtails tied with red and blue yarn, rushed in front of Paulie and Alex, beating them to the cart by a nose. Paulie grunted. The girl's mother appeared a moment later. She was easily half Paulie's age and wore a short white dress spotted with tiny bright sunflowers. She bent down to one knee beside her daughter and asked in a singsong voice, "What would you like, sweetheart?" The girl hummed in deep contemplation. Paulie shook his head in frustration. He had no patience on a good day; an excited Alex tugged on his arm, adding fuel to his annoyance.

"Stand still, for Christ's sake," he barked down at Alex.

Eventually, the little girl pointed to a pink balloon curled like a giant spring. The Toyman reached into some hidden crevice of his cart and extracted a handheld air pump. He twirled the black cylinder twice like a baton and then wedged it into the crevice beneath his armpit. The other hand dug into his pants pocket. A thin strip of pink latex snapped out, and, in one continuous motion, the Toyman had rolled the balloon's lip over the air nozzle tip and began pumping. It inflated quickly, first a bit of girth along the sides as the pink latex stretched, becoming almost transparent. Once it had spiraled to a sufficient length, the Toyman yanked the lip from the nozzle and, with surprising dexterity, knotted the tip with the stubby fingers of the same hand. The little girl clapped once before snatching the balloon from his outstretched hand while her mother dropped coins into his other. Mother and daughter, hand in hand, began to walk away.

"Finally," Paulie grumbled. The mother turned back and shot Paulie a dirty look, which he readily returned. She put an arm around her daughter and quickly ushered her away. Paulie nudged his son. "C'mon, pick something." Alex surveyed some of the treasures held within the cart: a bouquet of silver pinwheels, a battery of plastic machine guns, a larger-than-usual cluster of American flags. He soon turned to the pegboard that bisected the cart's interior. Upon it, tiny red clips held cellophane bags of miscellaneous plastic playthings: jacks, soldiers, kazoos. Paulie followed his son's stare. *What a bunch of junk.* He shook his head, but then something caught his eye.

"What about this?" Paulie said to Alex. He pointed to the cellophane bag that contained a balsa wood glider kit. Paulie smiled. He wasn't a man prone to nostalgia, but he had loved this simple toy in his youth. The design hadn't changed in four decades—tan pressed wood, red propeller, and a rubber band. Paulie remembered the fun of watching the plane take off from his hand, the thrill when it caught the breeze just right and sailed clear across a city street.

"I don't know . . ." Alex hedged, but Paulie had already gestured to the Toyman. The Toyman snatched the merchandise from the board and collected his payment. A long line of eager customers had formed. Alex began to grumble, but once the prize was placed into his hands, he smiled contently and ran back across the street. Seconds later, he sat cross-legged inside his gate and tore at the wrapper.

"Be careful," Paulie told him. "Let me open it."

"I know how to do it," Alex asserted, all thumbs in his eagerness. There wasn't much to assemble, just a few shafts of balsa to slide into one another, and then the plastic propeller. Alex spilled out the bag's contents onto the flat Bilco cellar door and unfolded the paper directions like a treasure map.

"Do the main wing first," Paulie suggested, hovering over his son.

"I can do it," Alex snapped, aggravating his father. Paulie threw up his arm and stomped back to the bench. Alex quickly slid the main wings into place, then the tail wing, and next popped on the propeller. He felt beneath his leg along the concrete pavement for the rubber band and, once found, looped it into the slots on the propeller. He stretched the band back beneath the wooden fuselage and secured it inside the designated slot at the tail of the plane. As he did so, the rubber band slipped out from between his fingers and snapped him in the wrist.

"Ow!" he shouted more in surprise than pain.

Dee shot Paulie a fierce look. "Help him before he takes his eye out!"

"It's a friggin' rubber band," Paulie growled back.

"I can do it, I can do it," Alex insisted, having already scooped it back up from the pavement. His second try went smoothly, and he proudly raised the plane overhead to admire the sight of his handiwork against the backdrop of a crystal-blue sky. He then bolted to exit the gate.

"Play with it inside the gate," his mother interjected, stopping him in his tracks.

"If he plays with it here, it's gonna crash and break," Paulie cautioned his wife as he unfolded his newspaper. "There's no room."

"It'll disappear out there," Dee insisted, gesturing into the crowded street. Paulie shook his head but didn't argue further. He'd said his piece. Alex, somewhat deflated, scanned the gate, his head darting from side to side, searching for the optimal site from which to launch his creation.

"Point it at the house," Dee said. Paulie shook his head.

Alex walked over to stand with his heels flush against the entranceway to the gate; he faced the front door. Gently, he pinched the bottom of the fuselage between his thumb and index finger of his right, and with his left index finger began spinning the propeller, twisting and twisting the band into a tight braid.

"Don't twist it too much," Paulie cautioned. The rubber braid knotted into itself twice over. Finally satisfied, Alex lifted the aircraft just above his head. Simultaneously, he released the propeller and flicked the plane from his fingers. The plane flew from his hand, and Alex's eyes fixed on its path.

The plane flew straight and fast for a whole second. Then it struck the edge of the aluminum awning above the front door. The tail kicked up and over the nose; it spun violently, still being propelled, unfortunately in a downward direction. It crashed into the concrete—the rubber band snapped, the propeller flew off, and the frame cracked in two like a hinge. Oh, the humanity!

"It broke!" Alex cried out.

"Let me check you for splinters." Dee waved her son over. Paulie shook his head again, not looking up from his newspaper. Alex, dejected, staggered over to the bench for examination, glancing back once over his shoulder to survey the wreckage. He frowned and pouted through his mother's quick, but thorough, evaluation.

"Everything broke today," he whined.

"What's broke?" Dee asked, her brow pinched tight.

"Everything! My tire, my plane, Zizi's thermometer. Everything!" Paulie, curious, looked up from the paper. Dee grabbed Alex by the shoulders, her face wild with concern.

"What thermometer? You broke glass?!" She grabbed her son's hands and scanned them intently. Had she somehow missed a hidden gaping wound that had been spilling out her son's precious blood for the last few hours? Alex pulled his hands back.

"I didn't break any glass. Zizi's thermometer, on the wall in her kitchen, wasn't working." Alex clarified. "I fixed it."

"How did you fix it?" Paulie asked, leaning closer. Alex thought for a moment, then noticed his father's radio still sitting beside him on the bench. He lifted the radio and pointed to the hashed and numbered tuning strip that spanned its width.

"The line was on the wrong number," Alex said. Then, he spun the tuning dial, the indicator sailed from left to right. "I fixed it," he smiled.

"Son of a bitch!" Paulie flung the newspaper down onto the floor. He bounded up from the bench and sped out the gate and up the block. Dee followed, red faced, walking as fast as she could, dragging her youngest by his wrist.

CHAPTER 14

Paulie and Dee rushed into Zizi's apartment; they felt a flash of heat across their faces as if they'd just dived into a blazing oven. They found Zizi in her armchair, muttering and moaning, semiconscious in a puddle of sweat and black veils, the apartment muggier than the deepest South American rainforest. Her skin was blotchy and red; a tuft of soaked white hair slipping out from its bun hung down over her forehead like a quail's plume. Before addressing his damp distant relative, Paulie ran into the kitchen. He cursed aloud upon seeing his son's handiwork and then quickly slid the lever from the ninety-degree hash mark down to sixty-five. Dee ordered Alex to stand in the corner as she rushed over to Zizi. She pressed her palm against the side of Zizi's clammy cheek and neck, then in front of her mouth.

"She dead?" Paulie asked from the threshold to the kitchen, seemingly hesitant to approach the body.

"You deaf? Can't you hear her moaning?" Dee shot back. She tried to nudge Zizi awake by lifting her chin and tapping the side of her face with increasing vigor, but the woman's eyes remained closed; incoherent guttural sounds still slipped from her mouth. "She needs the hospital."

"The car's parked by the OTB," Paulie disclosed reluctantly. He watched his wife shake her head.

"Then call Bensonhurst Volunteer," Dee shouted back. Brooklyn, like the other outer boroughs, had long suffered from lengthy response times to emergency medical calls. Over the past several years, local volunteer ambulance companies had sprouted up in many communities. Bensonhurst Volunteer Ambulance Company was located just a few blocks away, off the corner of New Utrecht Avenue.

Paulie rushed to the phone, grabbed the receiver, pointed his finger to dial, and froze.

"She doesn't have the sticker," he shouted. To introduce themselves to the community and, more importantly, publicize their phone number, Bensonhurst Volunteer workers had set out on a marketing blitz. In full uniform, the volunteers walked block after block, sliding custom-made ambulance-shaped stickers under the windshield wipers of parked cars and stuffing them into mailboxes. The stickers clearly advertised the potentially lifesaving phone number in thick white numbers set against a royal blue. Dee had immediately slapped her free sticker onto the kitchen wall, on a space immediately to the right of the rotary phone, beside the church calendar annually mailed by their parish, free of charge, as long as your envelopes added up right the year prior.

"You can remember what number came out last Tuesday, but you don't know the ambulance number?" Dee chastised before spitting out the memorized digits. Paulie dialed. Dee heard her husband nervously stammer into the phone, "It's an emergency . . . old lady . . . burning up . . . need help!"

A rare showing of teamwork between spouses marked the following minutes—Paulie soaked the checkered dish towels under the cold tap and handed one after another to Dee, who ran and draped them over

Zizi. They soon heard the first of the sirens approaching. Dee, tortured by visions of her youngest behind bars, ran to Alex and, holding him by the shoulders, commanded, "Keep your mouth shut! Don't say nothing!" A confused Alex nodded silently in response.

There was a hard and fast knock at the door, immediately followed by two paramedics bursting into the apartment. The two young men wore buzz cuts and white short-sleeve shirts with patches sewn into the breast pockets. With their navy shorts and duffel bags, Dee thought they looked like bellhops. The taller of the two took the lead.

"What happened?" he asked Dee as he approached and dropped his bag beside Zizi's chair. Dee stepped back several paces, ceding the space to him. She shook her head and said, "We found her like this." She turned away, gazing into the wall, and remarked, "I think it's the heat."

As the paramedic checked Zizi's pulse, he asked Dee, "Is this your mother?"

Dee's face soured. "My mother's dead," she spit out, and pointed toward the kitchen at her husband. "It's his family."

Paulie peeked his head out from behind the partial wall of the kitchen. He shot his wife a dirty look before emerging fully and nodding to the paramedics, almost in supplication. "She's related to me," Paulie admitted, half raising his right hand.

"Her pulse is steady," the paramedic reported. He felt her forehead and the sides of her face, causing Zizi to stir somewhat. "No fever. Probably just heat exhaustion." He furrowed his brow and scanned the room. "Why is it so hot in here?" Dee and Paulie both shrugged.

The other paramedic crouched over his duffel bag while sorting through its contents; he looked up and spotted a vent on the opposite wall. He sprinted over to it and held his hand against the slots. "Cool air's coming out," he said, somewhat puzzled. Both paramedics looked at Dee, then Paulie. Paulie stared back blankly.

"We have to get her out of these clothes," the taller paramedic said and began to peel the patches of damp washcloths from her, tossing them in a pile on the floor.

"The whole chair is soaked," the other paramedic said after patting the back cushions. The taller one turned to Dee in expectation of some assistance. Dee held her ground for a moment, but the paramedic kept staring until she stepped forward. He began to sort through Zizi's shrouds, searching unsuccessfully for something to unclasp.

"It's in the back," Dee commented. She watched the paramedic fumble around Zizi's back. *This is who comes to help in an emergency,* she thought. *Two kids that don't know how to wipe their own asses yet.* "Here," she said, and then reached around to unhook the top fastener. *More useless men.* Dee was mad at the paramedics, mad at Alex, still mad at Tony, always mad at Paulie. Yet pushing up through that anger, Dee felt a sudden sadness as she unhooked the clasps of Zizi's dress. She thought of her mother. Not the usual memories that Dee allowed herself to be lost in—cooking side by side in their narrow kitchen, sitting together at the table for morning coffee, or her mother's beaming smile from her perch at the front window, which Dee spotted the moment she'd round the corner returning home from work. Instead, she recalled the final months of her mother's life, bedridden, wasting away with cancer day after day. No conversation, no coffee, no smiles. Just the unveiling of wrinkled pale flesh to be wiped clean with washcloths, the bedpan emptied.

Dee shook her head and backed away. "You two do this." The paramedics shared a confused look.

"Does she have a robe or something around?" the taller paramedic asked her.

"I don't know what she has," Dee barked back.

"Please, could you look?" he said. "And some towels."

Dee looked at Paulie. Paulie threw his hands up. "I'm not going through her things."

Before Dee could reply, two cops barged into the apartment: all business, shouting questions, "Who? What? Where? When? Why's it so hot in here?" Alex recognized them immediately as the same two cops who had earlier escorted Chippy away. He feared a similar fate awaited him.

The paramedics had Zizi's dress peeled down to the waist. "We need those towels," one of them shouted. The cops looked at Dee. Dee turned to look for Paulie, who had retreated into the farthest recesses of the kitchen. Just as Dee heard Zizi moan, two firefighters barged in: one carrying an axe, the other, a tank of oxygen. Tony and Sally rushed in right behind the firefighters. This was something right out of *A Night at the Opera*. What they really needed was the engineer to turn off the heat, but truth be told, Paulie had already taken care of that.

Zizi suddenly stirred; her head rolled from one side to the other. "We could use a hand," the tall paramedic shouted to no one in particular. The four civil servants, eager to help, walked over and formed a semicircle around Zizi, awaiting further instruction. Dee disappeared into Zizi's bedroom to search for a robe.

Zizi's small bedroom was a spartan example of old Italian widowhood: a full-size bed bookended by single drawer night tables, no lamps, and a set of rosary beads spilled over a small dresser opposite the bed. The mauve bedspread with gold trim lay perfectly flat and unwrinkled, as if it had never been peeled back from the pillows. Dee wasn't thrilled about snooping around someone else's bedroom, let alone Zizi's. She was even less thrilled seeing Tony hanging around that boy Sally. Always up to no good, that one. She had never forgotten the time when Tony was probably no older than Alex, when she had let that Sally come upstairs to play with her son one rainy day. At first, the two boys had sat nicely at the table, playing Operation (though the boy was a twitchy mess even back then: *buzz! buzz! buzz!* every time he touched the damn tweezers). Dee had stepped into the kitchen to put a pot of water on the stove. She'd turned her back on Sally for barely a minute, and when she came back into the room, Tony was sitting alone at the table. She caught Sally inside her bedroom going through her dresser drawers. She hoped the boy's ear still hurt from her dragging him out of their apartment and up the block to tell his mother what he'd done. The mother wasn't home, of course. That was the last time she had let Sally into her house.

Dee returned from the bedroom, a gray robe draped over one arm, and handed it to one of the paramedics. Zizi's unwrapping was still slow going. The old woman was a tangle of wet black fabric. Growing frustrated, the taller paramedic tugged hard at a hem and suddenly Zizi's eye's pop wide open. Her head remained still, just two beady pupils, darting from side.

"STUPRO! STUPRO!" she screamed while her arms thrashed about. She kicked her feet with surprising force, sending the paramedics, still on their hands and knees, scrambling backward.

"Lady, calm down!" the officer with the bushy mustache barked. The other cop spun in front of Zizi and held up both hands in a calming motion. *"Signora, Signora!"* he pleaded. *Signore* and *signora* were the extent of his Italian, but it had historically been enough to get someone's attention in this neighborhood. When she swung at him with her free arm, he was ready and easily snatched it in midflight.

Overconfident, the officer held Zizi's arm in one hand and leaned forward, intending to use his other arm and upper body to immobilize her—for her own safety. As he leaned closer, he came face-to-face with her. He saw her eyes grow wild, her nostrils flare, and her mouth stretch open as she lurched forward, like a snapping turtle. The officer's head recoiled.

"She tried to bite me," he cried. Unbeknownst to him, Zizi's teeth were still sitting safely inside a glass of water on top of the bathroom sink.

Dee's first instinct at the onset of the spectacle was to spring across the room and act as a human shield for Alex. Alex cowered behind his mother, still fearing arrest but also freaked out by the confirmation of his worst fear—that the elderly were indeed undead zombies waiting for the chance to bite your face off. Suddenly, Dee saw Tony leap forward, yelling, "Hey, you're gonna hurt her!"

"Hurt *her*?!" the officer shot back.

"*Tutto bene, Zizi. Tutto bene,*" Tony repeated as he approached. Zizi's head wobbled from side to side, then straightened upright. She blinked several times then asked, "*Che cosa?*"

"*Tutto bene,*" Tony said, assuring the elderly woman that all was well. The paramedics, the cops, and the firefighters regrouped cautiously, not completely trusting the woman's new serenity. Tony turned back to Sally, who was fluent in Italian, and asked, "How do I tell her what happened?"

"Don't ask me. I have no idea what the fuck's goin' on," Sally said, shaking his head.

Zizi became aware of her bare neck and shoulders, flesh unexposed for the past several decades. Full of shame, she tried to pull her dress back up, but it was stuck beneath her. Tony spotted the herringbone-patterned afghan draped over the far arm of the sofa.

He reached over the end table to grab it, flung it open like a cape, and draped it over Zizi.

"Grazie. Grazie," Zizi said, and she turned her head and scanned all the faces in the room, those strange and familiar. Then she looked down, up at the ceiling, and then back to Tony. *"Così caldo,"* she said, and sank back farther into her chair, the adrenaline fading.

"Too hot," Tony agreed. "That's right. *Riposa*, rest," he urged. Zizi sighed, then suddenly bolted upright again. Her bare wrinkled arm snaked out from below the afghan, a bony finger extended straight at Dee, who glared back defiantly.

"Assassino!" Zizi said, stabbing an accusing finger at Alex, his head peeking out from behind his mother.

"She's delirious." Dee dismissed Zizi's comments. *What a fiasco,* she thought. She turned and saw her husband, still hiding in the kitchen, leaning against the stove. *The stove . . .* A new wave of panic swept over her; she'd left the ziti in the oven.

CHAPTER 15

Dee still felt the eyes on her as she sat alone, some hours later, under the diminishing shade of the oak. One by one, all the busybodies had paraded by her gate to stick their nose where it wasn't welcome:

"Did the cops take him away too . . . ?" Vivian Chipparetti asked.

"I heard he was playing with matches," Mrs. DeMarco accused.

On and on it went, for the past few hours. Even Mrs. Song had trotted out from behind her counter to interrogate. "Who die?"

She cut them all off, one by one, and sent them on their way. "Just the heat. She's an old woman. Go back to your fun. Enjoy yourself."

The worst indignity, though, might have been when Lorraine, Mario's show-offy wife, always with the makeup on and her hair blown out, hurried over to her, feigning concern—"I saw smoke coming out of your kitchen window," she said. "I was ready to call the fire department myself." Dee couldn't believe she'd burned the ziti. *Like a friggin' newlywed,* she scolded herself. She'd been forced to feed her children bologna-and-cheese sandwiches—on Wonder Bread! And the little one, after what he did, still had the gall to whine about it.

Dee glanced up at her front window. Alex sat alone, resting his head atop both arms folded across the windowsill, the frown of frowns upon his face.

She nodded once to herself, as if in reassurance. Holiday or no holiday, children needed to learn who was boss. Otherwise, as she often said, *You give them a finger, they take an arm.* Dee stood up to make sure she still had a clear line of sight on her oldest. There he was, still with that no-good Sally. Fine. It was the lesser of the evils, for the moment, she supposed. She checked her wristwatch and then looked up and down the block, her expression a mixture of annoyance and concern. And where the hell was her husband? Why wasn't he back yet?

★

Paulie stopped picking at the ripped upholstery as the car service slowed and pulled up to the barricades at the north end of his block. The driver, a middle-aged Puerto Rican man with bushy eyebrows and sideburns, honked twice. Paulie glanced at his watch. It was a quarter past four. He shook his head. *Happy effin' Fourth,* he thought. *What a joke.* Zizi, sitting to his left in the back seat, stared straight into the back of the driver's headrest with the rigid ferocity of a castle gargoyle. She hadn't moved or said a word since they'd left the hospital twenty minutes prior.

"You want to go move the barricades, *mijo*?" the driver asked. "Nobody's comin' over."

"Basta, basta! So camminare," a suddenly animated Zizi barked, and slapped the back of the driver's headrest. She abruptly popped open the passenger door and climbed out, pocketbook clenched in

her hand. She started down the block, one end of the tie from the bathrobe she still wore trailing behind her like a fuzzy tail.

"Forget it. We'll walk, I guess," Paulie told the driver. The discharge nurse had kindly offered Zizi some spare clothes before they'd left the hospital, trying to convey via pantomime that they were washed and clean. Zizi had scowled at the nurse as if she'd offered her a leper's tattered rags.

The car-service driver now turned and watched the tiny, shriveled old woman trudge down the block, clutching a bag half her size with one hand, the neck of her robe closed with the other, her flimsy hospital slippers scraping against the concrete with each small, but hurried, step.

"That your mother, *mijo*?" the driver asked Paulie.

"God forbid."

"Mother-in-law?" The driver looked up into the rearview mirror to check Paulie's response. Paulie shook his head. The driver gave Zizi one last glance. "Reminds me of mine," he mused, glancing back to Zizi. *"Bruja antigua."*

"What's that?" Paulie asked.

"Old witch," the driver said. "Fare's $4.50, *mijo*." Paulie grumbled something under his breath as he fished out five singles from his wallet, handed them to the driver.

"Keep the change," Paulie said. The driver let loose a sharp whistle as he counted the five bills.

"Cinquento centavos," the driver commented, adding a mocking whistle.

"Huh?"

"Feliz Cuarto de Julio—happy Fourth, *mijo!"* the driver said.

"Yeah, right." Paulie climbed out and swung the door shut. *What a fucking nightmare day,* he thought.

★

Paulie had almost vomited twice riding with Zizi in the back of the ambulance. His head had been spinning from the chaos that had just ensued—*Fucking Alex!*—and that was piled on top of the money he'd lost and the strike news. And the only place for him to sit was a ledge behind the stretcher facing the ambulance's back doors. Zizi, of course, had refused to lie flat on the stretcher and kept popping up like Dracula from his coffin. Every time the paramedic had tried to insert the IV needle, Zizi went for his eyes. As this went on, the ambulance rushed through the streets of Brooklyn, swerving in and out of traffic. Paulie rocked back and forth in his seat; through the twin windows on the back doors, the horizon constantly tipping and flashing by.

"Can't you just knock her out?" Paulie asked.

"What do you think I'm trying to do?" the frustrated paramedic barked back. Zizi hinged upright again, and at the paramedic's insistence, Paulie wrapped his arms around her bony frame. Zizi screamed curses in Italian. Finally, the paramedic, through skill or sheer luck, in one swift motion plunged the needle into a thin purple vein that snaked up the inside of her left arm. Seconds later she was out cold, and both men exhaled as if they'd just survived a plane crash.

The ambulance soon pulled up to the hospital's ER. The driver hopped out and sped around to open the back doors. The two paramedics then lifted Zizi, lying unconscious on the stretcher, up and out of the ambulance, making sure the IV and tubing came along. One paramedic noticed Paulie remained seated and shouted, "Let's go! You're coming too."

The ER's waiting room was packed. Paulie glanced around and cringed, seeing several men and teenage boys writhing and moaning in pain. Each appeared to be clutching a hand wrapped in a blood-soaked towel or gauze. *Christ!* Paulie thought. This was worse than anything he'd seen in the service. Mothers sitting with their sons would in one moment scream admonishments and the next tear at their own hair in self-flagellation. Thankfully, without pause, the paramedics rolled the stretcher across the waiting room, smashing through to double doors that swung open. The ER was a giant square room with observation and treatment units running along the perimeter, each sectioned off by blue curtains. The nurses' station sat in a square island at the room's center. Zizi was parked in what seemed the be the sole vacancy, labeled Unit 5. Paulie saw the number, was quickly reminded of the number-five horse he'd placed his doomed bet upon and silently wished he'd never eavesdropped that morning. The paramedics disappeared to confer with the staff. Paulie looked around, unsure of what do. After a few seconds, he sat himself in the lone gray plastic chair beside Zizi.

Surprisingly, in short order, a doctor soon entered the unit. He was holding a clipboard close to his face, squinting to read whatever notes were jotted on the page attached.

Great, another one with a clipboard, Paulie noted. The doctor was on the short side and wore a forlorn expression that seemed long acquainted with his face. An exhausted exhale escaped his mouth as he ran his hand up through his unkempt mop of curly hair. Draped in a slightly too-large lab coat, the doctor reminded Paulie of Harpo Marx.

"How long is all this gonna take?" Paulie asked impatiently.

The doctor looked up from his clipboard. "You in a rush?" The doctor shook his head and muttered mostly to himself, "Like I want to be here." Then he exhaled again and brought his voice back to normal level. "If it's just dehydration, two IV drips should have her back on her feet." He glanced up at the monitors. "Her vitals seem fine. . . . Better than mine, actually."

"How long's that gonna take?" Paulie repeated, matching the doctor's annoyance. He still hadn't received the answer to the question he'd asked.

"Two hours, maybe more, maybe less." The doctor shrugged and turned to leave.

"Fucking shoot me," Paulie said.

"Please, shoot me too," the doctor mumbled as he turned, pulling the curtain half-shut behind him as he exited, off to see the next patient.

Slumped in his chair, Paulie stared down at the floor. God, how he hated hospitals. He felt like his skin was crawling. But not even that could long distract him from his real problems. He had no idea what he was going to do about the tuition money, about the strike. What could he do?

Just outside their unit, a nurse strolling by stopped and asked no one in particular, "Who turned this off?" She reached up and turned on a small television that was mounted between the ceiling and facade above the nurses' station. Slowly, Walter Cronkite's image materialized on the screen. He was seated at a desk, multiple monitors playing on the wall behind him. The nurse raised the volume, and Paulie raised his head upon hearing Cronkite's voice. "And the celebration continues. . . ."

"Celebration?! You gotta be fucking kidding me," Paulie said. But despite his mood, he soon realized it was better to lose himself in what was on television than be assailed by his worries. For the next several hours, Paulie watched Americans across the country celebrating both their unity and their uniqueness. At 2:00 p.m. the feed switched to President Ford, after a short speech, kicking off the ringing of the bells. Video feeds from across the country followed—churches, schools, city halls, crowds of children, bells of all sizes, ringing in succession to mark the nation's birthday. Following that was a segment on Indian powwows and then the largest Civil War battle reenactment in the country's history. Paulie watched it all intently, at times curious and at others incredulous. There were "Olde Tyme Celebrations" featuring people dressed like hillbillies competing against one another in contests such as horseshoe pitching, tobacco spitting, and even husband calling. Here, he was unimpressed—none of these women could remotely match his wife in volume or tone. Finally, there were people racing buffalo, riding them like thoroughbreds across a dirt track. He wondered if there was wagering, though his pick would probably wind up goring its jockey midrace. Eventually, as if he were back home watching television from his spot on the couch, Paulie's eyelids began to droop, and for a brief few minutes, he nodded off.

He was jolted awake then by the sound of bells. "Again with the effin' bells," he said aloud, but soon realized the sound was monitor alarms blaring from the unit adjacent to theirs. Then there was shouting and people rushing by, and Paulie shook his head and felt his bowels spasm. He needed to go but swore he'd crap his pants before he used the hospital toilet.

Finally, the second IV emptied, and, almost on cue, Zizi's eyes popped open. Immediately she began tearing the wires from her and shouting, *"Voglio andare a casa adesso! Voglio andare a casa adesso!"*

Two nurses rushed into the unit, followed by Dr. Harpo. Paulie, unfazed by Zizi's antics, looked up from where he still sat.

"Can we go now?" he asked.

"Please do," the doctor replied.

Nothing about sitting in an emergency room for almost three

hours on the nation's Bicentennial had been fun, but at least that brand of misery had briefly blotted out the terrifying fact that he was unemployed. The moment Paulie stepped back onto his block, it all came flooding back. It felt like there was a little cash register in the center of his brain ringing up his expenses: rent, utilities, groceries, Tony's high school tuition. Just then the stomach cramps resumed. The down payment: he needed to pay that bill before Dee found out. Telling her that he'd lost his job was horrifying enough, but that he'd blown the tuition money on a horse? *Sweet Jesus.* He prayed he'd be spared the call until tomorrow at least, since he had more service time than most of the poor bastards. Just picturing Dee's reaction threatened to double him over. He needed to work, to earn money, fast. He could go to his brothers for money. They'd certainly help, but just the thought made him feel like he was a bug crawling on the ground.

The car-service driver honked twice as he pulled away. Paulie had a thought. Maybe he could drive some shifts? Every car-service storefront he'd ever seen had a Drivers Wanted sign taped onto it. Might not be so bad, just to help make ends meet; make some quick fares, short rides, driving a few old ladies to their doctors' appointments, the supermarket. He wondered if he could just sign up for the local rides. Probably not; the foundation of the idea began to crack. He shuddered at the thought of having to drive people to LaGuardia or Kennedy Airport. Jesus Christ, having to navigate the lunacy of the BQE and Belt Parkway during rush hour. He and Barney Short had seniority at their shop to work the 7:00 a.m. to 3:00 p.m. shift, gleefully avoiding the worst of highway traffic most days. Hell, driving car service, he'd probably even have to drive into Manhattan, take people to business appointments, Broadway shows. Even under the still-oppressive heat, the vision of him sitting in traffic in the middle of Times Square, horns blaring all around him, sent a chill up his spine. But what else could he do? He was almost fifty, had a sixth-grade education, and the only other job he'd ever held was working at his father's fruit and vegetable store. There weren't many options. Actually . . . maybe there was one, one he'd screwed up long ago. Maybe it was fate that Johnny Truz had suddenly popped up in the neighborhood today. Maybe that was the little bit of luck he'd been hoping for.

★

Alex was unfamiliar with the term *déjà vu*, but that was exactly what he was feeling, forced to experience another block party from the vantage point of his parents' front bedroom window. Last summer it had been the chicken pox that had remanded him to his mother's rocking chair, from which he'd spent the day watching other kids scream and laugh as they rode their bikes and ran through the street with reckless abandon.

At least last year no one was mad at him; in fact, everyone had acted extra nice to him because he was sick. His father bought him comic books from the candy store; Tony snuck him a cup of soft vanilla ice cream with rainbow sprinkles. Being in trouble, being punished, was way worse than being sick. He wished he were sick now.

It was bad enough that he couldn't play outside, couldn't have fun like everyone else. His mother insisted that he sit here in her chair, alone at the window, allowed to leave only to pee—and even then, he'd better get his rear end back in that chair fast, she had warned. He couldn't even sit in the living room and watch the Bicentennial celebrations on a color television. Hell, he'd be happy just to watch the Mets game, if allowed. He wondered if his punishment would be lifted in time for the first pitch of the Yankee game later that evening.

On his last trip to the bathroom, Alex had run as fast as his short legs would carry him, hoping to steal a few precious seconds of television on the black-and-white set in his parents' room. He figured if he heard footsteps coming up the hallway, he'd be able to quickly turn off the set and get his butt back to the rocking chair. He'd peed, raced back, and turned on the television. The old set hissed, and the black screen shimmered to reveal a brief glimpse of gray ships, on gray water, under gray sky, before the picture started to cascade like a waterfall. Alex frantically spun the vertical knob, then the horizontal knob, bent the antennae left and right, but all he did was make it worse. How did his mother watch this thing? He heard what sounded like the front door slam, and a bolt of fear shot down his legs. He quickly shut off the television and raced back into the chair; his mother was still outside, her eyes waiting for him.

What made the punishment suck even more was that more than half the block was hidden from his view. Three windows, arranged in a small arch, faced the front sidewalk from his parents' bedroom. From the window farthest left, where he sat now, he had a clear vista of the lower quarter of the block, as well as the avenue and under the El. However, the next two windows were mostly obstructed: a large steel window fan occupied the entire bottom pane of the middle window, while his father's dresser eclipsed most of the window farthest to the right. If Alex wanted to see what was happening anywhere else on the block, his options were limited. He had grown too large to squeeze his head behind the dresser, as he had in years past. He could press his face closer to the thin steel loops, an array of expanding circles, that formed the fan's outer shell and prevented foolish, curious children like him from having their fingers lopped off. But he was sure the moment he did, his mother would notice and quickly scream up at him from the sidewalk. He was in enough trouble already. Alex turned his head right. There was a narrow strip of daylight between the paisley window curtain and the edge of his father's dresser. He strained his eyes, unsure of what he was even hoping to see.

Alex had last glimpsed his father when the paramedics had insisted on taking Zizi to the hospital. He'd watched him begrudgingly climb into the ambulance, browbeaten by the two policemen to accompany his elderly relative. He was sure his father must be mad at him too.

For a moment, Alex thought he spotted Tony, clustered in a pack of older kids, but he really wasn't sure if it was his brother. There were a lot of teenagers with white tank tops and short black hair walking the street. They all looked alike from a distance.

He turned back to his window just in time to see Vito and Tommy ride their bikes into view. Tommy flashed him an empathetic smile as he labored at the pedals. Vito, instead of waving, recklessly raced his bike directly at a herd of pedestrians huddled close to the street barricade. At the last possible instant, he swerved and looped back around as the people he'd almost rammed shouted curses. On his return lap past Alex, Vito raised his right hand in both triumph and salute to his friend.

Alex glanced down at his mother. She still sat in her folding chair under the tree. She looked sad and angry, angry and sad, never letting more than a minute go by without glancing disapprovingly up at her son. Alex sighed.

CHAPTER 16

As Paulie made his way down the block, he purposely slowed his pace to keep some distance between himself and the robed crazy old lady his son had almost roasted alive. A slight lull had fallen over the block since they'd been away. Some folks still drifted across the sidewalks and street, but most revelers had receded into the front gates and onto their porches. Many settled into their folding chairs and benches, time to take a little break and digest. To the delight of many of the older residents, the DJ had exchanged thumping disco beats for Sinatra's soothing voice. "Summer Wind" sailed through the street, and Italians young and old smiled and swayed gently from side to side. Only the youngest children passed up the opportunity to recharge. A throng of boys and girls, some in swimsuits, others just stripped down to the waist, ran through the streams of water cascading from the fire hydrant. Paulie was sure the mayor, Mr. DeMarco, had made a production of turning it on.

The mayor was the sole possessor of the sprinkler cap and special wrench required to tap into the powerful New York City water flow. The frequency and way he'd relay what was required of him to obtain said items (filling out a one-sided form for the precinct desk sergeant) would make someone think that the accomplishment was on par with Jason retrieving the Golden Fleece.

"You know, they took down all my personal information and made a copy of my driver's license," he'd eagerly confide to anyone in earshot, each time he trekked the cast-iron sprinkler cap and wrench from his front door to a hydrant. "It's all under my name, you know." He'd look down to tell the children tailing him, as if they cared or were even listening. The mayor . . . there was something to do with the mayor that Paulie was supposed to remember. What was it? Whatever it was, the very question of it seemed to evaporate instantly under the hazy sun. Paulie gazed up at the sky for a moment, then back at the children splashing through the open hydrant. He'd love to take a run through. Jesus, how was it still this hot?

Paulie watched Zizi arrive at her front porch. As she started up the stairs, she tightened her grip on the front of her robe. Emanating from the porch's landing, he heard a commotion, a burst of raucous laughter.

"What, did you have a one-night stand?" Richie's voice could be heard over the laughter. As Paulie drew closer, he spotted Richie emerging from a huddle of friends. Many of them, like Richie, were shirtless and held cigarettes in one hand and a can of beer in the other. "Jesus, the guy couldn't even walk you home?" Richie continued, laughing at his own remark, and then took a sip from his can.

Zizi shot Richie the evil eye and barked *"Vaffanculo!"* as she stepped inside her home and slammed the screen door behind her. One of his friends laughed so hard that he spit out an entire foamy mouthful of beer, which just made the rest of the crew laugh harder. Even Paulie chuckled. Richie noticed his uncle down on the sidewalk.

"Hey, Uncle P., come up and have a drink," Richie shouted, and waved him up.

"Nah, I gotta get home," Paulie said, shaking his head. "My wife . . ."

"Aunt Dee is fine. I can see her from here, all happy sitting under her tree." Richie gestured down the block with his cigarette. "C'mon, have a drink with the boys." Richie's friends all chimed in, a chorus of voices egging on Paulie to join them. Paulie gazed down the block. He could just make out the specter of his wife seated across from their front gate. Paulie imagined the looks, the conversation that awaited him.

"Maybe just one beer," Paulie told his nephew. He climbed up the porch steps and exhaled upon reaching the top, as if he'd just scaled Everest.

Richie shouted back over his shoulder, "Hey, Bobby, toss my uncle a beer." Bobby was tall and lean with straight white-blond hair that stopped just above his shoulders. He had a thin mustache of the same color that seemed to vanish in direct sunlight. "You bet," he said. Bobby reached down into a blue cooler that sat in the only shaded portion of the porch, opposite a small hibachi. He fished out a can from the icy water and tossed it to Richie, who pulled the tab off and handed it to his uncle.

"*Salud*," Richie said. They clinked their cans together, and both took their sips. The beer tasted icy and crisp.

"Ahhhhhhhh," Paulie exhaled in delight. "Tastes good." Paulie, in truth, wasn't much of a drinker. Booze went straight to his head, but it was hot, and the last thing he'd had to eat or drink was coffee at breakfast. After taking another sip, he pressed and rolled the can over the side of his face, spreading tiny drops of chilled condensation across his cheek.

"Hey, Uncle P., you know the guys, right?" Richie pointed from right to left, "Bobby, Tony, Carmine, Vinny, Vinny."

Not one of them looked familiar, but Paulie nodded anyway. "Sure, sure."

Richie took a step closer to Paulie and whispered from out of the corner of his mouth, "So, Uncle P., what happened before?" Richie jabbed his thumb toward the front door. Paulie stared back, slightly confused. Now that he thought about it, during all that insanity, all the people rushing in and out of Zizi's apartment, he had never seen Richie's face.

"You weren't home before?" Paulie asked.

"I was home," Richie said. "Dead asleep. I like to take a little siesta after . . ." Richie popped his cigarette into his mouth, clenched his right fist, and pumped it sideways in short, quick bursts. "You know what I'm talking about," he said and plucked the cigarette from his lips. Paulie grinned like a schoolboy and took a long sip of beer that prolonged the moment. *Beer tastes good,* he thought.

"So, what happened?" Richie raised both eyebrows as he repeated the question.

Before Paulie could answer, they heard a series of sharp, toothy whistles. Paulie turned to see Richie's friends huddled together, leaning over the front of the porch wall. One of them whistled loudly again.

"C'mon, Uncle P., let's check it out," Richie said, whatever interest he'd had in Zizi gone. They sidled up behind his friends to try to get a better look.

Two Puerto Rican girls, maybe eighteen, maybe not, strolled by below. Both had long black hair that curled over their bare shoulders, their deep-brown tans putting the purest Sicilian blood to shame. The taller was all ass and legs, the former partially and the latter wholly exposed by her tiny denim cutoffs. Her friend wore a stretchy blue tube top that had two stitched white stars perfectly centered over both breasts. They continued their strut up the block, hugging the curb, drawing stares from both sexes—likely welcomed the attention, if the smirks across their bright-red lips were to be believed.

"Foxy!" one of Richie's friends shouted as they passed. *"You two like Italian sauseege?"* bellowed another. He pointed down to the grill, and then from the grill to his crotch. *"Right here!"* Another shouted, "Yeah, give her your Bicentennial Minute!" The guys laughed and whistled some more. Paulie giggled, invisible behind the wall of younger men.

Richie elbowed his way to the front. "Why you gotta say things like that?" he admonished his friends. Richie cleared his throat, his friends' laughter fading to snickers and chuckles. "Watch. Like this."

"Hey, wait, wait, wait," Richie spoke loudly but didn't shout. Both girls slowed. "You two said you'd have a drink with me." He repeated himself then, slightly louder, as if reminding someone of a broken promise—"You two said you'd have a drink with me."

"Oh yeah? When?" the girl in the tube top yelled, without looking back.

"When? Last week. We were dancing at Studio 54."

Tube Top stopped and turned. "We don't go to Studio."

"Sure, it was you," Richie said as he stepped sideways in front of his friends all the way to the far corner of the porch, hovering above where the girls now stood. The taller girl seemed less interested and urged her friend forward. Richie continued, "You said you were just in from Rio for the weekend to do a cover for *Cosmo*." Richie noticed Tube Top crack a smile. Paulie grinned, watching his nephew work. He took another sip of beer. "What's your name?" Richie asked.

"Gabriela," she said. "I thought you said you know me?"

"Not your first name," Richie shook his head. "How could I forget *Gabriela*? I couldn't remember your last name." Richie's friends nodded in assurance behind him. Gabriela stared back, eyebrows arched, her lips curled into an amused smile.

"What? You gonna mail her a letter?" Gabriela's friend barked. She bent down to whisper something intently into Gabriela's ear. The friend took a step to walk away, and when Gabriela didn't follow, she reached back, grabbed her hand, and yanked her forward.

"Ouch!" Gabriela said, and the two girls exchanged annoyed looks and heated words in Spanish as they began to walk away.

"Gabriela!" Richie called out. "Where you going?" He turned and pointed behind him. "C'mon back, I want you to meet my Uncle Paulie," he shouted. "C'mere, c'mere." He urged Paulie to join him at the edge of the wall. Paulie blushed and shook his head no. Richie's friend, Bobby, gently shoved Paulie forward. Richie threw an arm around his uncle's shoulders and shouted, "C'mon, have a drink with my uncle. He's lonely."

Paulie listened to the guys laughing and felt their hands slapping across his back. He took another sip of beer; he looked left and right, soaking in the camaraderie.

He gazed out at the girls walking away, held up the can, and shouted, "The beer's cold." Everyone laughed a little louder.

CHAPTER 17

Many years ago there was a boy named Paulie who, when he wasn't in school (which was quite often), worked in his father's fruit and vegetable store. Paulie had three older siblings—two brothers and one sister, who was the closest to him in age, five years his senior. Paulie had a best friend, too, named Johnny Truzino, who lived in the four-story dirty-brown-brick walk-up that sat atop Paulie's father's storefront. Johnny had no siblings, nor a father, just a mother named Agnes; she was still a looker in bad light and worked at a bar that was always dark inside. She wasn't home much, and even when she was, she wasn't alone. These men, of whom Johnny would catch only occasional glimpses, would quickly turn their faces or, worse, wink and grin.

Paulie's parents, despite already having enough mouths to feed, frequently welcomed Johnny to their table at mealtime. When Paulie's mother grew tired of seeing the boy looking so disheveled, she began splitting her oldest sons' hand-me-downs between Paulie and his friend. Soon, she began to cut Johnny's hair, just as she did for Paulie. One day, a squat elderly woman who bought one ripe banana every morning ambled into the fruit store. She took one look at Paulie and Johnny stacking pears in an empty stand and muttered *"Gemelli"* to Paulie's mother. Twins. The name stuck, and deservedly so. They were inseparable.

Truth was, despite having siblings, Paulie's older brothers, because of the age difference, didn't bother with him much, aside from bossing him around at the store. Both were chasing skirts by the time Paulie had graduated from diapers, and they regarded him no more than they did the family mongrel, which was kept chained to a gas pipe in the back alley.

The twins got into their fair share of hijinks, though they were careful not to get caught, as Paulie's father wasn't shy with the belt. For kicks, they'd swipe an occasional piece of hard licorice from Mr. Grimaldi's candy store on the next block. Johnny always took the lead:

"Hey Mr. G.," Johnny would shout. He'd then step up onto the bottom ledge of the soda counter, press his hands into the green marble top, and lift himself up like a gymnast so his sneakers dangled a few inches above the tiled floor. "How long you think I can hold myself up like this?"

"Get a-down!" the always agitated Mr. Grimaldi would shout.

"I bet I can do this for five minutes."

"No! You get a-down now. Little bastard!"

Johnny smirked. He also knew Paulie already had a pocket full of candy waiting to be divvied up as soon as they got outside. At first, Paulie, who never liked to think too hard about things, never minded how Johnny always took the lead, whether it was suggesting they hop the turnstiles to catch a game at Ebbets Field, sneak into a gangster picture, or climb the fire escape up to the apartment building's asphalt rooftop to smoke a few cigarettes they pinched out of someone's unguarded pack.

But as they got older, Paulie noticed the ramifications of always taking the back seat. When you let someone else pick which two girls to chat up, you never seemed to get the prettiest one. What started to fester at some point in time, though, was that Johnny's suggestions stopped beginning with the words "You wanna" and instead led with "We're gonna." Paulie already had a father and two older brothers who barked commands around the fruit store: *Do this! Do that!* He didn't need someone else telling him what to do all the time.

Then one Tuesday morning, when the boys were well into their teens, a truck delivering crates of bananas pulled up onto the sidewalk in front of the fruit store. Johnny barked to Paulie, "Go get the unloading ramp."

"Hey, Johnny"—Paulie raised his voice—"don't tell me to get the unloading ramp."

"Huh?"

"I know to get the unloading ramp. I've been getting the unloading ramp since I was born."

"I didn't mean nothing,'" Johnny replied matter-of-factly. "I saw the truck, so I said get the unloading ramp."

"Yeah, I see it too. It's right there." Paulie pointed to the truck. "How come you're always saying we should do this or do that? Like just before, you said, 'Let's go fishing off the pier tomorrow morning.'"

"You don't wanna go fishing, we won't go fishing."

"That's not the point. You always pick what we're gonna do."

"Okay, you pick. Whatta you wanna do tomorrow?" Johnny pushed his bottom lip out and shrugged. He waited for Paulie, who was staring back blankly, to respond.

"Let me think about it," Paulie said and went to get the unloading ramp.

They went fishing the next day. Voicing his displeasure was

enough of a victory for Paulie, who never brought up the subject again, and Johnny, who never meant anything by it to begin with, made sure it didn't sound like he was bossing his friend around. He was grateful to Paulie and his family for their kindness and generosity, as well as smart enough to realize his place in the pecking order around the store—the three sons would always come before him. By this point in his life, Johnny's mother no longer tended bar. The only drinks she still poured were for herself, sitting alone and staring out the alley window, coughing out one cigarette after another. Johnny got a job busing tables most nights at an Italian restaurant under the El. His friendship with Paulie went back to what it had always been.

Three months to the day from his nineteenth birthday, Johnny's number came up, and after several unpleasant weeks of basic training in the Texas heat, he was off to Korea. One day he was collecting plates dripping with globs of marinara sauce, and the next he was trekking through the hills of a foreign country, the thunder of enemy and friendly shelling drawing ever closer. Several weeks into his tour, Johnny's squad was making its way through a thick brush of trees. Johnny was chatting with his best new pal, Jimmy Schliffka, from Piedmont, Tennessee. Piedmont had a population of 875 residents, one traffic light, and half a stop sign (Jimmy bragged about his older brother blasting off the top half with a shotgun on his prom night). Despite growing up in different places, they seemed to have shared similar lives. Jimmy's mom hit the bottle more than a little too often, and he'd also spent his youth working from dawn till dusk (on a poultry farm) and had almost nothing to show for his effort. They'd chat as they walked in loose formation, about what they were going to do when they got out of this mess.

Jimmy had this idea for a chain of ice cream stores fronted by a big white rabbit named Fluffer, which he'd eagerly sketch for anyone who'd stand long enough to watch. Jimmy said he had so many ideas that sometimes it felt like they were all stuck together in his head. One day as they both trekked up a hill that had supposedly been cleared, Johnny heard a buzz and felt a sharp sting on his right ear. "Damn mosquito," he cursed as his hand went to his ear. Something felt wrong. He stopped dead in his tracks; his earlobe was missing. In a panic, he turned to Jimmy, who was no longer standing beside him; the same sniper's bullet had also blown a hole out the side of Jimmy Schliffka's skull.

Once back home, Johnny would sometimes tell people about the bullet that cost him an earlobe: the bullet that had won him a Purple Heart, which he kept in a small black box alongside a worn black-and-white photo of his mother cradling him as an infant in her arms, a bright smile across her face; the bullet that seared into his heart and mind the realization that one's life could be snuffed out in an instant. He was determined to make the most out of his own.

There was this one idea Johnny always had. For so many years, he'd unloaded truck after truck after truck of fruit and vegetable de-liveries at Paulie's father's store. Those trucks would have to trudge all the way from the Bronx Terminal Markets, through Manhattan or Queens traffic, with crates of produce stacked upon blocks of ice. The rare truck that had refrigeration seldom lasted a whole route without breaking down. What if there were a closer hub, one that purchased in bulk from the wholesalers and then sold smaller quan-tities to nearby mom-and-pop shops, grocery stores, and restaurants? Johnny figured that if he picked the right spot, where he could oper-ate also as giant retail store, he could make a killing. Pre—World War II, this idea would have been a turkey, but with the suburban sprawl and the surging sales of automobiles, he knew he had something.

He just needed to save a little more money to get started—unless he brought in a partner.

Now, Paulie had also been drafted, but fortunately the cease-fire was signed a month before his squad was set to ship out from their barracks in Amarillo, Texas, the farthest he'd ever strayed from Brooklyn. Paulie, to this day, still liked to brag about how all the fellas loved his spaghetti sauce, which he prepared every Sunday at the mess. He wouldn't tell the story if Dee was within earshot, because she'd just ruin it with a sneer or remark about how she'd never seen him boil water. By the time Paulie was discharged, Johnny was waiting at home for him with the opportunity of a lifetime. Johnny knew that, say what you will about Paulie, no one had an eye for produce like him. Not his father or brothers, and certainly not Johnny. The twins could grow rich together. All Paulie had to do was say yes.

But he hadn't.

CHAPTER 18

Paulie nursed his second beer while he sat over the ledge of the stoop. Richie was telling some story to his friends that he had trouble following. He kept thinking about Johnny.

"Paulie. . . . Hey, Paulie!" Hearing his name shook Paulie from his reverie. Paulie turned and saw the mayor shouting up at him from the sidewalk. "Paulie. It's time for the races." The mayor held his clipboard out and jabbed his index finger precisely at the spot of his strict schedule that read "4:30 p.m.—Races—Paulie A." Despite the prolonged heat of the day, the mayor's shirt was still a crisp white, not betraying a solitary wrinkle or errant drop of perspiration.

"What?" Paulie barked back, more annoyed than inquisitive.

"The races," the mayor exclaimed. He shifted the clipboard from one hand to the other. What had been hidden beneath the clipboard was a tangle of novelty gold medals dangling from red, white, and blue ribbons. The mayor lifted and shook them, assuming the visual aid would serve as an effective reminder.

What the hell is this ball-breaker talking about? Paulie thought; he took another sip of beer. *Jeez, it feels like it's still getting hotter.* He gently wiped the cool condensation from the can across his forehead, the sensation granting him some small taste of relief.

The mayor held his ground, staring up at Paulie, his eyes like two black ink spots in contrast to the silver of his eyebrows. He lifted the medals slightly higher, as if he were lifting a lantern to further cast its light.

Crap. A hazy memory coalesced inside Paulie's brain. It wasn't enough that he'd shelled out ten bucks to sit in his own gate like he would any other Sunday. Now he remembered: he was also expected to help with the block party, to work. The mayor, after collecting Paulie's cash, had read from his clipboard the available tasks and activities that Paulie could assist with. "Well, your choices are setup, cleanup, water balloon fights, bouncy house . . ."

"Whatever." That's what Paulie remembered saying: "Whatever." Whatever it took to get rid of him. *Crap.* Paulie sighed, and his shoulders slouched. The mayor gazed down at his clipboard, then scratched a checkmark beside the line that read "4:30 p.m.—Races—Paulie A." A victorious grin flashed briefly across his face.

"I gotta go do this race thing," Paulie turned and said to Richie as he searched for a place to toss the empty can. Richie took the can from his uncle's hand and tossed it into an empty plaster planter.

"What kind of races?" Richie asked. Paulie shrugged. He had no idea.

Paulie climbed down the steps to stand in front of the mayor, who was lost in deep thought while he pondered the top sheet of his clipboard. He made small humming noises, as he scanned the page from top to bottom, then left to right, making sure all was in order.

"Just hurry up and tell me what I gotta do," an impatient Paulie said, interrupting the mayor's musings.

"Why? Are the police and fire department coming back for

another visit with your family?" the mayor cracked. Paulie's face flushed as he gritted his teeth and jutted his jaw forward. He took a sharp breath in through his nostrils, but before he could speak, Richie bounced down the stairs and grabbed the clipboard right from the mayor's hands.

"Hey!" the mayor barked and tried to snatch it back. An amused Richie spun around and held the clipboard at arm's length as he furrowed his eyebrows, feigning deep interest while reviewing the notes.

"Uh-huh, uh-huh, I see." Richie nodded to himself. He hummed, "Mmmm-hmmmm," then looked up and said, "Uncle Paulie, it's time for the races," and handed the clipboard back to the mayor without sparing the man another look. The mayor snatched it back. He ran a palm over the top clipped sheet like he was trying to smooth over a shirt wrinkle.

"That's what I said," the mayor mumbled and shook his head. Paulie stood watching the whole exchange, his expression a strange mix of amusement and festering anger. He pressed a thumb against his temple. His head felt tight. Maybe it was the beer, or the heat of the sun, or both. He didn't care. He didn't have time for this bullshit. He wanted to think some more, decide what to do.

The mayor regained his composure, squeezed the metal clamp of the clipboard, slid his thumb between the sheets of paper, and pulled out a smaller clipboard from the bottom of the stack with the quick snap of a wrist.

Richie arched an eyebrow. "How many more clipboards you got in there?"

The mayor paid him no mind and instead reached behind his back and produced a small megaphone, which he handed Paulie along with the tangle of ribbons and medals. "Give out the medals, make sure I get the clipboard and megaphone back," he told Paulie, then pushed out his lower lip, turned, and started to walk down the block, his eyes falling back to once more study his schedule.

As the mayor walked away, Richie's friend Bobby leaned over from the top of the porch and shouted, "Hey. Hey!" The mayor looked back. Bobby, in a serious tone, asked, "What time do the hookers get here?" The mayor shook his head and walked away as laughter erupted behind him.

Paulie looked down. He held the megaphone and medals in one hand, the clipboard in the other. He stared, trying to mentally fit the pieces of the puzzle together, but with his head spinning he may as well have just been handed a bouquet of flowers, a hamster, and a clarinet. Richie quickly noticed his uncle's struggle and said, "No worries, Uncle P., we'll help you out." Richie relieved his uncle of the megaphone and the clipboard and left him holding the medals. "Grab the cooler, boys," Richie shouted to his friends. "We're going to the races."

One guy grabbed the cooler while another harpooned the hot dogs off the grill and hastily stuffed them into buns. In less than a minute, Paulie, along with Richie and his friends, marched down the block, hot dogs and beers in hand, like they owned the place, while a tiny voice in the back of Paulie's head whispered, *Johnny.*

★

Alex sat at the window and kicked his legs back and forth, the tips of his sneakers sometimes grazing across the linoleum floor. Though the plume of white smoke from Mario's last round of grilling had already dissipated, the smell of charred hot dogs clung inside his nostrils. He salivated, imagining himself biting into a juicy frank dripping with mustard. He suddenly heard what sounded like carnival music emanating from somewhere beyond his limited view. Was it Mister Softee? Had someone set up a merry-go-round just out of sight? He was devastated that he'd already missed out on riding the Whip and the King Kong. Well, if he was being honest with himself, he didn't really miss out on the Whip. The one and only time he'd ridden it, he'd vomited all over himself after being spun violently for thirty seconds. Still, he could have ridden the King Kong—maybe even sat in the second bench from the bottom this year. The King Kong ride, like the Whip, was a steel monstrosity on wheels. But instead of whipping soon-to-be nauseated children around in circles, the King Kong swung its riders like a pendulum while they were strapped (usually) inside what looked like three-quarters of an open wheel. The higher level you sat in, the greater the sensation that you may be launched halfway across the avenue. None of that mattered now anyway. The rides had come and gone.

A sudden crescendo of exploding firecrackers distracted Alex. Unconsciously, he reached and felt for the outline of the box of snaps he still had tucked inside his pocket. The box was still half-full. He thought for a moment of launching them down into his parents' linoleum repeatedly in the same spot, as if the repeated inconsequential pops might, in sum, scar the brown and black interlocking hexagons. He could leave a mark in protest. *Here is my mark,* it would say. *Don't tread on me!*

But Alex didn't dare. He just sat there and cycled through the many stages of childhood grief: dumbstruck silence, whiny crocodile tears, full-fledged tantrum, whimpering asthmatic sobs, indignation, and finally depressed resignation. *This stinks, this stinks, this stinks, this stinks, this stinks, this stinks, this stinks, this stinks, this stinks, this stinks,* like a metronome over and over in his head.

He heard a loud buzzing then, its source, unsurprisingly, beyond his limited point of view. The noise grew closer, the buzzing turning into a distorted voice over a loudspeaker or megaphone. He couldn't make out the words, but looking out into the street, he saw new patterns in the crowd's movements. He craned his neck to see where everyone was going, what was happening, but it was all out of frame as he pressed his face flush against the wired mesh of the storm screen window. Alex struggled so hard to see beyond his horizon line that he hadn't noticed his father just outside the front gate directly below him. Only after his father called his name for a third time did Alex hear.

"Alex, for Chrissakes, whatta you, deaf? Get the hell down here," his father shouted. Alex smiled.

Liberty!

★

Paulie tapped his foot, staring at the front door, until Alex finally emerged. His youngest melodramatically shaded his eyes from the sun's glare as he stepped outside, like a political prisoner freed following years of incarceration.

"C'mon!" Paulie grabbed hold of one of the boy's thin wrists and began dragging him into the street. He didn't bother to glance back at his wife; he'd already been treated to a solid two minutes of Dee's disapproving glare.

Alex had made a mistake, fine. Punish the kid, but not today—it was the freakin' Bicentennial. It wasn't right to lock the kid inside on a day like this. Paulie was the one who had been stuck in the ER for three hours. If anyone had a right to be pissed off at Alex (besides Zizi), it was him.

But that's how his wife always was—spiteful. Paulie's mind flew back to an evening, months ago, when Tony had just started working at the deli. The kid was a few minutes late coming home. Dee had marched right to the store and found her son just hanging out with some friends on the corner. Wasn't drinking, wasn't smoking—just hanging out. Fine; say, "Tony, time to come home," or "Come here, I have to talk you." Nope, Dee, as Tony later described to his father, started yelling at her teenage son and, catching a smirk on one of Tony's friends' faces, then turned her anger on them. Paulie shook his head; his parents were guineas off the boat who couldn't speak ten words of English between them, but they were smart enough to know you don't yell at a boy like that, you don't embarrass him that way in front of his friends.

Enough was enough! Dee had Alex sitting at the window like he was an old lady. Christ! Plus, if Paulie was stuck running these stupid races for everyone else's kids, hell if he wasn't going to have his own kid participate.

Paulie, with Alex still in hand, made his way through the horde of children who had congregated in the middle of the street, awaiting further instruction. Paulie looked around for his nephew. He'd entrusted the clipboard and megaphone to Richie while he'd gone to fetch his own son. One glance at the list was enough to make his head spin. There must have been a dozen different races listed on the sheet: boys aged five to seven, girls aged five to seven, boys aged eight to ten, girls aged eight to ten, and so on. *This guy thinks he's runnin' the fucking Olympics.* Paulie shook his head.

If he wanted to track down Johnny, it was best to do so before it got dark and the fireworks started, assuming his estranged friend was still even in Brooklyn. Paulie had a hazy recollection of Johnny always taking his family down by the Promenade to watch the fireworks. When Paulie would turn down the invitation, his friend would chastise him: "C'mon, ya wooden Indian. Get off the block for once."

Paulie would just spout his usual litany of excuses: traffic, Tony was too young, he didn't like to drive at night. The single truth was that Johnny's world was a bigger place than his. Paulie shook his head again; the skin on his forehead still felt tight from the sun and beer, though, quite frankly, he was thirsty for another.

Paulie spotted his nephew just beyond the cluster of overeager children. Leaning against the Rizzo gate, Richie chatted up both mother and daughter, nonchalantly twirling the megaphone around one finger like it was a gunslinger's sidearm. Paulie walked over and tapped him on the shoulder.

"One sec, Uncle P.," Richie said over his shoulder. He took a few moments to wrap up another of his stories—they all seemed to end with him swiveling his pelvis. The Rizzo ladies giggled in delight. Paulie turned and surveyed the miniature crowd, a gallery of small round sunburned faces awaiting instruction. Richie handed the clipboard back to his uncle. Paulie squinted down at the small print. He raised his head, looking up then down the block, unsure where to even begin.

"Where should they race?" he asked Richie.

"I don't know." Richie shrugged after lighting a new cigarette. "Up the block? Around the block?"

"We'll be here for an hour," Paulie looked back down at the clipboard, flustered. Alex, standing behind him, tried to peer around his father's hip to see what was so interesting on the clipboard, but Paulie shrugged him off.

Richie stepped forward, took a drag from his cigarette, and surveyed the street. The owners of the restaurant where he worked loved

Richie because he kept the guests happy *and* turned over the tables fast. He nodded decisively and turned back to his uncle.

"Go hydrant to hydrant. We can bang this out quick." And with that he winked back at both Rizzo women, took the clipboard from his uncle's hand, and marched through the cluster of children to the middle of the street. He raised the megaphone to his lips and belted out his rendition of the thoroughbred racing bugle call—"Bep bep bepbepbep bepbepbep bepbepbepbep"—and then shouted, "It's post time!"

A few of the adults within earshot cracked a smile while the children either stared, confused, or just laughed at the silly sound. Richie's friends were having a good laugh as Richie flashed a quick pose with the megaphone like he was giving a concert. Richie glanced down at the clipboard for a quick check, then spoke into the megaphone. "Oooookay, let's see. Boys. No, girls. Ladies first, right? All girls . . ." Richie swayed his head back and forth for a few seconds like he was weighing a tough decision. "Hmmm . . . all girls . . . twelve and younger, line up by the hydrant next to the DJ."

Richie turned toward his uncle, who had followed him up the street, and said, "Figure we speed things up." Richie raised his right fist and extended a finger as he rattled off, "Little girls, little boys, older girls, older boys. Done. We call it a day." Paulie nodded. Whatever. He couldn't care less. Richie turned and began walking toward his impromptu starting line, his friends in tow. As they strolled, Bobby distributed beers from the cooler that one of the Vinnys carried, cradled in his arms. Richie saw his uncle following and said, "No, Uncle P.—you have to wait by the finish line." Paulie's face contorted into confusion and annoyance. "You're the judge," Richie said, which somewhat softened the look on Paulie's face. Richie shouted to Bobby, "Hey, toss my uncle a beer—he's empty handed."

A silver can came spinning Paulie's way. It was slippery with condensation, and a surprised Paulie fumbled the first attempt at snatching it from the air. The can flipped forward, and Paulie batted it from his left to his right hand before finally seizing the cold aluminum. Richie and his friends cheered as they strutted up the block. Paulie headed toward his assigned hydrant. As he passed Alex, he grabbed him by the arm. "C'mon. This is the girls' race. Stay with me."

Paulie did his best to plant himself at a spot in the middle of the street that looked perpendicular to the fire hydrant. Opposite it, at the starting line, the racers were still getting themselves settled. Paulie squinted upward. The powder blue morning sky had given way to a metallic haze that still seemed intent on scorching all that lay below. He surveyed the block from left to right. A handful of parents and some older kids lined up at the curb to watch the race. He noticed much of the star-spangled bunting and decorations that had been meticulously draped across gates and homes had already come loose and either littered the sidewalks or were crumpled into large misshapen balls and stuffed into garbage cans. One end of the string that secured the massive banner over the middle of the block had snapped; the sheet now hung wrinkled and limp from a streetlight. This, of course, paled in comparison to the mess and carnage that Chippy's annual fireworks show would leave once darkness fell. On a normal Fourth of July, Chippy's handiwork was sure to leave the asphalt street battle-scarred beneath piles of tattered paper. Still, Chippy and his friends always cleaned up their mess, and the first summer thunderstorm postholiday would wash away the brand left by the celebration.

Paulie's gaze fell upon Mario, who was entertaining some guests sitting inside his front gate. Mario's linen shirt remained crisp and white, unblemished, not a bead of a sweat or grease on him. Paulie looked down at his own shirt, damp with sweat from underarm to underarm. He should have run upstairs to change it, but what did it matter? He watched Mario, who now pointed back to the facade of his house, extended his index finger, and slowly directed his guests' attention from floor to floor, as if he were a geologist explaining the origin of each piece of masonry cemented to his home.

Paulie shook his head and inadvertently swung his gaze to the next gate, his own. He spotted his wife gazing back skeptically at what was unfolding. Paulie wrinkled his nose, raised his beer in hand, and cracked open the tab. There was a spray of foam that surprised both husband and wife. Dee snorted at the spectacle. An indignant Paulie tilted his head back, raised the can above his mouth, and spilled its contents down his throat. Dee shook her head. Paulie straightened up and promptly let loose a loud belch. Alex laughed, and from the middle of the block, Richie shouted into the megaphone, "Ready. Set. Go!" catching Paulie unaware; he again almost dropped his beer.

★

Moments after redheaded Theresa Murphy crossed the finish line by a retainer's length over the lanky-legged Linda Montefiore, the boys were called to the starting line.

"Alex, go! What are you waiting for?" Paulie shouted at his son. Alex's preference was to remain at the finish line. He'd enjoyed standing beside his father during the girls' race, mimicking his father's wide-legged stance, arms outstretched to the sides to mark the finish line. Alex began to protest his forced participation in the race, but his father's impatient look suggested not to bother. He scurried after the other boys who were already at the starting line.

The rambunctious herd of boys elbowed and shoved each other, trying to jockey for a spot in front. Richie did his best to straighten them out into something that looked like a line. As Alex arrived, he sheepishly glanced over at Zizi's porch and front door, half expecting to see the old woman's angry face, her long shriveled arm and finger still extended in accusation. He jumped as he felt someone grab him by the elbow. It was Richie.

"Get in front." His cousin bent and whispered as he used his hip to relocate some other kid. Richie winked at him and ran toward the curb. The boy that had been bumped shot Alex a dirty look. Alex felt an elbow poke him in his opposite side. He turned and saw his friend Vito smirking back. When a heavy paw fell over his shoulder from behind, he didn't have to turn to know it belonged to Tommy. He smiled, happy to be with his friends, and then someone shouted, "Go!" and everyone was running past him. Alex hurried to follow. He pumped his arms and legs as hard as he could, only to watch the field quickly pull away. He heard people laughing from the sidewalks behind him and turned to see only Tommy lumbering behind him, the boy's girth heaving up and down with each laborious stride. Alex slowed to a jog to allow his friend to catch up. Alex dropped into a walk for the last few yards so they could cross the finish line simultaneously.

As Tommy hunched over, held himself up by the knees, and caught his breath, Alex watched his father hang a medal over Vito's head. Vito flashed a cheesy smile while his father shot him back a disappointed look.

CHAPTER 19

Tony and Sally watched the race from the curb. Tony never expected his brother to win; he was surprised Alex didn't trip over his own two feet and skin his knees. The family had made enough of a spectacle of themselves for one day. Since the incident, he'd kept a low profile, spending most of the last few hours on Sally's stoop, where he kept vigil for Maria.

Following the first race, Tony laughed when Richie barked into his megaphone, "Teenage girls. I want teenage girls." Several of his buddies shouted, "Us too!" Then, after a dramatic pause, Richie clarified, "I want the teenage girls to line up." Tony saw then that his cousin was waving him and Sally over.

"Here, you're in charge," Richie remarked, handing the megaphone to Tony and running off before he could protest. Richie shouted back over his shoulder, "I want the front view." Tony looked over to Sally, who shrugged and said, "Why not?"

Only a half dozen or so girls appeared at the starting point. Two hardcore tomboys in silk shorts and T-shirts were first to line up. They both folded over to stretch out their hamstrings while the other participants milled around, some snickering, some already looking bored. Tony, with a look of disinterest, offered Sally the megaphone, but his friend shook his head.

"This is all you," Sally assured. He then slid behind his friend and dug his thumbs into Tony's neck and upper back in encouragement.

"Ow!" Tony squirmed out from under Sally's rough kneading. "Do yourself a favor and don't ever become a masseuse," he told Sally. *Might as well get this over with,* Tony thought. He raised the megaphone to his mouth and cleared his throat. He was surprised when every one of the girls quickly turned their eyes to him. He found himself not disliking the attention. He began to speak. "On your mark . . ."

"Hold up, hold up," Sally interrupted, tapping Tony roughly on his shoulder. Tony spun his head and saw the two girls in hot pants from this morning running over to join the already assembled racers. Tony watched them slide into the lineup. Red Hot Pants flashed him a smile before turning to whisper something into her friend's ear. Tony watched her turn back and smile at him again, a smile he this time returned. He cleared his throat again and confidently raised the megaphone to his mouth. Every racer had turned their head to stare at Tony, waiting for his signal.

"On your mark, get set, go!" Tony shouted.

Sally immediately jabbed Tony in the ribs as the girls sped away, unnecessarily reminding his friend to admire the view. Tony looked back over both shoulders, suddenly concerned that Maria might have chosen this moment to appear, only to catch him ogling other girls' rear ends. By the time he turned back, the race was over. He spotted Richie grabbing one of the medals from his father. Tony didn't recognize the winner, one of the tomboys. Whoever she was, she stood somewhat apprehensively as Richie came up on her from behind and draped the ribbon and medal slowly over her head. Richie took great care in making sure the ribbon fell flat over the girl's chest.

"Your cousin giving her a medal or fitting her for a bra?" Sally remarked in Tony's ear. Tony laughed. "You see that one chick checking you out?" Sally jabbed Tony in his arm for emphasis.

"What girl?" Tony played dumb.

"C'mon." Sally rolled his head back. He straightened up and slapped Tony against his back as they strolled to the finish line. "See, this is what happens now that you're not walking around all day in your little Catholic-school outfit. You can show off those muscles." Sally reached over and pinched Tony's biceps. Tony shooed him off as Sally continued. "You're like a zoo animal released back into the wild."

The girl was probably just smiling because he was holding the megaphone, Tony figured. Who knows?

Tony and Sally had almost reached the finished line when they noticed Richie galloping back toward them. Tony handed Richie the megaphone and turned to head for the sidewalk.

"Where you going?" Richie asked. Tony turned back and gestured to the sidewalk. Richie shook his head, then beckoned his cousin over to him. He wrapped his arms around Tony's shoulder and whispered in his ear, "What's wrong with you? Go race. You got all these girls watching you now."

"No one's watching me," Tony said dismissively. Richie wrapped his arm tighter around Tony and said, "You got a lot to learn. C'mon." He led Tony up the block.

★

"Let's go, Tony!" Paulie shouted as his son bolted toward him, quickly distancing himself from the other runners. Paulie noticed Sally, trailing the pack, run a quarter of the way, then abruptly brake off his pace, toss one arm in the air, and begin walking nonchalantly the rest of the way. As Tony sped closer, Paulie bent his arm at the elbow, signaling his son for a high five as he zoomed toward the finish line. Seconds later, father's and son's hands slapped together, race won.

Paulie turned to watch his son slow his pace. For the first time since this morning, he felt something positive, a surge of pride. Maybe not all his life was a flop. He noticed Tony scanning the crowd, like he was looking for someone specific. Paulie separated a medal from the bunch he'd stuffed in his pocket. He walked over and tapped a distracted Tony on his shoulder. His son spun around, and Paulie proudly placed the medal over Tony's head. His truncated responsibilities fulfilled, Paulie walked over to the curb and dropped the remaining medals and clipboard down onto the sidewalk. He was all done.

Paulie started walking to his gate, thinking about giving Barney a call to see if there was any additional news about the strike. His mind kept going in circles regarding Johnny, a gray cloud obscuring a glimmer of sunlight each time it sparked. Maybe what was done was done. The more he thought about it, the more his head hurt, though that might be the beer. He should probably drink some water and eat something too. He hadn't eaten a bite since breakfast.

Unexpectedly, Richie again barked into the megaphone, "One more race! One more race!" Paulie, half-annoyed, half-confused, glanced back toward his nephew, who flashed a smile, then announced, "Forty and over." Richie vigorously waved him over. Paulie shook his head. Richie decided to go public with his encouragement. "C'mon, Uncle Paulie," he urged through the megaphone. Paulie winced at the attention. "Pau-lie! Pau-lie!" Richie chanted. Paulie shook his head as the amplified chanting of his name echoed through the street. Tony and Sally, still meandering around the finish line, joined the chant.

The children that lined the curb and some neighbors began clapping their hands in unison. He allowed himself a chuckle as he glanced back to his gate. Dee and Alex stood under the shade of the oak. Alex smiled and chanted, "Dad-dy, Dad-dy!" Dee just lit another cigarette. Paulie looked back to Tony, who urged him toward the starting line. Reluctantly, Paulie began to jog up the block. He wasn't sure if he wished he'd had one fewer beer or one more.

At the starting line, Paulie sized up the competition. Of the five male competitors present, only Yosef and Giovanni, like him, were not yet old enough to qualify for social security. Mr. Orsini and Mr. Bonello, who rounded out the field, couldn't beat a dead bird in a race. He eyed up Yosef. The man could probably lift him effortlessly over his head, but Paulie doubted he was fast. As for potbellied Giovanni, he'd never even seen the man walk quickly. This was silly. But fine, he'd run. Who knows, maybe a win would snap his bad luck? The lenses of his rose-colored glasses cracked as he spotted Mario sauntering up the middle of the street to join the runners.

Effin' Mario. The glorified grease monkey strutted onto the line, looking like he'd just stepped off the set of a Pellegrino commercial: his linen shirt still pristine, his chinos unwrinkled. Paulie looked down at his neighbor's feet. Was this SOB racing him in sandals? He looked up at Mario, who winked back. Paulie felt his face flush.

A new round of cheers mixed with laughter as Teddy and Paddy Rispoli, eighty-three-year-old twin brothers, both widowed for several years, hobbled toward the starting line. Teddy carried his cane; Paddy, a piece of pound cake he wished to finish. Neighbors and visitors who'd ignored the initial races rose from the benches and folding chairs from their front gates and backyards and began lining the curbs to witness the spectacle. Richie ran in front of the runners and made the time-out sign with his hands while everyone waited for the

Rispoli brothers to bridge the remaining short distance to the starting line.

As Paulie took a moment to adjust his pants at the waist, Mario leaned over and said, "Atta least you won't come in last."

Before Paulie could respond, Richie was back on the megaphone. He'd jogged down to assume his uncle's place at the finish line.

"This is it—the race of the century," Richie shouted. "Or should I say, the race for people older than the century." He chuckled at his own joke as several in the crowd booed. Paulie gritted his teeth and muttered some final curses under his breath for Mario. He locked eyes on his nephew. Richie raised his arm in the air.

"On your mark, get set, go!"

Paulie sprang forward. In horse racing terms, he felt he'd gotten a good jump out of the gate. He pumped his arms as he galloped over the asphalt. He was tired of losing, tired of his own bad luck, tired of being shit on. Onlookers took note of his ferocious expression, the wild look in his eyes as his feet pounded the blacktop and he pulled away from the field, all except for Mario, who was running at what seemed to be a leisurely pace with a comfortable lead. Paulie chased him, chased him as hard as he could, ignoring the hammering of his heart, his lungs aching for air. Sadly, he gained no ground. Paulie reached inside for one last burst, a burst that would have been to no avail had Mario's left sandal strap not suddenly snapped off at the sole. The sandal, expensive and fashionable but not made for racing, twisted sideways and flew off. Mario stumbled, but still staggered forward, half-barefoot, toward the finish line.

Paulie, spotting his nemesis falter, surged; they were neck and neck as they hurtled toward the finish line, both men reaching forward for Richie's arms, extended out like two signposts. Richie's right hand fluttered forward, like a hummingbird's wings, almost too fast for the naked eye, and slapped his uncle's flailing hand. As both men raced past him, Richie lifted the megaphone he'd tucked between his legs and proclaimed, "The winner—Uncle Paulie!"

Mario regained his balance and immediately began protesting the call. Paulie thrust his arms up in victory. Someone in the crowd restarted the chant "Pau-lie! Pau-lie! Pau-lie!" Richie grabbed a medal from the pile and raced over to drape it over his uncle's head. Tony and Alex ran over to congratulate their father, who was still jogging in a circle, pumping his arms in the air. Someone jumped out from the crowd, holding up a Polaroid camera. "Let's get a picture of the winners." Paulie threw his arm around Tony—father and son, both adorned with red, white, blue, and gold. The neighbor brought the camera to his face, and as Alex tried to join, stepping in front of his father as he often did for family shots, Paulie shoved him out of frame just as the camera flashed. Paulie launched himself in another victory lap, the crowd still chanting his name. As he ran toward the avenue, arms pumping in the air, he decided not to loop back around. No, this time he kept running, forward, to his car, to Johnny, to victory.

Paulie ran and ran, the cheers of neighbors and strangers alike still echoing in his ears. He ran and ran, both arms thrust upright, raised in triumph, dripping with sweat. He did not break stride until he'd swerved around the blockade at the end of the block and, dropping his arms into a pumping motion, was forced to run in place for a moment as one lone vehicle approached, a wood-paneled station wagon. The driver eased off the accelerator at the sight of the running man, likely fearing he might attempt to rush across the avenue in front of him. Paulie noticed the driver slow, that he stared at him a little too long; he saw the man's wife in the front passenger seat crane her red head forward to do the same, and in the back seat, two children pressed their chubby faces against the rear window, staring at him like he was some oddity. Half the neighborhood was exploding, literally, and these people want to stare at him like he was an escaped circus gorilla. Well, he wasn't a gorilla, or some homeless bum wandering the streets. He was a winner. Paulie charged the vehicle, arms punching into the air, and roared, "Yeaaaaaaaah!" The children in the back seat recoiled from the window; the driver's eyes widened with surprise, and he quickly floored the gas pedal. His wife's hands flapped over her head as the station wagon lurched forward in a sudden burst of acceleration and sped away.

Paulie continued across the street and down the next block. Hearing the rumble of an approaching B train, Paulie turned right onto New Utrecht Avenue to shadow its path. As the train roared overhead, the daylight shining through the tracks vanished and flashed again. Paulie felt like he was running through lightning and thunder, like he *was* lightning and thunder, his heart beating harder now, the alcohol he'd consumed dripping out through every pore. He ran faster, trying to keep up with the powerful engine above, but it soon pulled away, leaving him to run alone through the quiet, broken shadows beneath the tracks. At the end of the next block, Paulie saw the familiar wooden barricades of another block party. He turned a sharp left onto the block, still running, arms alternating between being held up high and pumping at his side.

He ran down the block, a block barely distinguishable from his own. There were the same crowded gates, the same bridge tables covered with paper and plastic tablecloths emblazoned with the stars and stripes. Paulie weaved his way through the crowd, eyes intent and focused; he repeatedly pumped his fists above his head in anticipation of continued smiles and cheers. Instead, the smaller children scattered at his approach, some elderly revelers sitting close to the edge of the curbs to better watch their grandchildren play shot the strange running man dirty looks, but most failed to even no-tice him. Midway down the block, Paulie reached for the gold-tinted aluminum medal that hung from his neck. He pinched it between thumb and index finger, then lifted and flashed it to those he passed like it was a police shield. After a few paces, he dropped it and let it swing back and forth like a pendulum over his belly, his eyes focused straight; he'd run to his car and then find Johnny. It wasn't too late.

CHAPTER 20

"Yo, your pops is nuts," a grinning Sally told Tony, slicing his arm and hand through the air in emphasis.

"I guess." Tony wasn't quite sure what to think. He'd never seen his father drink beer—he'd barely seen him drink at all. He'd only spied him at the occasional holiday dinner fill half a glass with red wine and then the remainder with Coca-Cola. To his knowledge, the only alcohol they even kept in the house was a bottle of Dewar's White Label solely for when Uncle Frank paid a visit. As a matter of fact, Tony remembered that Uncle Frank gave his father that bottle when Alex was born. It remained half-full.

Just ahead, the DJ cued up a new record, dropped the needle onto the vinyl, and the screeching of electric guitar clawed out of the massive speakers.

"For all you rockers out there," the DJ bellowed into his microphone, *"KISS!"*

"Yeaaaaaaaah!" someone shouted over the music. Suddenly, there was a gaggle of denim and black T-shirts crowded around the speakers, people hopping up and down, someone playing air guitar, another a set of air drums, one gangly kid with pimples and glasses strumming an air bass. Sally bobbed his head along to the beat with increasing speed, pumping his fist into the air.

"Since when you like rock?" Tony asked.

"I don't give a fuck." Sally grinned. "I like anything that gets me pumped." Sally began to jump and spin around, arms flailing in what looked like the culmination of some orgasmic tribal dance. Tony laughed. His friend never seemed to have a care in the world. Sally could walk through a buffalo stampede during an earthquake and hailstorm looking like he was taking a morning stroll across a beach. Must be nice not to give a fuck.

Tony went back to scanning the crowd. He wondered if Maria was even still planning to come by or if she had gotten lost in the affairs of her own block, her own family, her own bullshit too? Maybe she'd just changed her mind. Why bother with a guy who's still treated like a toddler by his own parents? Suddenly there was a *pop!* in front of him, and he felt something brush by his leg. He looked down and saw Alex run by, flashing a mischievous smile, clutching his little cardboard box in his hand.

Speaking of not giving a fuck . . . maybe he had it backward. Maybe he was better off like his brother—content with a toy that cost a quarter and the thrill of running through the street, chasing his friends. What would Alex's greatest challenge be when third grade started after summer had passed—learning long division? All you had to do in grammar school was just sit there and try not to piss your pants until recess, when the nuns would let you use the lavatory. Maybe that was the life—no worries, no job, girls still just something to be annoyed by, to avoid crashing into while playing in the schoolyard; no worries about having to keep your grades up in a new school to maintain your scholarship; no worries about having to impress a new coach, trying to hit the ball harder and farther than everyone else; not having to work five nights a week so you had some money in your pocket and wouldn't have your mother looking over your shoulder twenty-four seven. No pressure. Not feeling like you were on fire, like you were about to explode every time you thought about holding Maria in your arms.

"You good?" Tony heard Sally's voice, knew he was being addressed, but didn't turn. His breathing had become rapid, his chest noticeably rising and falling. Sally repeated, "You good?"

"What? Yeah, yeah," Tony replied. "I'm . . . It's just too fucking hot."

"You're overheated." Sally pointed his finger at a spot right between Tony's eyes. "Look at you. You're all wound up from the race. You're like a fucking thoroughbred once you get started. You gotta work that off." He sprinted ahead a few steps, his elbows and knees jutting out at odd angles like they did whenever he tried to run. He spun around, backpedaling in a slow, clumsy jog while facing Tony. "C'mon, man, want to race me?" Sally cajoled him. "You know if I kept running in the race, you wouldn't be wearing no medal." Sally gestured with the point of his chin toward the shiny circle that Tony, like his father, still wore around his neck. "I'm like fuckin' Secretariat once these legs get stretched out," Sally insisted, slapping the sides of his thighs as he pumped his knees high, almost losing his balance. He transitioned midstumble into a boxer's dance, circling Tony, who continued his aimless march up the block. "You want to box instead? Huh? Huh?"

Sally threw clumsy jabs that fell safely a foot short of his friend, his long flailing arms looking more like he was trying to shoo a fly away than land a punch. Try as he might, Tony couldn't suppress his smirk as Sally windmilled one arm, crouched down, popped back up, and almost hit himself in the mouth.

"You're gonna knock yourself out," Tony told his friend.

"I'm the only one who can," Sally said, bobbing and weaving. Tony held up both his hands, palms flat, pressing down against the humid air, urging Sally to take it down a notch. Just then, one of Sally's errant roundhouses grazed the shirt of a passerby.

"What the fuck!" the person shouted.

Sally, lost in his own world, still danced and feinted, unaware the shout was meant for him. Tony's muscles tensed immediately as he recognized the face attached to the voice. It was Marco Lombardi, red faced with a bit of spittle hanging from his mouth, and just off Marco's shoulder, his brother Benny, smiling like the devil.

"Huh," Sally said quizzically, unaware of the incidental contact.

"What the fuck," Marco shouted again and got in Sally's face.

"Get the fuck outta my face," Sally shouted and shoved Marco, who stumbled back a step but quickly recovered his footing. "What's your fucking problem?" Sally flung his arms out in emphasis.

"You fucking sucker punched me!" Marco screamed. He pointed at Sally with his left hand, his right balled into a fist at his side. Tony's eyes darted between Marco, Sally, and then Benny, still smirking.

"Who the fuck are you? Get the fuck off my block." Sally slung his hand dismissively through the air.

"Yeah. You make me," Marco spat back, his mouth twisting into a sadistic smirk. "C'mon, you fucking pussy!" Sally lunged forward to oblige him, but Tony's arms were already wrapped around his waist, holding him back.

"Easy, easy." Tony tried to calm Sally down. He shouted around his friend at Marco. "Relax! It was an accident."

The spectacle soon drew notice. The crowd milling around by the DJ had heard the shouts, and in seconds, a circle of spectators surrounded the teenage standoff.

Marco feigned charging several times, taunting Sally. "Tell your girlfriend to let you go. C'mon!"

Sally tried in vain to shake Tony loose, shouting, "Let me fucking go! Tony, let me fucking go!"

The number of onlookers swelled, their ranks now bolstered by younger kids screaming, "Fight! Fight!"

Tony wasn't even sure why he was holding Sally back, but that was his first instinct, to stop something bad from happening. Besides, just about every "fight" Tony had witnessed mostly involved guys shouting at each other and puffing out their chests. In the rare times the situation escalated to physicality, it more resembled a dance than a brawl—the dual headlock tango. Two red-faced kids wrapping an arm around the other's skull, twisting themselves into a pretzel, never throwing a punch, just waiting for people to pull them apart. It all seemed silly.

The present standoff with Marco continued. The middle Lombardi looked around and dropped his fists to his side. Marco wasn't stupid—he was taunting someone on a block that wasn't his own; he was a foreign aggressor, and folks in this neighborhood looked out for their own. He lingered still, though, held his ground and ignored the shouts to get off the block. Sally, still held back by Tony, had calmed somewhat. Marco pivoted and began to turn to walk away. That's when Benny chimed in.

"Hey, Tony!" Benny shouted. "Maybe this is why Maria just blew me. She knew you already have a boyfriend."

Tony's arms fell away from Sally. He stepped in front of him.

"What did you say?" Tony asked, head turned and cocked as if to listen better with one ear. Benny grinned wider.

"You heard me. She just sucked me off again," Benny said, pointing to his own groin. "You're a joke, begging for my sloppy seconds!"

All that heat, the burning restlessness coursing through Tony's blood all day—that was little more than a cool spring breeze compared to what blazed inside him now. Tony felt a smoldering heat behind his eyes and at the base of his neck. It flared, expanded, pushed right through his skin. He wasn't even aware he was already in motion, charging forward, away from Sally, pouncing on Benny, a wild fist swinging, grazing his chin. He swung with his left, then right again, but he was already being pulled away, arms wrapped around him, restraining him.

Benny turned to Marco and laughed. They both pointed and laughed. Tony lost it. He struggled violently to shake loose; silver streetlights, brick, and concrete spun by as he whirled around. Free, he charged at Benny.

"Tony, stop! Tony!" He heard someone shout but ignored it. He clawed at Benny once, threw a wild punch that sailed right in front of Benny's chin. Marco lunged at Tony; Sally dove at Marco. Then they were all pulled apart again, restrained. Tony panted like a bull, eyes glazed over, struggling to free himself. Suddenly he felt a hand slap his face. Awareness returned. He blinked once, twice, eyes focusing on who it was that had just struck him. It was his mother, who, with tears in her eyes, lifted her right hand to strike again.

CHAPTER 21

Paulie, drenched in sweat, finally reached the avenue where his car was parked. Good thing too: he was running on fumes, panting heavily; the trek up the last block was more of a lumber than a sprint. Despite the fatigue, Paulie willed his legs forward, a drunk-like stagger, causing more than one parent to pull their child from his path. His forward progress came to an abrupt halt, as the sidewalk and street in front of him were packed with cheering people. Paulie took the opportunity to catch his breath. He glanced around, confused as to why such a crowd had gathered. It was still bright out, way too early for any fireworks show. He heard some occasional muffled popping nearby, but that certainly wouldn't draw a crowd like this—not today, at least. He tried to slip through the crowd, but the weariness of his legs left him unable to navigate with any precision. He decided instead to let the weight of his exhausted body teeter forward and ignored the dirty looks of people he expected to move out of the way. More than one annoyed person shoved him back, shouting, "Watch it!" Undeterred, Paulie let that momentum drive him forward. One final push allowed him to break through to the front of the crowd and, unfortunately, directly into a parking meter. His right knee bashed into the steel pole, the leg buckled, and he dropped hard to the pavement. A jolt of pain shot up his right side as he grimaced and cursed out loud. An elderly woman who stood nearby with her grandchildren quickly reprimanded him for his language. *"Disgraziato,"* she said as she sneered down at him.

Paulie shook off the initial pain from the fall. If nothing else, the tumble had shaken the cobwebs from his head—the combination of fatigue, alcohol, and sun. He needed to remain on mission. He just had to make it to his car.

Paulie pulled himself upright, his right knee throbbing in pain. He winced and turned his head. He spied the reason for this congregation. Slowly approaching down the avenue was the procession of a saint. Which saint, he wasn't quite sure yet. The neighborhood was filled with Italian American "social clubs," sponsored by a certain segment of the population. Each of these clubs had adopted a Catholic porcelain statue and shrine. The Manhattan and downtown-Brooklyn clubs had laid claimed to the Blessed Mother, San Gennaro, and the other major saints. Bensonhurst was left with the D-list of heavenly hosts, statues named for the patron protector of long-abandoned Sicilian villages. Paulie was somewhat suspicious; some of the saints' names sounded made up, but the people who ran the clubs weren't the kinds of characters that took kindly to questions. So, on occasions when horns and cymbals were heard and a social club's doors swung open and a barge and shrine emerged, everyone just lined up. The masses cheered and held up whatever bills they had in their wallets and purses, waving them high over their heads as the gentlemen bearers in their green and red sashes passed, their silent stares seemingly commanding the onlookers:

Approach and offer homage, tens and twenties preferred, but all cash denominations accepted.

As the procession paused, the saint hovered directly in front of Paulie. He gazed up at its porcelain visage, which had a certain androgynous air to it. The eyes and nose seemed distinctly male, yet the lips were painted a bright shade of red and had the slightest hint of a pucker to them. The saint's yellow curls fell upon the shoulders of a sky blue robe. The base of the shrine was piled high with white carnations, obscuring the contour of its torso. What did all this have to do with the Bicentennial? Who knows? Everyone needed to wet their beaks.

Paulie then flinched as arms flew up around him, hands stretching forward to slide their cash offerings under the red and green ribbons snaked around the shrine, while those farther back simply balled up their dollar bills and tossed them onto the bed of white flowers. Paulie again winced, the pain in his knee growing in intensity. Turning his head, he recognized the shrine bearer closest to him by the white linen cap he still wore. Paulie's face flashed with anger; he opened his mouth to speak. Instantly, the man in the cap's expression morphed into one of intimidation. Paulie turned away, the challenge unaccepted. Paulie then waited a few moments before glancing back; he mistook the sway of the crowd for movement, and when he turned back, the man in the cap still stared. Paulie froze until, slowly, the man in the cap's gaze slowly lowered to Paulie's hip, the bulge of Paulie's wallet. The man in the cap raised an eyebrow, and Paulie found himself digging out his wallet. He fished out the sole remaining dollar bills in its fold. He reached forward to slide the offering onto the Shrine of Saint Him or Her. The man in the cap turned forward, muttered something, and the procession continued. Paulie took a deep breath, praying the march was almost over. His car was parked just across the street, and it was getting late. He needed to get to Johnny.

CHAPTER 22

Dee had rolled her eyes the moment she heard her neighbor Frances Magliavo call her name repeatedly as she waddled over to where she sat. The afternoon sun's path left her with just a sliver of shade. Soon even that would vanish.

"Dee! Dee!" Frances called again, in a voice like a strangled cat. On a block full of busybodies, Frances was probably the worst of the bunch, always trying to dig into other people's business, looking to stir up trouble. Dee shook her head. This woman was the mother of an eleven-year-old dullard of a son who had already been held back twice—in public school—and a thirteen-year-old daughter who painted her face like the Whore of Babylon. Certainly, this was someone who should mind her own house before poking her nose into other people's affairs. Dee sighed as Frances's faded red slippers slid to a stop just a few feet from where she sat in the shade. Despite her disdain for fireworks, a part of Dee wished a rocket would come whistling down from the sky and fly straight into this woman's big mouth.

"Dee, your son, your son!" Frances bellowed, her hands flapping in emphasis at her side.

"What about my son, Frances?" Dee growled back without meeting her neighbor's gaze. "Old people can't take the heat. Alex had nothing to do with it." Dee shook her head, annoyed. Couldn't she just have one moment's peace?

"Not Alex." Frances flapped her hands so rapidly that, had she been a few dozen pounds lighter, she might have lifted from the pavement, like some giant Sicilian hummingbird. "It's Tony. Tony!" Frances exclaimed.

Dee's head snapped around, and she shot out of her chair and snatched Frances's wrist midflap. The woman's hand twitched and fell limp in Dee's grip.

"What about Tony?" Dee yelled.

"He's fighting up the block. He's fighting!"

Dee flung Frances's wrist away as she rushed past her and marched up the block, her heart pounding in her chest. She really had the horns on her today, Dee told herself again; she really did. The heat of her pooling tears stung her eyes as she scanned the crowded street, searching for her son.

The crowd swelled thickest around the DJ; there were still too many damn kids flying around on their bikes. (And where was Alex, for that matter? She'd taken her eyes off him for two seconds. He should still be punished, locked upstairs in their apartment, for what he'd done. Why did she ever listen to Paulie? The man was useless.) The first tear streamed down her cheek as she charged forward, not pausing for anyone, adult or child. It felt like there was a great weight pressing down against the back of her neck and shoulders, trying to crush her into the pavement, but still her legs carried her forward: she would not fall; she would not crumble. It was up to her, always up to her. She couldn't take her eyes off her children for a second, not one second. Oh, to have a clear head, like the greaseballs from the other side, the ones that, as soon as the sun rose, tossed their kids out into the street like they were dogs. How she wished she could go around with a clear head like the women who were always dolled up, always with the makeup on and their hair set. Not one of them could bear her responsibility. They'd trip and fall over their high heels; that's if they weren't already one of the broken ones—the ones whose husbands and children came and went as they pleased, the ones who were trampled over like they were doormats. Those women couldn't hold a candle to her, let alone her own mother, may she rest in peace. And the children knew; that's why those women got no respect, why their kids talked back and acted like animals, why the boys left them for the first *buttana* who came along and spread her legs. Dee would have never left her mother. Ever. If Dee could have clawed her own chest open and ripped out her lungs to give them to her mother, she would have, without hesitation.

Dee's face was a deep scarlet by the time she reached the outskirts of the altercation. A circle of animals, shouting and screaming. She elbowed her way between two teenage boys—both tall and gangly and in her way. As one was shoved aside, he turned to bark a complaint, but the sight of Dee, red faced and teary eyed, gave him pause. Unbeknownst to her, Dee's presence had caused an immediate receding of spectators, specifically the residents of the block who knew it was best to make way.

Dee spotted Tony, thrashing around like some wild animal. There was her Tony, spit shooting from his mouth as he shouted threats and obscenities, his face as red as her own. There was Sally, struggling to restrain Tony as he whirled around, his fists swinging wildly. Dee paid no attention to whoever was the intended target. What did it matter what louse was on the opposite side? He wasn't her son, her own flesh and blood.

Though her path was now unobstructed, Dee's final steps toward her son felt as if she were trudging through deep water. Drawing closer, she saw how her son's face had twisted in anger to something horrific. The fear in her heart—in her whole being—felt like it was going to crush her, but she was too outraged to give in to it. She had labored every single moment of the past fourteen years making sure that her son didn't wind up like every other punk in this neighborhood; making sure he was in the right school, that he went to church; making sure she kept him off the streets away from the trash, all the lowlifes and tramps. To Dee, it had all come unglued in one day.

Sally was the last to be tossed aside. Instinctively he'd cocked his fist as he felt someone grab him from behind, but upon turning to see Dee, he immediately withdrew. Sally faded from her view like the rest the crowd, the rest of the block. There was only her son, tensed and coiled, the epicenter of the colors and noise that blurred and swirled along the fringes.

The instant she swung him around, her open palm struck the side of his face. The second and third slaps followed with a speed so alarming it wasn't until the fourth swing that her son was able to throw his own hands up to shield himself. Dee would later admit that she never intended to hit him once, let alone again and again. She never meant to embarrass him in front of so many people. In the span of a few seconds, the crowd cheering for violence chuckled at the overprotective mother and then winced and turned their heads away from the public humiliation.

But it was her son. That was Dee's only excuse. It was her son.

CHAPTER 23

Many years ago, on the Lower East Side of Manhattan, lived a little girl named Dorotea. She was born to Italian immigrants, Ciro and Pietra, who spoke little English. Ciro was the youngest of four brothers, all born in Casoria, Italy. He'd defied his aging parents and overbearing brothers by forgoing the life of a pig farmer to instead cast his lot in America. Pietra was an only child, a rarity at the time. The two met, fell in love, and were married shortly after they'd each arrived in America. They tried for almost a decade to have a child, but Pietra's first three pregnancies never survived the first trimester. The couple held their breath every minute of Pietra's fourth attempt—nine months of novenas and lit church candles. On a sunny June day, their baby girl was born. They named her Dorotea—"gift of God." Ciro, of course, had wished for a son and secretly hoped his wife might still be able to provide him with one. A gender preference never crossed Pietra's mind; the first time she held her daughter, her heart swelled so that she thought it might explode in her chest.

Not long after the child's arrival, a half-deaf Irish nun marched into their hospital room. She introduced herself as Sister Mary Catherine and began asking questions to complete the birth certificate application. In fairness, she did her best with Ciro and Pietra's accents, but in the end, she penciled the name *Dolores* on the application. It was the name of another girl born in the same hospital the night before. If only Sister Mary Catherine had been a cinephile—and less deaf—she might have at least Americanized it properly to *Dorothy*. The mistake was irrelevant for years, as her parents always addressed and introduced her as Dorotea.

The transmutation of her proper birth name was not discovered until some years later when Pietra walked her daughter by the hand several blocks from their Mott Street tenement building to the imposing brick castle that was PS 130 to enroll Dorotea in school. The young girl squeezed her mother's hand tightly as their footsteps echoed through the empty hall that led to the main office. Once inside, Pietra extracted the birth certificate from her purse and unfolded it flat on top of the tall, wide counter that split the narrow office into two narrower halves. Mother and daughter stood unnoticed by the school receptionist, busy typing away at her corner desk, until Pietra cleared her throat several times to gain her attention. The receptionist, fighting a summer cold, rose slowly. As she crossed the floor, she dabbed her nose with a tissue and, once at the counter, stood up on her toes to peer over. She regarded little Dorotea, standing shyly, adorned in a dress her mother had sewn. The receptionist glanced at the name on the birth certificate and back to the girl.

"Hello, Dolores," the receptionist addressed her in a nasal voice. Dorotea stared back blankly, unsure who the woman was speaking to. The receptionist repeated herself once more to the same result. Fearing the girl was deaf, the receptionist reached over her desk and loudly snapped her fingers directly beside Dorotea's right ear. The girl immediately flinched and stepped back to hide behind her mother. The receptionist shrugged, then swiveled in her char to pull a mimeographed clip of paper from a stack sitting in a wire mesh tray. She began scribbling down the child's information while continuing to dab the tissue at her runny nostrils.

Once finished, the receptionist handed the bottom yellow copy to Pietra. She folded it several times and then tucked it, along with the birth certificate, back into her small black purse that she held close to her breast, and mother and daughter turned to go home. The purse blended into the black of Pietra's dress, the only color she'd worn for the past several months since the tragic death of her son, Dorotea's baby brother. It would be the only color she'd wear for the remainder of her life. And though Pietra's face betrayed no sign of joy, she was pleased that her daughter would soon start school. It would be good for her to have someplace to go.

On the day of the fire, a frigid but bright Tuesday in late February, Dorotea was kneeling in the hallway of her building, just several doors down from her apartment, playing jacks with the Lowenstein twins, two girls her age who lived on the floor below, and a little boy who followed the twins around like a lost puppy. She was quite pleased that the boy regarded her with complete disinterest. It was bad enough that she had to contend with her baby brother. Dorotea had thought having a sibling would be fun, like having a new doll to play with. Instead, all the eight-month-old did was cry all day and pull at the hem of her dress as he crawled by, like she was some stepladder to be climbed. Dorotea had bounced the little red rubber ball high into the air, swept her hand across the dusty floor, and scooped up a fistful of eightsies, when she heard her mother call for her. Despite being a dutiful child, she grunted in resentment, knowing what she was being summoned for. She told her friends she'd be right back. Sure enough, as soon as Dorotea stepped foot into her apartment, Pietra charged her with minding her brother. Pietra's recovery from her second child's birth, even these months later, remained difficult. Not that the discomfort and fatigue afforded her any respite. She was a wife and mother of two children; there was work to be done. Pietra set a pot of water to boil on the stove as she finished cleaning the chicken and chopping vegetables. Soon, Pietra carefully dropped the chicken and vegetables into the rolling boil and set the burner to simmer. She was suddenly overcome with fatigue; she almost felt faint. She called for her daughter.

Inside their apartment, Dorotea lamented to her mother that she was about to win her game, and Pietra reassured her that she'd just be a few minutes. *Watch your brother,* she told her in Italian. *Stay out of the kitchen.* Pietra disappeared into her bedroom and fell into a deep sleep the moment her head hit her pillow. Dorotea stood with her arms folded, watching her little brother, Antonio, crawl in circles. After several minutes ticked by, both siblings tired, and Antonio now sat still, fumbling a wooden block from hand to hand. Dorotea had plopped herself down several feet away, crossed her legs Indian style, and waited impatiently. When she heard her friends' shouts echo through the hall, calling for her to finish their game, she contemplated a small defiance. Antonio now lay on his side, his eyelids heavy. He was probably going to conk out any second. She bet she could win her game and be back before either mother or brother had even noticed. Slowly she rose, careful not to make a sound. As she tiptoed toward the front door, she had another idea. For safe measure, Dorotea carried, as quickly and quietly as she could manage, two chairs from the dinner table over to block the kitchen's open entranceway. The eight wooden legs seemed more than an adequate obstacle. She'd be right back anyway.

As soon as Dorotea stepped out of the apartment, Antonio grew curious as to where his sister had gone. He began crawling for the door, but halfway there noticed the strange obstruction his sister had built. He scurried across the floor and navigated around the chair legs and onto the cold kitchen floor. He started toward the stove and, once there, managed to pull himself up by a dishtowel looped over the handle of the oven drawer. Then, either out of pride in his accomplishment or simply for amusement, the child tore loose the dishtowel and began whipping it up and down. One grease-stained tip sailed too close to the flames and caught fire. The chubby legs of the startled child collapsed beneath him, and he fell on the small runner that ran the length of stove and sink. The blazing cloth fell over him. He screamed.

Pietra woke in a panic and rushed out of the bedroom, into the smoke-filled living room. Inside the kitchen, the child's cotton dress, a Dorotea hand-me-down, and the narrow small rug were completely in flames. Pietra charged into the kitchen, and in her haste, she tripped over the chairs blocking her way and crashed hard into the floor. Despite the pain slicing through her right arm, she crawled and threw herself over her child, trying to smother the flames.

Dorotea was about to go for tensies when she heard her mother's scream. It froze her completely. She turned and looked down the hall; smoke billowed from the open doorway of her apartment. Seconds later there was a great commotion, doors being swung open, people shouting and running past. Someone kicked the red ball and sent it careening down the hall. Someone stepped on her foot, and Dorotea screamed, and suddenly she was scooped up into the arms of a neighbor who was part of the stampede rifling through the hall into and down four flights of the narrow stairwell and finally into the cold winter air. Dorotea, set down on the sidewalk, struggled to see above the heads of her neighbors now crowded along the sidewalk. There was a collective gasp, and a flame exploded from Dorotea's kitchen window, followed by plumes of black smoke spiraling into the sky. A freezing and frightened Dorotea looked around for her mother. She flinched at the piercing scream of approaching sirens. Soon there were policemen and firefighters barreling into her building. Dorotea wormed her way to the front of the swelling crowd just as two firemen emerged from the front door carrying her unconscious mother, the hem and sleeves of her dress still smoldering, out the doorway and down the front stoop. Then another fireman emerged, hunched over, cradling something small and burnt in his arms. Dorotea felt dizzy; everything went black.

In the hours immediately following the fire, most residents agreed that as far as tenement fires go, this one could have been much worse. The fire had somehow stubbornly refused to spread beyond the kitchen. That fact did little to lessen the tragedy of the lone casualty.

When Dorotea woke, she was curled in a fetal position in a chair inside a hospital room. She was unsure of how she'd arrived there and blinked several times, trying to shake away the cobwebs. She noticed her mother lying unconscious in the bed beside her. As her head began to fill with questions, from the hallway she heard a growing commotion and one familiar voice. She turned and spotted her father amid several other men, all covered with the dust and sweat of a full morning's work. Ciro, his face ashen, grave with concern, rushed into the room, the other men remaining just outside the doorway.

Upon his arrival in America, Ciro had been fortunate to have been befriended by a family of bricklayers who taught him their trade, one that would serve him better in New York City than pig farming. Ciro worked whenever and wherever he could. To not work, even for a day, was to risk your spot. Truth was that father and daughter saw relatively little of each other. He was often off to work by the time Dorotea woke and frequently did not return home until after she'd been put to bed. Most of their interaction was limited to the rare nights Ciro returned home earlier than usual from work. Pietra had taken up the habit of allowing Dorotea to carry the small cup of espresso from the kitchen to her father after he'd finished his supper. Dorotea treasured these moments, her father's attention fixed solely on her. She carried out her task with solemn responsibility, glancing nervously up at her father and then back down to the surface ripples of the espresso as the small cup rattled within the saucer, despite her careful steps. Dorotea watched her father inhale deeply through his nostrils, savoring the rich aroma of the espresso. She loved the way he gazed back intently, his lips pressed together with just the hint of a smile at the corners. Finally, without spilling a drop, Dorotea would lower the cup onto the frayed lace placemat in front of her father. Espresso delivered, Dorotea swelled with contentment at the sight of her father's small grin, the nod of his head, and the gentle pat that she received on her head. This was the greatest expression of joy that she ever witnessed her father exhibit. That was until her brother was born, and then Dorotea watched her father's eyes fill with wonder, watched him smile so wide and laugh so loud each time he bounced his new baby boy on his lap.

Ciro rushed into the hospital room only to halt abruptly at the sight of his wife, lying unconscious and bandaged. He recovered and continued to the foot of her bed, only then noticing his daughter seated in the chair beside her mother. He glanced over to Dorotea and nodded his head once in reassurance, much like he did after she'd successfully delivered his evening espresso. Ciro turned, hearing a doctor enter the room. The other men, still huddled at the doorway, parted to make way for him. The doctor cleared his throat once before tersely introducing himself and launching into his summation of the situation. Seeing Ciro's blank expression, the doctor sighed and looked up at the ceiling as he asked if anyone in the room spoke English. The question was intended for the men still huddled at the doorway, but it was Dorotea who answered first.

"I do," she said.

The doctor turned and regarded Dorotea, holding her hand up straight like some circus oddity—a seal balancing a ball on its snout. The corner of his mouth twitched as he stared down at her. One of the men in the hallway then took a solitary step into the room, cleared his throat, and in broken English offered his services. Dorotea recognized the man. It was Giacomo, her father's padrone. The title just a decade or two earlier carried with it expectations of fealty and indentured servitude for immigrant workers. Those times had ended, and it was now mostly used as a term of respect for a bricklayer or mason's foreman, always a somewhat-bilingual man who answered to the real bosses. Her father had brought Giacomo home for dinner more than once, bragging that his wife made the best *pasta con le sarde*, pasta with sardines, anchovies, and fennel, on this side of the Atlantic.

The doctor now crossed the room and spoke in a low voice to Giacomo. Dorotea saw something grim flicker in Giacomo's eyes. The doctor finished speaking and took one step back. Giacomo drew closer to Ciro. He opened his mouth to speak; his right hand rose and began to spin in small circles at the wrist as he visibly struggled to find the right words. His gaze strayed sideways for a moment, and he locked eyes with Dorotea, who stared back intently. He quickly turned away from her and back to Ciro. Giacomo drew in a deep breath and began to speak. Dorotea shuddered as her father's face flushed, and his right hand shot forward and seized Giacomo by the throat. Ciro swung his head to his wife momentarily before turning back to Giacomo, who stiffened in his grasp like a small animal in the powerful jaws of a predator. Ciro's mouth opened like he was about to roar, but there was no roar; there was no sound at all. Dorotea couldn't quite understand what she was witnessing: one moment her father was ten feet tall, the next it looked as if he were being broken in quarters. His knees buckled first; then he folded at his waist and finally fell backward into the steel frame at the foot of the hospital bed where his wife lay and then onto the white tile floor. As he hit, his head sloped forward with such finality, Dorotea feared him dead. No one moved or spoke a word; Dorotea was scared to even take a breath. A few frozen seconds passed, and Dorotea saw her father stir. He brought his arms and hands up over his head as if he were trying to muffle some terrible noise that only he could hear. Then he let loose an anguished howl that sent shivers up Dorotea's spine. The howl faded and gave way to long, harrowing sobs. Just as Dorotea began to feel dizzy once more, she heard her mother call her name.

Dorotea turned. Pietra now sat upright in bed. She was pale and bandaged but held her chin high and wore a look of steely resolve that instantly anchored her daughter. As her father continued to sob, her mother called to her once more, in a familiar tone suggesting she was in no mood to be kept waiting. Dorotea immediately stood up and walked to her mother's bedside. Her mother patted the mattress beside her, and Dorotea climbed up into the bed to sit beside her. Her mother flinched slightly as she lifted her arm and curled it around her daughter and pulled her close. Dorotea closed her eyes, the sounds of her father's sobs now turning to gasps. He still sat crumpled at the foot of the bed. The doctor and Giacomo tended to him while Dorotea sat cradled in her mother's arms.

Dorotea spent the following three days with the twins' family, sleeping in one bed while the sisters shared the other. When Dorotea asked about her parents, the twins' mother, Mrs. Lowenstein, assured her that they were fine and would soon come for her. (And while Mrs. Lowenstein thought the omission curious, she was quite relieved to not have to field any questions regarding the deceased brother.) On the third morning, there was a knock at their door. Dorotea smiled as her mother, wearing a simple black dress, entered the apartment. Dorotea ran over to embrace her. Her mother whispered down into her ear that it was time to go home.

Downstairs in their apartment, Dorotea quickly noticed that her brother's basinet, which had sat in the living room during the daytime, was gone, along with any reminders that the child had ever existed. It seemed strange, as if some vast cover-up had been perpetuated. It was only the last vestiges of the acrid stench from the charred floor that betrayed any sign of the tragedy, even after a small battalion of housewives had scrubbed the black stain for two days. Another family's donated rug covered the scarred section of wood. Despite the efforts, Dorotea understood perfectly what had happened. And despite her youth, she realized that she should have felt worse about it than she did. The little boy that screamed and cried all the time and pulled her own toys from her hands, the boy who made her father's eyes light up, her brother, was dead. And yet it was not his death that distressed her. What distressed her instead was the sight of her father sitting at the table staring vacantly through the open doorway to the kitchen. She had no idea how long he'd been sitting there. His face was unshaven, his clothes crumpled. Dorotea slowly approached him.

"Poppa," she said, but he did not respond. Pietra summoned her daughter and told her to go play.

For two days, Ciro continued to sit at the table. He did not go to work; he ate no food set before him. He did not even ask for espresso at night; he just sat and reached for a bottle of wine that never seemed to empty. When her bedtime came, Dorotea would approach her father to say good night only to have her mother suddenly appear in her path, spin her around, and shoo her to bed.

On the third evening after returning home, Dorotea sat cross-legged in the corner of the living room, playing with her jacks. Her father was still at the table, her mother inside the kitchen, stewing a pot of escarole and cannellini beans for dinner. Pietra soon emerged from the kitchen carrying a large bowl that she set down on the table. She called for Dorotea to sit for dinner. Ciro said nothing; he did not even look up as his wife and daughter joined him at the table. With a ladle, Pietra filled everyone's bowl with steaming portions, dripping in olive oil, and then sat herself to eat.

The room was silent except for the sound of Pietra and Dorotea chewing and swallowing. Dorotea ate quickly; this was one of her favorite meals. Her bowl half-consumed, as she reached for the salt-shaker she noticed her father's forearms and hands, which had been lying still on the table in front of him, begin to tremble. Dorotea turned and gasped. It looked like some unseen force had seized her father by the shoulders and begun to violently shake him. His head rolled to one side; his eyes clenched closed—the way he vibrated, it looked to Dorotea like he was trying to keep something horrible trapped inside. Suddenly Ciro's eyes flew open, and he leaped from his chair with such great velocity that Dorotea snapped back in her chair. Ciro seized the two edges of the table closest to him with his hands and loomed menacingly over the table, which now shook in his white-knuckle grip. Dorotea nervously glanced up, saw her father panting like a bull about to charge; then his mouth twisted into a brief snarl before it cracked open.

"HAI UCCISO MIO FIGLIO!" he shouted across the table. *You*

killed my son! Dorotea froze, too scared even to breathe. The table still shook in her father's grasp, the tremors edging it closer and closer to her mother until it was flush against her chest. Frightened for her mother, Dorotea mustered the courage to reach out and take hold of her father's arm. Ciro's head spun to his daughter. His face, Dorotea would never forget his face, the way his features contorted, first in rage, then in fear, and finally in disgust. He recoiled from the table, turned, and fled out the door.

"Poppa!" Dorotea shouted. But he was already gone.

Pietra neither moved nor spoke. Dorotea briefly feared the same paralyzing disease that had struck her father had now infected her mother. But then Pietra raised her hands from her lap to carefully push the table away from her, back to its rightful place. Then she turned her head to Dorotea and told her to finish her dinner.

Dorotea hoped that when she woke the following morning, she'd find her father at the very least sitting stoically back at the table, but he was nowhere to be seen. She wondered, perhaps, if instead of returning home, maybe he had gone back to work. But when evening came, there was no Poppa. The fire was an accident, so she didn't fully understand why her father was so angry. She was still here, still alive. Her father was still a daddy, still *her* poppa. Wasn't he? She wondered the same on the following day, and the day after that, and the day after that, when there was still no sign of him. Dorotea's mother ignored her husband's absence; it was as if he, like Dorotea's baby brother, had never existed. Pietra didn't even set a plate for him at dinner. Maybe that was the problem, it occurred to Dorotea later that evening. Maybe if Poppa smelled the espresso brewing on the stove, he'd return home. Dorotea sensed the idea would be unwelcomed by her mother. Though forbidden to touch the stove, Dorotea thought it was worth the risk.

She waited until after dinner, when her mother retreated to the bedroom to fold the day's laundry. Dorotea lightly tiptoed into the kitchen and opened the doors to the cupboard beneath the kitchen sink. Slowly and carefully, she liberated the small espresso pot from the pile of other pots and pans. She set the pot down on the kitchen table and quickly disassembled its components and laid them out on a dishtowel. She carried the pot's bottom chamber to the sink and held it just beneath the faucet. She was careful to turn the cold-water handle just slightly so the water quietly filled the chamber. She shut off the water, returned to the table, and replaced the stem and filter basket inside the chamber. Dorotea then scurried over to the narrow pantry and scanned for the short can that read *Medaglia d'Oro*. She found it on a high shelf and had to stretch to reach it.

At the table, Dorotea mimicked the nightly routine she'd watched her mother perform, spooning generous tablespoons of grains into the basket, then (quietly) shaking the stem until the pile leveled off just below the second hash mark. She replaced the cover into its slot, carefully carried the pot to the stove, and placed it on the front burner.

Dorotea took a deep breath and turned the burner lever. The burner clicked twice, and just as it ignited, Dorotea heard footsteps. She turned and saw her mother standing in the kitchen doorway.

"No!" Pietra screamed and rushed over to the stove. Pietra grabbed her daughter by one shoulder and flung her back from the stove. She quickly shut off the burner, and then spun and slapped Dorotea across the face. Dorotea, at first, was more stunned than hurt. Her mother had never raised her hand to her, had never had reason to. Again and again, her mother struck, still screaming, "No! No! No!" Instinctively, Dorotea brought her hands around her head, but her mother's smacks continued to fall, crashing against her arms.

Finally, the slaps slowed. Pietra staggered and fell to her knees; her arms flew around her daughter. For a brief second, Dorotea thought to flee, but instead, feeling the force of her mother's embrace, hearing her mother sobs, she wrapped her own arms around her mother. Mother's and daughter's tears and apologies mingled together. They sat there on the floor, holding each other, holding each other as if they were the only two people left in the world.

CHAPTER 24

Paulie muttered curses while he rubbed his throbbing knee as the procession crawled by at caterpillar speed. His fingers found a significant tear in his pants. Some skin had been scraped from his kneecap along with the polyester; several thin streams of blood streaked down his pant leg.

Images of Alex suddenly flashed into his mind. His youngest always seemed to suffer similar wounds on alternating knees from May through September. The boy would annoyingly sob and flail, like an infant, while Paulie tried to clean the scrapes with a peroxide-soaked cotton ball. There was no peroxide on hand, so Paulie dug into his pants pocket and pulled out a white silk hanky, the sole survivor of a set of three he'd received as a Father's Day gift some years back; he held it up to his mouth and lapped saliva over a spot of fabric with his tongue and then crouched over to dab his wound. Those closest in the crowd had already distanced themselves, wary of his disheveled appearance and agitated grumbling, so he had sufficient space to hunch over and clean his wound.

After a few dabs he straightened up, just as the crowd began to stir and slowly press forward. *Thank God,* Paulie thought. He glanced at the folded hanky as he was about to stuff it back in his pocket and saw it was now stained in red blotches. "Crap," he blurted, then tossed the hanky into the steel mesh trash bin. The silk unfolded midarc and floated like a bloody parachute into the depths of the bin. An exhausted Paulie then joined the crowd as they, thankfully, headed in the direction of his parked car. He grimaced as he stepped down off the curb and began to hobble forward with a pronounced limp.

Soon he'd comfortably plop down in the Olds's front seat, maybe allow himself a few minutes of well-deserved rest as the crowd dispersed and the Holy Shrine of Whoever was tucked away, its likely place of hibernation the back room of some social club. There it would wait until once more summoned forth, at the next feast, block party, or whatever occasion presented itself. If you had a dollar to buy a bag of *zeppoles* or bet on a number at a spinning-wheel game, then you had a dollar to offer in tribute.

An olive-skinned boy walking beside Paulie waved a tiny American flag in one hand, the Italian flag in the other. On the opposite side, two men in brown marched reverently, in full suits and fedoras, not a drop of sweat on either's brow, despite their attire and heat of the day. In contrast, visible patches of perspiration adorned Paulie's shirt; it clung to his sides and underarms and just below his sternum where his belly began to slope outward. He peeled the shirt from the places where it stuck to him and flapped the fabric in false hope that the small current of air might quickly dry both flesh and fabric. The act yielded little result, but it didn't matter; he was almost at his car.

Again, the procession halted. Paulie craned his neck up over the crowd, searching to see why. The shrine had indeed come to find a resting place, but unfortunately it wasn't within the walls of the social club. Instead, the bearers had decided to set it down atop the roof of Paulie's car. The squared roof of the Olds made for an excellent pedestal as the saint regarded the crowd beneath it. Paulie nudged through the crowd, emerging beneath the shrine where the bearers stood, two by two, at opposite ends of the car.

Paulie needed his car. He needed these men to bear the shrine back up over their shoulders and continue on their way. He turned left to meet the gaze of the man in the ivy cap once again. Paulie opened his mouth to speak; the man in the cap stared back, his eyes widened. The two stood suspended in this expression, eyes locked for several seconds until Paulie dug back into his pocket for his last dollar. He crumpled it in his hand and tossed it onto the shrine, where it rolled forward and came to a stop beside the exposed holy porcelain toes. Paulie turned and began to hobble away from his car as the crowd pressed forward all around him. *"Viva Italia!"* they chanted.

CHAPTER 25

One would imagine that the last place Alex wanted to be was near Zizi's house, but once more, there he was, happy as a clam. Of course, this time he wasn't abandoned inside Zizi's apartment, stuck to her plastic furniture, and left alone with her sagging and wrinkled flesh and hateful stare. And though he did occasionally glance back to the front door, still fearful that her grim, accusing face might suddenly appear, he seemed quite content sitting at the highest tier of the low porch wall shared with the adjoining house. His skinny legs dangled over the wall as he kicked his feet, the back soles of his Pro-Keds bouncing off the bricks. In one hand he held his box of snaps, with maybe a half dozen left to enjoy; in the other he held the true source of his contentment—a hot dog he'd already half devoured. It was delicious, perfectly charred, and it rested inside a real bun, the way people ate hot dogs in commercials, not wrapped inside a thin slice of Wonder Bread that immediately turned soggy and pink. The crisp skin exploded in a juicy burst, and Alex couldn't help but smile wide as he chewed.

"Chew with your mouth closed! You're gonna scare the girls away," Alex heard his cousin Richie say. His cousin had peeled away from his group of friends that huddled in the opposite corner of the porch and walked over to him. Alex's eyes widened, and he closed his mouth immediately, his thin lips pressing together. Richie chuckled and gently nudged his cousin with an elbow. "I'm just messing with you."

Alex raised his eyebrows in acknowledgment that he got the joke. He nodded, smiled, and resumed chewing.

Alex never knew what to make of his cousin. Compared to himself, Richie was obviously a "grown-up" but acted more like a kid than like his parents. He couldn't remember ever being alone with Richie without the rest of his family. Most of their interactions revolved around Richie asking him to "slap him five" whenever they crossed paths. Alex would slap his palm with all his strength, and Richie would always feign injury, shaking his wrist as if it had been harmed by the intensity of Alex's slap.

Alex suspected his mother wasn't a fan of Richie, but that hadn't stopped her from barking at her husband's nephew to "Watch Alex!" after the whole Tony incident. Alex tried his best to think about what had happened. All the screaming and shouting was bad enough, but he'd never seen his brother act like that, way worse than the time Alex had accidentally spilled a full glass of milk on an essay Tony was just finishing. Even worse, their mother's terrifying anger; sure, he and Tony had been swatted across their bottoms on more than one occasion, but neither had ever been struck in the face. Alex had felt like he wanted to cry even though it was his brother who had been struck. Tony had fled down the block, and his mother took after him, pausing briefly to bark her orders at Richie. Alex couldn't tell if she was running after Tony to catch him or chasing him back into their home.

Another mouthful of hot dog helped dispel the bad memories.

Richie and his friends even used the good spicy mustard, not the tasteless yellow stuff his mom bought.

"How you doing? Good?" Richie asked. "You thirsty?" Alex tilted his head from side to side; he wasn't *not* thirsty. Richie looked around, curious, then down to the aluminum can in his own hand, "You're legal, right?" he asked Alex, half in jest. Alex shrugged his shoulders, not understanding the question. He really didn't even like soda— the bubbles got up his nose and made him sneeze. He was more a Kool-Aid man, grape preferably. Alex swallowed what was left in his mouth and asked Richie if he had any.

"Uh, no. No Kool-Aid," Richie said. "Hold this anyway." He handed Alex his beer and then reached into his pocket and pulled out a new pack of cigarettes. He slapped the edge of the box into his palm several times before peeling away the cellophane and tapping out part of a cigarette that he fully extracted with his lips.

"Why do you do that?" Alex asked, curious.

"What?"

"That." Alex pointed.

"Who?"

"You," Alex raised his voice, confused at the confusion.

"When?" Richie teased back.

"Right now," Alex shouted. "The cigarettes!" He put the beer down next to him so he could mimic how Richie had slapped his cigarette pack into his open palm. Richie laughed at his young cousin's growing exasperation. He lit his cigarette, took a drag, reached for his beer, and took a big sip. "I'm joking," he told Alex. "Don't you watch *Welcome Back, Kotter*? You know—Vinnie Barbarino?" Alex shook his head. Richie rolled his eyes.

"I think your mother puts you to bed too early. Here, take a little sip, live a little." When Alex hesitated, Richie added, "Trust me, with your mother, you're gonna want a drink." Alex wasn't sure what Richie meant but cautiously accepted the cold can. He nostrils flared as he took a sniff. "Don't smell it, sip it!" Richie chided.

Alex took a small sip and immediately grimaced. "Blech!"

"It's an acquired taste," Richie said and took back his beer. "You'll see."

Alex quickly took his last bite of hot dog to get rid of the bitter taste in his mouth. As he chewed, Richie's friend with the mustache waved his hand to signal the rest of his crew and, gaining their attention, lit a single firecracker. He tossed it in a high arc over the sidewalk. It tumbled through the air, a thread of spiraling white smoke trailing it.

Descending, the firecracker barely missed landing on two chubby boys, neither older than ten, walking past. One boy, with red-stained lips, sucked on a Bomb Pop while his shorter friend urgently lapped dripping vanilla ice cream from the rim of his cone. The firecracker bounced once off the asphalt, spun, and detonated, startling both boys. They jumped at the blast, and the boy with the ice cream cone jerked his arm, which dislodged his remaining scoop of vanilla and sent it plummeting to the ground.

Richie's friends burst out into hysterical laughter as the boy stared down into the sad sight of his glob of ice cream rapidly dissolving on the hot pavement. His friend braved an angry look at Richie's gang before ushering his teary-eyed companion on their way.

Alex watched Richie shake his head, trying to suppress a chuckle; then he glanced down the block, searching for any sign of his family. Neither Tony nor his mom were visible, and he had no idea where his father had gone—the last Alex had seen of him, his father was running wildly across the avenue. Now, a young boy approaching on his tricycle came into Alex's view. He couldn't remember his name but was pretty sure he lived up the block on the opposite side of the street. Alex dug his fingers into his box and pinched out one of his last snaps. The young boy labored at the tricycle's pedals, as the block rose on a slight incline, invisible to the eye but noticeable on bike. Just as he was about to roll directly past the porch, Alex cocked his hand and fired the projectile but realized quickly that he'd miscalculated. He was too high up and the snap too light, so halfway down its sharp trajectory the snap straightened, then simply floated down to the pavement. The boy pedaled happily over it without a sound.

Directly behind the boy a mass of people followed, and Alex heard a muffled pop. When the crowd cleared, his flattened snap lay there like a trampled moth. Alex frowned.

"Kid!" Alex heard one of Richie's friends call out. "Kid!"

"Hey, he's my cousin," Richie reminded him. "He has a name." Richie turned to Alex with a serious expression and asked in a low voice, "What's your name again?"

"Alex!" Alex shouted, confused and annoyed. His cousin knew his name.

"Alex." Richie nodded. "That's right."

"Alex. Whatever." The friend stumbled over. He was taller and broader than Richie. He was shirtless also and had more hair on his chest than Alex did on his head. Around his neck were several gold chains of various lengths.

"You like comics, kid—I mean, Alex?" Alex's eyes immediately lit up. He smiled and nodded. Richie's friend pulled a magazine from out his back pocket. "Here you go. Enjoy!" He tossed it onto Alex's lap, coughed up a laugh, and stumbled back to the others.

Alex eagerly unfolded the magazine. Alex tried to flatten the creases of the front cover to admire the artwork. This didn't look like any comic book he'd ever read. The cover centered on a bizarre caricature of Superman. Alex recognized the red-and-blue uniform and cape, though it bulged with exaggerated muscles, especially around the hero's groin, stretching the red tights to their limit. Said bulge seemed to be the intended target of the cover's villainess: an anthropomorphic cat woman with orange fur, seductive eyes, and a painted-on black leotard, which barely contained her heaving furry bosom. Alex was most confused by the fact that he knew full well that Catwoman fought Batman and not Superman. He thought everyone knew that. Still, there was something appealing about this comic book, so Alex turned to ask Richie if it was okay for him to read it. But before he could get the words out, a young woman standing across the street wearing a blue bikini top under a suede leather vest caught his cousin's eye. Richie was already trotting down the porch steps and crossing the street. Alex shrugged and turned the page.

CHAPTER 26

Paulie limped down another block. He'd become selective on his trek, preferring streets that did not host any festivities. These blocks felt like ghost towns, like the entire residential area had been transported to somewhere more fun. Paulie half expected a tumbleweed to roll past him. He did resemble a wild man who'd stumbled in from the desert—his bald spot beet red, his pants torn and bloody, and, unbeknownst to him, a black grease smudge up the back of his shirt from leaning against a beat-up van to catch his breath. At least the dull throbbing at his temple now served to distract him from the pain in his knee. Five more avenues to Johnny, he told himself. Five more.

At the next corner, he noticed a nice big blue mailbox sitting under the shade of a tall tree. It seemed the perfect place to pause for another moment or two, maybe rest his head against it for a moment. Just as his forehead touched the cool painted steel, he heard a loud honking and jerked his head back up.

"Pauuuuul-iiiee!" Paulie turned and saw a black Monte Carlo stopped in the street right in front of him, its engine revving.

"Chippy" was all Paulie could muster, along with a nod of his head.

"What's happenin', m'man?" Chippy leaned sideways and lowered his head so he could better see out the front passenger window. He wore sunglasses with green-tinted frames. Paulie tilted his head once to each side, pondering an answer. After a few moments of waiting for a response, Chippy asked, "You need a ride or something?" Paulie nodded and pushed himself off the mailbox.

Paulie opened the car door and waited for Chippy to sweep a pile of crinkled fast-food wrappers off the black leather passenger seat before he could climb in.

"Sorry for the mess. Today I'm like Santa on Christmas Eve. A lotta last-minute shoppers. Gotta eat on the run."

"Hey, you're doing me the favor," Paulie said gratefully, finally taking a seat and closing the door. He would have been happy to ride in the back of a sanitation truck. He took in a deep breath and exhaled, his muscles relaxed, the throbbing in his knee, for the moment, quiet. "Thanks," he said to Chippy.

"That's what neighbors are for," Chippy said, his head bopping in a nod. "Happy to give you a lift home."

Paulie shook his head no. "I actually need a ride to Bay Ridge," he said and told Chippy the address.

Chippy wrinkled his nose at the news. He turned his head to look out his own side window and then looked down into his lap as he scratched the stubble under his chin. "Uh . . ." He began to say something but noticed the tear in Paulie's pants, the trickle of blood down the fabric. He turned toward Paulie and, with his index finger, lowered his sunglasses slightly down the bridge of his nose. Paulie could tell Chippy thought he looked like he'd been put through the ringer. Chippy turned back and looked out the front windshield. "Yeah, sure. I can do that. . . . I just gotta make one stop first." He shot Paulie a knowing look, adding, "If you don't mind."

"No problem," Paulie replied. He was sure this would get him to

Johnny faster than walking, regardless of wherever Chippy needed to stop first. Quite frankly, he wasn't sure how many blocks he still had in his legs. He took another deep breath in through his nostrils. The Bicentennial wasn't over yet. Paulie still had time to make things right. What was it he had heard President Ford say on TV when he was fidgeting in the hospital waiting for Zizi to be discharged? Something to the effect of "Americans are always improving. It is not only right—it is necessary."

Paulie, his head rolled right to better enjoy the breeze, started a chuckle that never materialized. Instead, he sighed. When was it that he'd stopped improving? He knew the answer wasn't last year or the year before, or even the year before that—it was a question of which decade. Both front windows were completely rolled down, and Paulie, eyes closed, relished the breeze. It wasn't a cool breeze, but it still felt good. Paulie opened his eyes and stared blankly as the street signs whizzed by. As Paulie's gaze returned forward, he noticed the passenger sun visor was cluttered with an array of metal and enamel button pins of varying shapes and sizes. One was a simple smiley face pin; another depicted a tiny cartoon devil holding a pitchfork, with "I'm Horny" lettered above; one asserted "Disco Sucks." Paulie's eyes went to what looked like an election pin spotlighting Donald Duck: "Get Down, America" curved along the pin's upper edge.

"Heh, Donald." Paulie could still muster a chuckle. Chippy heard and shook his head.

"Nah, man, not Donald. That's Howard," Chippy said, turning to Paulie. Paulie looked closer, and sure enough, the bottom of the pin, in thinner letters, read, "Vote Howard the Duck in '76." Chippy added, "You know Howard? *Trapped in a world he never made!*'" His right hand released the steering wheel, and he gestured with his thumb toward Paulie, then himself. "Just like us."

"Uh . . . right," Paulie replied and turned to face out the passenger window as he rolled his eyes.

Chippy accelerated down the next avenue. If you went fast enough, you could make it through each dangling traffic light just before it blinked from yellow to red. The neighborhood was a stark contrast of celebration and desolation from block to block—quick flashes of colors and noise, stars and stripes and joyful yelping of children one second, a completely deserted street the next. The motion of the car began to make Paulie a little drowsy. He checked his watch.

The volume on the car radio grew louder as a song trailed off and a commercial began; some pitchman that sounded like a carnival barker hawked cheap electronics. Paulie's temple throbbed, but thankfully Chippy took one hand off the wheel to change the channel. He poked at one silver button after another as the red-line channel indicator bounced from left to right, hopping from one preset station to another. Chippy's final selection landed on the Lovin' Spoonful's "Summer in the City," and he smiled and bit his bottom lip. "Excellent tune," he said. Then he turned to Paulie and asked, "You know what my favorite season is, Paulie?"

"Summer?" Paulie guessed. Chippy held up one finger and shook it back and forth like a scolding schoolteacher might.

"Nope," Chippy said. Paulie turned to face Chippy as he waited for the correct answer. Chippy bopped his head and looked slyly at Paulie with that little squint in his eyes, knowingly trying to inject some drama. A wide grin then sprouted across his face, and Chippy said, in his best Elmer Fudd voice, "Wabbit season."

Chippy slapped the steering wheel as he broke into wild laughter. Paulie smiled and nodded politely. Maybe accepting this ride hadn't been the best idea.

CHAPTER 27

Tony hadn't cried in years, not like this, hyperventilating, leaking saliva from his nostrils and lips like a child. The tears had subsided, but he still sucked in long, deliberate breaths through his nose, his exhales broken and trembling. Alone, he paced the length of his family's apartment, fists clenched, his head swinging absently from side to side.

Images of the fight, his mother, faces in the crowd overwhelmed him. He couldn't think straight, not since he'd fled his mother, run down the block as fast as he could, trying to hold it together, to spare himself further humiliation. She'd yelled at him, slapped him in front of everyone: Sally, all the other kids on the block, that fucking Benny, everyone. Tony was most haunted by the image of one face, the one face among all the blurred faces that had become crystal clear as he spun away from his mother—the one belonging to the girl in the red hot pants, whom he'd traded smiles with earlier. She had laughed at him.

If spontaneous human combustion were truly a thing, he would have left a nasty scorch mark back on the asphalt. But nothing metaphysical intervened to spare him; he had felt paralyzed for several

seconds that seemed an eternity, until he felt as if he was falling forward; he took one step to balance himself, then another and another,
and he was soon running as fast as he could. He wasn't sure why
he hadn't kept running, off the block, run to anywhere else but his
home. That's what he should have done; he should have run right past
his goddamn house, turned under the El, and kept running under its
shadow and broken light. He should have run and run as the steel
trains thundered overhead, rumbling so loud that he wouldn't be able
to hear himself think. But, instead of escaping, like a little boy he'd
run home.

CHAPTER 28

At a stoplight, Chippy reached one hand into the small tray behind the T-shift and dug through some loose papers and wrappers. Not finding what he was looking for, he furrowed his eyebrows and began to pat his front pants pockets, still steering with his left hand. "Ah-ha," he exclaimed after discovering his cigarettes in the breast pocket of the flannel shirt he wore like a jacket over a camouflage tee. He tapped out a cigarette halfway and offered it to Paulie. "You want a smoke?"

Paulie, sunk back into soft leather, shook his head. "No thanks."

Chippy nodded, fully extracted the cigarette with just his lips, and tucked the pack back into his pocket. He lit it and took a puff. Chippy spun the steering wheel left at the next corner, turning down the block without slowing down a stitch. All of Paulie flew to the right. He winced as his bad knee thumped into the passenger door.

Paulie straightened himself in his seat then and glanced at the homes they drove past. He wondered if he knew anyone who lived on this block. This was something of a habit of his when driving through the neighborhood, asking Dee or the boys, "You know who used to live on this block . . . ?" The answer was often a name neither of his children had ever heard. Dee usually quipped, "You shoulda been a tour guide." Paulie glanced overhead: a dozen or so pairs of old sneakers, each pair knotted together at the laces, dangled from the phone and electrical wires above.

"You know who used to live on this block?" Paulie asked Chippy. He leaned forward slightly and pointed to a gray apartment building on their left.

"Who?" Chippy played along, shrugging both shoulders.

"Joe Pepitone," Paulie said. "Right there, the gray building."

"Yeah?" Chippy gave a look back over his left shoulder as they drove past it.

"I think so," Paulie said, fully turned in his seat, squinting out the back window. He sounded like he was trying to convince himself. Eventually satisfied that he had the right building on the right block, he spun back in his seat. "Joe Pep. They don't make ballplayers like that anymore." Paulie shook his head and smiled. He reached up and felt the top of his head. "I used to have a head of hair just like him."

"Ha!" Chippy laughed. "Yeah, I remember." Chippy took another drag off his cigarette. "Didn't you smoke?" he asked Paulie.

"Long time ago," Paulie answered without turning or opening his eyes.

"Ah, I knew it," Chippy said, steering with his left hand while gesturing toward Paulie with the lit cigarette in his right. He raised the same hand up to his forehead and tapped a spot just above his temple. "Memory like an elephant," Chippy boasted. "Dee still does, right?"

"Like a fucking chimney," Paulie said as Chippy flicked ashes out his window. After speeding down another block, he made a right turn at the corner and gave his rearview mirror a glance once he'd straightened out the steering wheel.

"Why you quit?" Chippy asked and took another drag. He made

another right turn at the next corner, his eyes again darting to the mirror while he waited for an answer.

"God," Paulie said.

"God made you quit?"

Paulie shook his head as he looked out the front windshield. He admired the dedication of whoever was responsible for tying thick red, white, and blue ribbons in a bow around every tree on the block.

"So," Paulie began, "it was the week before Christmas. Tony was two and a half. He woke up crying with a fever of a hundred and one. By the time the pediatrician was in the office, it was a hundred and two. By the time he got to the apartment—this is when they still made house calls—it's a hundred and three. So, whatever, he gives the kid a shot, I go to the pharmacy and get whatever antibiotic he prescribed, nothing happens. Two hours later the fever's a hundred and four; Dee's cryin', screamin' at me; my brother Frank drives us to Maimonides Hospital in his squad car. ER is packed, Frank's in uniform. You know my brother Frank?"

"Yeah, sure. The cop." Chippy made another right turn.

"So, anyway, there's this big colored woman sitting at the desk, and she drops a clipboard down and says, 'Fill out these forms, sign this, sign that.'" Paulie made a nasty face as he mimicked her tone. "And the waiting room, the door had one of those buzzers, so she had to buzz you into the examination rooms. *Whap!*" Paulie exclaimed as his fist slammed down against the top of the dashboard. "My brother slams his baton down against the desk and tells her, 'You fill the forms out. Now open the fucking door.'" Paulie, reenergized by his own story, chuckled. "Whole room was packed; we go right in."

Chippy forced out a laugh that sounded more like someone clearing their throat. "Cops" was all he said as he nodded and flicked his stub out the window.

"Anyway," Paulie continued, "they take Tony inside and throw him in a big sink filled with cold water. They start dumping ice into the sink, trying to get the fever down, and they send us all back into the waiting room. I'm praying, saying Our Fathers. I'm all nerves, so I'm about to light a cigarette and—it just popped into my head—I promised God that I'd never light another cigarette if . . . if he would make Tony okay again. So, I tossed the pack into the trash, and a half hour later the nurse came out and said the fever broke." Paulie looked over at Chippy, who was staring up into his rearview mirror. Paulie wasn't sure how much of the story Chippy had heard. He took a breath and turned to gaze back out the passenger window as the houses, parked cars, and streetlamps streaked past.

Chippy made a final right turn, his eyes again darting up to the rearview mirror. Coast clear, he pulled into an open spot on the right side of the block. He turned off the ignition as Paulie regarded what was a fine parking spot, right beside a large oak, plenty of shade above.

"Hey, Paulie. You mind giving me a quick hand? This way we'll do this in one shot." Paulie nodded, and they both climbed out and walked to the back of the car. Paulie again felt a sting in his right knee when he climbed out of the car, but it seemed to subside after a few steps. Chippy popped the trunk, and Paulie's eyes went wide at the sight of the cache of explosives. There were several brown grocery bags—some with the tops crumpled shut; others overflowing with pointed tips of rockets bundled together like bouquets of roses; others piled high and tight with mats of firecrackers. Visible inside one bag was a colorful assortment of round and square explosives— some in cellophane, some not; all with thin white fuses sprouting from them. Wedged in the back of the trunk were milk crates filled with Roman candles and one ominous wooden crate with the word *Mortars* stenciled across its lid. Paulie suddenly wondered how wise it was for Chippy to be smoking in the front seat while they chauffeured an H-bomb's worth of explosives in the trunk.

Chippy reached into his back pocket and pulled out a folded piece of loose-leaf with little symbols and numbers scribbled on it. He looked back down into the trunk and nodded as if he were counting. He bent over and unfurled one closed bag, lowering his face into its mouth. He straightened back up, rolled it back shut, and handed it to Paulie. He grabbed two of the overflowing bags for himself, cradled them with one arm momentarily while he slammed the trunk down with his free hand and gestured with his head for Paulie to follow.

Paulie's leg hurt less, but the limp was still there. He quickly fell a pace or two behind Chippy as they strolled casually down the block. Carrying the grocery bags, he felt like a boy again, making deliveries for his father.

Paulie told himself this would all be a good story to tell Johnny, a nice little icebreaker, not that he thought he needed one. Johnny wanted to see him, after all. Barney had said so just hours ago. Johnny was technically not angry with anything Paulie had done. Technically. It was Dee's snide remarks, her inability to just keep her mouth shut, that was responsible for the estrangement—fifteen months after his first wife passed, Johnny married a woman named Sharon, ten years his junior, who'd managed his company's payroll for the past five years.

"You got right back up on the horse, didn't you, Johnny?" That's what Dee had said to Johnny at his own wedding reception, within earshot of his new bride. That was what she had said to a man who had watched his first wife of fifteen years, the mother of his children, waste away.

The look on Johnny's face after Dee's comment—Paulie could still picture it, and it made him sick to his stomach. On the way home that night on the BQE, Paulie lit into his wife. A defiant Dee asserted, "I call it like it is. I'm no phony." Only when Paulie became so incensed and started swerving toward then abruptly away from the guardrail did his wife finally acquiesce to her husband's wishes and shut her mouth. After Johnny had returned from his honeymoon, Paulie should have picked up the phone to call his friend to apologize, but he had been too embarrassed. He had hoped Johnny would forgive and forget, that his phone would ring at the next holiday or birthday, but Johnny's call never came.

"Back here," Chippy said over his shoulder to Paulie. Paulie followed Chippy down a shared driveway between two red-brick homes. Chippy stopped midway, still a few paces ahead of him, and whistled loudly through his teeth—three sharp notes. Something akin to a muffled birdcall echoed back from somewhere unseen. Chippy whistled again—this time a wolf's call responded. Paulie spotted a shadow emerging from the rear of the driveway, stretching out and away from the edge of the wall, followed moments later by the large man who cast it.

"Chippyyyy!" the large man bellowed in a deep, gruff voice. To Paulie, he looked like a cross between a biker and Santa Claus—heavyset, clad in denim and leather despite the heat. His beefy arms were covered in tattoos; an American-flag bandanna wrapped around his head. And when he smiled, his bearded face flashed a jovial, almost elfin grin.

"Aaaabe!" Chippy shouted back gleefully.

As Paulie watched the two men exchange an urban handshake, then embrace, he was filled with the increasing and overwhelming desire for someone to relieve him of his bag of explosives. Chippy, almost sensing what Paulie was thinking, turned back and reached to grab Paulie's bag. Paulie eagerly stretched his arms forward, but before he could unload his parcel, he saw Chippy's eyes flash wide.

"Shit!" Chippy blurted. In a flash, Chippy and Abe spun and bolted away.

Paulie turned and looked over his shoulder; his heart almost stopped at the sight of two cops racing up the driveway toward him; his legs, almost instinctively, began to carry him forward, but as soon as Paulie planted his right foot to propel himself in the same direction as Chippy and Abe, his knee buckled, and he tumbled to the ground. One cop was soon standing over him.

"Don't fucking move!" the cop commanded. Paulie's heart raced; he struggled to catch his breath. Pressed flat against the concrete, he felt his stomach gurgle, his intestines spasm. He feared he'd shit his pants.

CHAPTER 29

Dick Pole tumbled in a downward spiral. The long strands of his light-brown hair flowing out from under his Boston Red Sox cap appeared to flutter back over his left shoulder as he spun through the air. He landed face up, his eyes squinting, almost in challenge, at Alex. Alex squinted right back down at him. He wasn't going to let a Red Sox player look at him that way. He raised his left hand, a narrow deck of 1976 Topps cards clutched within his grip. He flicked the middle finger of his right hand against the deck, *whap whap*, just like he'd watched Tony do many times. He was never quite sure of whether this was technique or ritual, but he liked doing it just the same. He peeled the top card from the deck with the grace of a Las Vegas blackjack dealer and spun it around in his hand to hold it delicately, glossy side in, thumb along one long edge, the tips of his middle and ring finger along its opposite. He glanced at Tommy, his opponent, who had flipped first.

Tommy's meaty countenance seemingly could only ever reflect one of two expressions—infectious happiness or grave concern. Either the muscles of his face had yet to learn subtle or overt reflection of the remaining spectrum of emotions or Tommy truly possessed only two states of being. The look of worry now crossing his face was quite clear. Under usual circumstances, neither Alex nor Tommy, nor most kids in the neighborhood, would waste a bead of sweat at the prospect of losing a Red Sox card while flipping. Maybe, if pressed, they'd begrudgingly admit to the value of a Rice or Yaz card, but otherwise any Red Sox card was as disposable as the backup shortstop on the Milwaukee Brewers. In fact, as loyal Yankee fans, the fewer Red Sox cards you held in your stack, the better. But this was no ordinary card—next to the Chicago Cubs' Pete LaCock, Dick Pole of the Boston Red Sox had, to children of all ages, the funniest name in baseball.

Alex bent his arm like the letter *L*, his elbow creased into an almost perfect ninety-degree angle; then he snapped his wrist back. *"It's all in the wrist."* He could hear his brother's voice in his head, lecturing on the proper technique. The card spun several times, almost suspended midair at the point of release before whirling down toward the pavement. It struck the ground edge first instead of landing flat. It teetered for a moment, then fell face down.

"Crap," Alex said, as Tommy exhaled a deep breath.

"This is soooo boring," Vito whined. He sat on the curb beside his two friends. Alex shrugged in response as Tommy struggled, folding over to scoop up both cards. "When are they going to start blowing shit up?" Vito further clarified his grievance.

"When it gets dark, I guess," Alex said.

"I have some sparklers," Tommy suggested as he added the two cards to the top of his deck.

"Sparklers are for babies," Vito blurted, more in disappointment than insult.

"I have some snaps left," Alex quickly offered. Vito just stared down at the laces of his sneakers and shook his head.

Alex shrugged. It was his turn now. Before reaching for the next card, he looked back down the block. He and his friends had slowly drifted a few yards away from Zizi's porch. He could clearly see his cousin, huddled with his friends, some girls having joined the party. Alex wasn't sure if Richie had even heard him when he'd tapped him on his arm to ask if he could go and hang out with his friends. Not that he wasn't grateful for the hot dog and, quite frankly, would have been happy to scoff down another. But the sip of beer left a bitter taste in his mouth, and that was no comic book Richie's friend had handed him. There were naked pictures inside that magazine—naked, hairy men and women who looked like they were hurting each other. He'd tossed the magazine aside after looking at just a few pages.

Alex remained concerned that his mother would be upset if she came looking for him, but as long as he was within view of his cousin, he thought it would be all right. He stared down into his deck of baseball cards and gazed upon the glossy photo of the next man up in his deck, New York Yankee Dick Tidrow—another Dick. It was his turn to flip first, so he flicked his finger twice against Dick and peeled the card from the top of the deck. Just as he carefully centered the card in his fingers, he was startled by the sound of screeching tires. A bike skidded to a stop just behind Tommy. Tommy's entire torso sprang upward in surprise, his bottom half not quite elevating from the pavement. Alex leaned sideways to look around Tommy to see who it was. Vito had already sprung up from the curb and was greeting the kid on the bike.

Ugh. Alex knew the kid, Dennis something or other; he went to public school with Vito. He lived up the next block and was a real jerk. Dennis had a dark complexion and narrow face that made him look like an eel. He did have a nice bike, though. Alex admired it—a Schwinn Sting-Ray, red, three speeds—the Corvette of bicycles.

Dennis paid neither Alex nor Tommy any mind as he began an animated conversation with Vito. Alex and Tommy glanced at each other, shrugged, and decided to continue with their game.

Alex flipped, and his card landed face up. Tommy gleefully stared down at the potential prize—he was eager at the prospect of scooping up a Yankee. Alex watched Tommy slide a card from the deck into his wide paw. As Tommy readied to flip, Alex looked down at his card. Dick Tidrow looked slender and sharp in his pinstripes, standing perfectly in the set position, about to go into his windup, Yankee Stadium arching behind him under a bright-blue sky.

Alex held his breath, anticipating Tommy's card to come fluttering down any second now. Instead, a bicycle tire rolled into view, stopping alarmingly close to the pristine edge of his card.

"Hey!" both Alex and Tommy shouted in unison. Alex looked up and saw Dennis sitting on his bike, smirking back at him.

"We're playing," Alex protested.

"We're playing," Dennis mocked. He was roughly the same size as Alex but always acted like he was ten feet tall. Alex stared into his beady, sunken eyes and then shot a look over at Vito, who just stood there, his thin lips pressed together in a straight line, arms folded.

Dennis slid off his bike and popped the kickstand out all in one motion. He stood with a gunfighter's stance, legs apart, directly above the baseball card lying prone below him. He held his arms away from his sides, his eyes darting back and forth between Alex and Tommy. The music bursting from the DJ's speakers, loud conversations, and laughter—all the ambient sounds of the block—faded until there was a tiny bubble of silence surrounding the boys.

For a moment, Alex thought of darting forward to snatch his card back. Who knew what this Dennis was going to do? As if reading Alex's mind, Dennis dropped his gaze to the card. Alex held his breath. Dennis's hand dipped into his back pocket as he pivoted ninety degrees, swinging his body back into the spot where Tommy stood. Despite being twice, if not three times, Dennis's weight, Tommy gave way, stepping back to stand beside Vito.

"I'll flip you," Dennis said to Alex. He held out his fist and opened his fingers to reveal a stack of forty—no, *fifty*—baseball cards. Alex stared at the top card facing out at him: Thurman Munson, the first captain of the NY Yankees since Lou Gehrig. Munson's imposing visage, even when just a few inches tall, reflected authority. He wore a full beard, his jersey unbuttoned, no undershirt, wild chest hair spilling over onto the pinstripes. He had a look in his eyes, almost daring the photographer to snap the picture. Munson was Alex's second favorite player next to Mick the Quick. Not only that, but the Munson card was also one of the few Yankee cards that had eluded him this season. Alex had somehow collected seven Rick Dempseys, a player who had been traded to Baltimore in June, but not one Munson.

Alex's eyes widened—he feared he might be salivating. Still, he hesitated, remembered Dennis bragging once that he'd stolen the Sting-Ray from another kid. He didn't believe the story, but that was the problem: he didn't trust this kid. Alex turned toward Vito, hoping to see some look of reassurance, some sign that the challenge was on the up and up—this Dennis reeked of sneaky. Vito looked away.

A voice in the back of Alex's head urged him to pick up his card and walk away. Yes, that was the smart thing to do. Alex noticed the fading rays of sunshine glinting off the Munson card, almost putting a twinkle in the captain's eyes.

Okay, what was the harm? He was pretty sure he had Dick Tidrow in doubles anyway. Worse came to worse, what was one fewer Dick Tidrow card in his collection?

CHAPTER 30

As the squad car pulled up to the wooden horse barricade, its siren wailed, and three teenagers scrambled from the corner stoop. The officer at the wheel nodded in satisfaction as two of them ran to opposite ends of the blue barricade while the third took it upon himself to supervise. He barked, "Grab it by the support and beam. Grab 'em both." His friends complied and lifted the entire wooden structure an inch off the ground. One teen stood still while the other pedaled backward as the barricade swung like a hinge. The supervisor flashed a congratulatory thumbs-up and turned to direct the officers through the newly opened path. The squad car was already rolling forward, causing the supervisor to hurry out of the vehicle's way.

The officer jabbed the siren button again. One abrupt buzz and a quick flash of the lights was enough to drive the rest of the revelers and pedestrians from the street and onto the sidewalks as the car continued its slow roll down the block, drawing both curious and annoyed stares from the crowd.

"Address is ten-fifty, you said, right?" the officer driving asked, squinting at house numbers.

"I think so. You really could have dropped me on the corner,"

Paulie said, sunk down in the back seat, a hand at his brow to shield his profile from the curious stares.

"Nah, this was the least we could do," the officer sitting in the passenger seat insisted as the car came to a full stop in the middle of the block. "Remember to tell your brother that Bobby and Eddy from the Sixty-Eighth send their regards."

Paulie gave his assurances and said his thanks. He tried to exit the vehicle, but the door remained locked.

"Hang on," the officer in the passenger seat said. "I'll let you out." Paulie slumped back into his seat and exhaled while he waited for the officer. While Paulie wished he would have been let out on the corner, this was much preferable to being hauled down to central booking—which is exactly where Paulie thought he was headed when he was lying face down on the pavement just a short time ago. Despite Paulie's motionlessness, the officer had kept yelling at him, "Don't move!" Paulie was amazed that he hadn't had a coronary or crapped his pants. It felt like he had been lying on the ground for hours, but it was probably no more than a minute before the other officer returned. He'd heard the heavy footsteps approach, the officer panting, "Faster than . . . they looked. . . . Got . . . away."

"We got one of 'em," the other cop said to his partner and then ordered Paulie to get up slowly, to keep his hands on his head, which, with his injured knee, was a slow and painful process.

"I got nothing to do with those guys," Paulie pleaded as he staggered to his feet.

"Naturally," one officer responded while the other walked over to the brown paper bag Paulie had dropped when he fell.

"The guy was just giving me a ride. I hurt my leg," Paulie gestured with his head, down to his torn pants and bloody knee. He turned and winced as he watched the other officer unfold the top of the crumpled bag and peer down into its contents. The officer shook his head, lifted the bag in one hand, and carried it over to his partner. He tilted the opening of the bag toward the other officer, who craned his neck to give a look inside. They both shook their heads.

"Let's see some ID, pal," the officer who had chased Chippy and Abe commanded. The officers watched closely as Paulie slowly reached for his back pocket. He extracted a beat-up brown leather wallet and began fumbling through the plastic inserts, looking for his driver's license.

"Stop!" one officer shouted. Paulie froze. "Whose shield was that?" the office asked.

A flustered Paulie stared down at the mini gold shield pinned to one of the wallet's plastic photograph flaps.

"My brother," Paulie blurted, as if he had just remembered the fact that he had a brother. "My brother, Frank. Frank A—"

One officer smiled, and the other chuckled.

"Frank? I was at his retirement party," the officer who had chased Chippy and Abe said. He shook his head, still chuckling, and told Paulie to put his wallet away. "What are you messing around with those guys for?" he asked, his tone more conversational now. Paulie tried to explain his day. After half a minute, the officers waved Paulie silent, having heard more than they cared to.

"Can we give you a ride?" one officer asked. Paulie nodded and thanked him.

The same officer now released Paulie from the back seat and then climbed back into the passenger seat. He held up his hand in farewell as the squad car pulled away. Paulie looked around at all the gawking faces, strangers wondering about the identity of this disheveled man emerging from the back seat of a squad car. Paulie lowered his head to avert rows of staring eyes. As he turned, about to make his way across the street, he locked eyes with Johnny Truz, emerging from a crowd of onlookers.

CHAPTER 31

Alex was still in shock. He'd lost almost his entire stack to Dennis. Every single card, one after the other. He held his last card, a Graig Nettles with sharp, perfect edges, desperately pinched between his thumb and index finger. Directly opposite Alex, Dennis smiled, raising his now much taller stack of cards in torment of his opponent. The shock of the loss would be bad enough if it was just an unbelievable streak of bad luck to blame, but that wasn't the case. Alex was sure that Dennis had cheated. Instead of flipping like a normal person, making the card spin several revolutions in the air, Dennis crouched down slightly, and somehow, inexplicably, made the card spin only once before landing flat.

"Cheating!" Alex had cried out after his opponent's first unorthodox flip, to which, of course, Dennis took immediate exception.

"You calling me a cheater?" Dennis stepped right up to Alex, who reflexively stepped backward.

"That's not how you flip," Alex shouted, regaining his moxie.

"Says who?"

"Says anyone!" Alex answered. "It's called flipping. The card has to flip." Alex extended an index finger and spun it in a tight circle to further illustrate his point.

"It did flip."

"Once."

"Once is a flip. Who made you the flip boss?"

Alex was flustered by the challenge. The rules governing playground and sidewalk games were quite provincial and subject to wide variations. He looked to Tommy and Vito for support. Tommy had defaulted to his troubled countenance and would be no help. Vito just shrugged his shoulders and looked down at the ground. *Thanks, Vito!* Alex thought. *This jerk is your friend.* With a clear absence of substantiated evidence to prove the technique illegal, the contest continued. Alex was so flustered he could barely make a match. Even when he tried to imitate Dennis's method, he failed—the card either spun and came up on the losing side or fell flat, and he was the one forced into a do-over. Soon every card was lost save for Nettles, whom Alex now reluctantly slid between his fingers.

"Maybe you should kiss it goodbye before you flip it," Dennis teased.

Alex took a deep breath and then flipped his last card. It landed backside up. Dennis flipped. Backside up. A victorious and smirking Dennis collected both cards from the ground and added them to the top of his deck. He spread his cards out like a fan in one hand and grinned wide, seemingly impressed with his winnings.

The tears began to well in Alex's eyes, and he turned, ready to head home. It was bad enough that Dennis had just won all his cards; he wasn't going to give the jerk the satisfaction of calling him a crybaby too.

"Hey, wait a sec," Dennis shouted. Alex turned back.

"What?"

"Flip me again."

"You won all my cards," Alex shot back. *Jerk!*

"I'll give you a chance to win them all back. One flip."

"I'm outta cards!"

Dennis shuffled through his fat stack, extracted one card, and handed it to Alex. Alex cautiously snatched the card from him. His eyes widened as he stared down into the glossy cardboard—it was the Munson.

"You flip me. You win, you keep that card and every card I already won from you," Dennis said smugly. Alex again stared down at the card, as if in consultation with the Yankee captain.

"Why would you flip me for your own card?" Alex shot back.

"I like those buttons," Dennis said, pointing to the two Bicentennial buttons pinned to Alex's shirt. "I win, I get the buttons." Dennis then raised an eyebrow. "And your shirt too." Dennis smiled and pointed directly at the eagle emblazoned across Alex's chest. He nodded and repeated the terms for clarity, "Shirt and buttons for Munson and all your cards back."

Alex took a deep breath in through his nose. He looked at Tommy. His poor friend looked like he was about to have a stroke. He looked at Vito, who just tilted his head to one side and looked away. He looked back down at the card, deep into Munson's fearless eyes. Alex could swear he heard a voice whisper in his ear, *Flip him, kid.*

CHAPTER 32

"Jeez, Paulie," Johnny said, trying in vain not to chuckle. "You look like the shit. What the hell happened to you?"

Paulie started to answer. He opened his mouth yet had no idea where to start. Thankfully, instead of being left to stand there, mouth agape, Johnny approached and wrapped his arms around his old friend.

"Too long, Paulie," Johnny said. "Too long." Johnny patted him hard on the back several times before releasing his embrace.

"You look good, Johnny." Paulie smiled, standing face-to-face with his best friend for the first time in almost a decade. Sure, maybe Johnny, like him, had packed on a few, but otherwise the guy looked like a million bucks with his dark tan, fancy silk polo, paisley-embroidered golf shorts, and thick brown leather sandals. He looked like a movie star, like he'd just finished playing golf with Bob Hope. Paulie also noticed that his friend wore his hair longer at the sides, so his missing earlobe was now completely obscured.

Johnny reached forward and gently rubbed his open palm over Paulie's scalp. "Where'd it all go? Your feathers got plucked." Johnny laughed. Paulie winced under the head rubbing, but he let his friend kid him.

Paulie noticed most of the crowd behind Johnny had dissipated during their greeting, but from the corner of his eye, he spotted Johnny's second wife, Sharon. She stood just a few paces off her husband's right shoulder, arms crossed in front of her. *Christ!* Paulie thought—she must be pushing forty by now but barely looked thirty. Hell, twenty-five. Her shoulder-length feathered blond hair framed her face, dominated by a pair of oversize sunglasses that she still wore despite the fading daylight. She sported a half-sleeve floral print blouse, buttoned only halfway and tied in a knot above her exposed midsection. Paulie was confident a stomach that flat had never provided Johnny with children.

Johnny noticed Paulie noticing Sharon. He turned to his wife. "Sharon, look who's here." Sharon tipped her head forward so she could gaze out over the tops of her large frames. Paulie began to raise his hand to offer both a greeting and, finally, an apology for his own wife's behavior years ago.

Before he could say a word, Sharon raised her head upright, looked at her husband, and remarked from the side of her mouth, "I'll be in the backyard helping my sister." Without sparing her husband's friend a solitary look, Sharon spun around and strutted back up the long driveway.

"Anyways . . . ," Johnny continued after his wife had disappeared into the backyard. "How are Dee and the kids?"

"Good, good." Paulie nodded. There was a sudden loud hissing noise. Paulie turned to see some teenagers scurrying away from a just-lit Roman candle, which sparkled, ready to erupt. The candle spit a glowing red ball into the air, a stream of white smoke trailing behind. It flew high and burst into a shower of red embers, which quickly faded into the twilight.

"What are they doing?" Johnny said to Paulie. "It's too early. Right? You can barely see it." Johnny pointed up to the sky.

"Ahhh, they don't know what they're doing." Paulie quickly parroted and waved his hand.

"Why don't you come in the back?" Johnny jabbed his thumb over his shoulder. "I just put some fruit on. You gotta taste these kiwis I got my hands on."

Paulie took a moment to take in the facade of Johnny's sister-in-law's house. He remembered Sharon's sister was married to some guy that imported or exported something or another. Their home looked like an immense Italian villa. An array of perfectly manicured junipers framed the property, which included a slick slate driveway and a working three-tier marble fountain centered in the front lawn so ornate that it looked like Michelangelo himself had chiseled it.

"Some house, right?" Johnny said as Paulie admired it. "They had it imported stone by stone. Guy makes me look like a pauper." If Johnny was a pauper compared to his brother-in-law, Paulie wondered what that made him.

"So, how's the old neighborhood? I saw your buddy Barney at OTB. I wanted to come by the block, but half the streets are closed. What a pain in the ass to drive today. Thankfully, coming in from the Island, traffic was going the other way."

Paulie blew out a hard breath in agreement. *Traffic.*

Johnny looked his friend in the eyes. "So, what's new? Jeez, what's it been, six, seven years?"

"Almost ten, I think," Paulie said and looked down.

Johnny looked away in the direction of the Roman candle spitting out another burst. He turned back to Paulie. "You still with the phone company?"

"Yeah," Paulie said, and then paused and thought for a moment. "We're on strike." It wasn't a lie, after all.

"Right, right. I saw that in the papers. You get something from the union, right?"

"Yeah," Paulie said. "I get something." Again, the rent, all the bills, Dee, the weight of his reality hung over him, threatened to crush him at any moment. It took all his will to straighten his posture, look his friend in the eye, and go on. "That's what I wanted to talk to you about, actually. When Barney said you were in town . . ." Paulie gestured with both hands in front of him as he spoke, as if he were trying to reel the words out of himself. "Remember how you always busted my chops to come and work with you?"

Johnny's eyebrows raised, and he gave a slight nod in response.

Paulie went on. "You know no one picks fruit like me, right? Remember when what's-his-name—the Irish guy that used to try to sell us the overripe bananas . . . ?"

Johnny looked somewhat confused but smiled and nodded back.

"Anyway, I was thinking, since this strike's going on, maybe I could come and work with you . . . for you. You know, make sure all the fruit's top notch. . . ." Paulie trailed off as he stared at his friend smiling blankly back at him.

"Paulie . . ." Johnny paused, visibly struggling to find the right words. "You know, it's a big, complicated operation now. Not like when I started it." Johnny cleared his throat and glanced back over his shoulder. He turned back and leaned a little closer toward Paulie, and said in a hushed voice, "We haven't even told Sharon's sister yet, but we just bought a place down in Boca. She can't stand the winters.

Next, she'll want me to buy a boat so she can sunbathe on the deck all day."

"You sold the business?" Paulie asked.

Johnny shook his head. "J.J.'s been running the shop practically since he got out of Cornell. It's all fancy management this and that now. I don't understand half the crap that comes out of his mouth." Johnny laughed.

Paulie tried to laugh but could only manifest a weak smile. J.J.—John Jr.—was out of college already? Paulie guessed he must have been around Tony's age when he'd last seen him. Johnny continued. "Yeah, come next winter, Sharon and I are turning into a pair of snowbirds."

The color was quickly draining from Paulie's face. His friend seemed to notice and interjected, "Hey, you need to make some extra bucks, I'll make sure J.J. finds something for you." Paulie watched Johnny's eyes furrow, as if his friend were silently searching his thoughts, trying to conceive of some menial job for his old friend Paulie. Charity.

Almost on cue, a young man emerged from the shadows of the long driveway and shouted, "Hey, Pop. Sharon wants you."

"Hey, J.J. C'mere. You know who this guy is, right?" Johnny called back to his son. The young man walked over. He was tall and lean and wore a crisp red-checkered button-down with the sleeves rolled up to the elbow. Except for his blue eyes, the son was the spitting image of his father at his age. Staring at J.J., Paulie suddenly felt like he'd been transported back in time and was standing once again in his father's fruit store, Johnny staring back at him and about to tell him what to do next.

"Paulie" was all J.J. said.

What happened to Uncle Paulie? Paulie thought. Paulie smiled and stepped forward to embrace the young man, who instead offered his hand. Paulie shook it and then watched J.J. check his wristwatch for the time.

Johnny began, "Paulie and I was just talking—"

"You know what, Johnny? Hold off on that. I'll call you in a few days. Let me see how things go," Paulie interrupted.

"You sure?" Johnny said, sounding genuine.

"Yeah, don't worry. Forget about what I said," Paulie said, slowly backing away from Johnny and his son. "I really got to get back to the kids."

"You going already? Take some fruit back with you, at least. I brought too much." Johnny gestured back into the dark recesses of the driveway.

"Nah, I'm good. I gotta go." Paulie began to turn away, but Johnny stepped forward and gave Paulie a farewell hug, just as Johnny's son turned and walked back up the driveway without uttering another word.

"You need a ride or something?" Johnny asked, as Paulie turned again to walk away.

"Nah, I'm good. I'm good," Paulie repeated.

"Hey, Paulie. Don't be a stranger," Johnny shouted as his old friend began his long walk home.

JULY 4, 1976

EVENING

CHAPTER 33

Darkness overwhelmed the hazy twilight. Dee hated nighttime, always had. Not that she was ever someone who woke up singing "Zip-a-Dee-Doo-Dah" every morning to begin with. At least everything was out in the open during the daytime; less places for things to hide. Standing alone in her gate, the street was now filled with shadows drifting past one another. Even the surviving decorations—the flags, bunting, and banners—had dimmed from bright red, white, and blue to muted bands of gray at nightfall. The DJ still hijacked power from the block's center streetlight, the lamp's glow replaced by an unsteady flicker. The loudest of the explosions had subsided momentarily, a détente, replaced by the sounds of skyrockets zipping into the air and bursting into a shower of colorful embers raining down from above. These were just random projectiles, though; the more elaborate fireworks displays were still to come. By now, Dee would usually just be annoyed with the oohs and aahs from the crowd, people gaping up at the sky as if they'd never seen a firework before, but she was too livid with every member of her family to care about anything else. What they had done to her today! She couldn't wait for this day, this torture, to end.

Not long before, Alex's friend Tommy had lumbered down the block to ask if Alex could have ice cream cake at his house.

"It's Carvel," Tommy shared with great joy. "They made an Uncle Sam Cookie Puss."

Dee barely acknowledged the child's presence as she weighed the request. For the last hour, she'd been engaged in a glaring match with her oldest: she planted firmly at the entrance to the front gate, Tony at the front window. Dee's initial inclination was to demand Alex get his little ass back home. When Tommy added, "Then we're going to watch the Yankee game on television," she reconsidered. *At least that keeps the boy away from the rest of these animals,* she thought. Tommy was shocked when she acquiesced without any other questions. Any other time, the chubby boy would have cracked like an egg under the usual interrogation—*Where is my son? Why isn't he with you now?* With a noticeable look of relief, Tommy hurried away to deliver the good news.

Almost immediately after Tommy departed, Tony decided to end his self-imposed exile. Dee had glanced away from the window just for a moment, to make sure Tommy was heading toward his home. When Dee turned back to the window, it was empty. Seconds later, Tony shot out the front door and walked right past her without sparing a word or look. Dee started to say something as he flew out the gate, but for once, she was unsure of her words. She technically had never ordered Tony up into the apartment. He'd fled there on his own. Despite her rage, her disappointment, the impulse to shout at him, to demand he get back upstairs, never came.

"Stay on the block" was all Dee could come up with as her son walked away.

"Fine," Tony snapped back without turning his head as he

marched into the street. Dee quickly lost sight of him in the swirling crowd.

Almost on cue, Mario sauntered across his own gate to stand opposite Dee on his side of the short wall.

"Where's your husband? He has my medal." Mario spoke in a teasing tone; he shot a resentful look down at his sandals. And where was her husband while all this was going on? The last time she'd seen him, Paulie had been running through the street like a real schmuck, and then he'd just disappeared.

"You need a medal, too, Mario?" Dee snapped back. "You don't got enough?" A skyrocket exploded in the sky above the El, a burst of orange embers showering down over the empty tracks.

"You see, that's the fireworks I like." He tapped his own chest with the tip of one finger. "So pretty." Dee turned reflexively to look, but the embers had already dimmed and vanished.

Mario cleared his throat, his expression turning more serious. "I would say this to Paulie, but I . . ." He paused for a moment and looked down, searching for the right words. He raised his head back up, looked Dee in the eye, and said, "No joking around, he ever need to make a few extra dollars, I could always use some help in the shop."

"My husband has a good job," Dee said, a puzzled and annoyed look on her face.

"I know, I know," Mario said, throwing his hands up defensively. "I just mean . . ." Dee didn't wait for Mario to finish his sentence. She turned her back to him and walked to the other side of the gate.

★

Alex felt guilty about lying to his mother but felt he had no choice.

He knew he'd get scolded just for flipping baseball cards; it wouldn't be the first time. Dee's frequent refrain: "I don't buy you things so you can gamble them away." And if his father were in the immediate vicinity, she'd add, "This is because all they watch you do is play horses!"

Alex was scared to death over what might happen to him if his mother found out that he'd literally lost his shirt. He looked down at the plain gray tank top he now wore—Dennis's tank top. Too snug at his belly, it made him look like an overstuffed sausage. The worst part was Dennis made him say "Pretty please with sugar on top" before he finally flung the shirt in his face. Well, Dennis *was* doing him a favor, as exchanging shirts hadn't been a stipulation of the bet. Alex hoped now he'd get the opportunity to wipe the smirk off that jerk's face.

Alex just needed some time to think. He had to come up with some plan to get his shirt back, assuming Dennis reappeared again. Alex pictured him riding his bike from block to block, swindling kids out of their baseball cards. The furthest Alex had come with his plan so far was the story he'd charged Tommy to deliver to his mother to buy him some time. It wasn't a complete lie. He was now standing inside Tommy's front gate. Tommy's mother had shouted about ice cream cake on her way back inside her house, and, through the curtains of Tommy's first-floor window, Alex had just watched the Yankees take a three-run lead on four singles.

He turned away from the game—he didn't have time to waste on distractions. Any moment his mother could come up the block looking for him. She'd slapped his brother across the face, in front of everyone, and Tony hadn't even done anything wrong—the other kid had started the trouble. Alex feared, especially after the whole Zizi incident, what might lay in store for him if he couldn't somehow reclaim his shirt from Dennis.

Alex looked to his friends in hopes of inspiration. Vito was searching along the street curb, looking for duds—an activity usually reserved for the day after the Fourth, when many children would comb the cracks and crevices of the street and sidewalks scavenging for undetonated fireworks. Tommy hovered by the front door, standing on his tippy-toes so he could peer through the upper windowpane for the first signs of his mother and ice cream cake. Alex hung his head. He wondered where Tony and his father were right now, though he doubted either could help him out of his predicament.

"Found one!" Vito shouted. He ran to his friends, holding high in one hand a solitary bent firecracker.

"It's all wet," Tommy said, momentarily abandoning his dessert-spotting post to examine the firecracker.

"So what? I'll make a genie," Vito said, referring to the act of igniting the insides of a dud firecracker. One touch of a match and *poof*—a sudden bright flash that resembled the burst of smoke that, legend had it, immediately preceded the appearance of a summoned genie.

Vito peeled away the damp outer wrapping. Then he carefully pulled the inner layers apart, exposing a thin stripe of black powder packed inside. Vito slowly and carefully laid the unraveled strips of damp paper atop the sidewalk, careful not to spill any of the powder inside.

"The powder looks all wet too," Tommy observed.

"Don't jinx me. Go look for your cake."

Alex watched Vito reach into his back pocket and pull out a book of matches. He wondered for a moment what would be worse for him—his parents learning that he'd lost his shirt, or his parents catching him playing with matches. Vito struck the match and pressed the flame to the powder. He let the flame burn down almost to his fingertips. Nothing. Sometimes a dud was just a dud. A disappointed Vito tossed the match away.

"I say we jump him," Vito suddenly blurted, leaping to his feet.

"Huh?" Alex responded, confused at how his friend could switch mental gears so quickly.

"We jump him and take the shirt." Vito's hands flew excitedly as he simultaneously pantomimed and voiced the plan he had concocted on the fly. "One of us can be the lookout. Then, when we spot him, I'll wave him over like I gotta tell him something." Vito added a beckoning wave, then immediately, violently, shoved both hands out. "And then Tommy comes over and knocks him off the bike and sits on him." Vito pointed at Alex. "Then you come over, pull the shirt off him, and we make a run for it." Vito smiled and folded his arms in front of his chest, quite pleased with the prospect of his plan.

Alex stared back silently; then he turned and looked over to Tommy, who had walked back to his door to check on the cake situation. He turned back to face Vito.

"I don't think it'll work," Alex said. Vito stared back with an exasperated look, his attempt at atonement falling short.

"I think I saw my mother go in the kitchen," Tommy cheerfully reported. Alex wasn't feeling very hungry anymore, even for ice cream. He looked back into the street and noticed the crowd had grown denser. He walked over to the gate and peered down the sidewalk. A steady stream of people filtered in his direction.

"I think the fireworks are gonna start," Vito said, an excited look on his face, suggesting he'd now moved on from Alex's shirt dilemma. Alex's enthusiasm for the fireworks display had all but evaporated, but he was a sitting duck to be spotted in Tommy's front gate if his mother was indeed making her way up the block with the rest of the masses. He could better hide in the crowd. Alex and Vito headed out the gate.

"Hey, what about the ice cream cake?" Tommy shouted after his friends. He glanced back nervously between his own front door and the direction his friends now walked before sighing and jogging after them.

CHAPTER 34

Paulie felt like crap. His knee throbbed, his head hurt, and he was probably dehydrated. Happy fucking Fourth of July! He looked like shit too—at least the darkness somewhat masked the heat blotches dotting his face and hid his torn clothes, now completely soaked through with sweat. Despite wanting nothing more than to take a shower and lie down in his bed and let the shit stain of a day be over and done with, he stopped one block from his home. He thought about continuing, turning onto his own block, but the image of Dee, with cigarette in one hand, glaring back, quickly dissuaded him. So, instead of pressing forward, he turned and began walking up the preceding block that ran parallel to his own.

He walked slowly, passing other men with their families. Some bent over to light sparklers for their young children; some clustered in the corners of their front gates and chatted with neighbors. He heard two men in polo shirts swapping summer vacation plans. At least there was no DJ blasting music on this block. Instead, some families had taken their portable radios into their front gates. Parents and children sat around bridge tables or on benches listening to an oldies station or the ball game. Paulie imagined, for a moment, what the rest of his extended family was doing at his brother's house right now: they were probably all sitting in the backyard, eating pastries, maybe playing bocce ball on the little court Vic had cleared across from his tomato plants. Paulie's thoughts then swung to Johnny and his family. He could imagine what they had to say about him once he'd left. It didn't really matter, anyway, he supposed.

Paulie reached the opposite end of the block. The avenues were absent of traffic. Most people were already where they wanted to be by this point of the night. Want—that was a funny concept, Paulie thought. What did he want? Was it the admiration of his wife and children, or at least something that resembled a modicum of respect? Was it to go back to work in a job that meant only a paycheck to him, doing what he was told to do by men in short-sleeve button-downs day after day? Did he want a house in Boca and a woman half his age on his arm? He stood there for a few moments, staring blankly into the streetlight's glow. Nobody cared what he wanted—that was the truth of the matter. He wasn't sure if *he* even cared anymore. Paulie turned right and began walking home. He had nowhere left to go.

★

A brooding Tony leaned against the brick wall of the narrow alleyway beside Sally's building. He stared down at the laces of his sneakers. Sally leaned against the same wall a few feet away. Tony could tell his friend was trying to be silent and still, but it just wasn't in his nature. Every minute or so Sally pushed himself away from the wall, paced a few feet toward where the garbage cans were stacked, then paced back. He was biting his nails now, while staring at Tony.

"Stop looking at me," Tony said.

"Where you want me to look? The wall? Here, fine, I'll stare at the wall for you." Sally spun and stared at the wall, his legs lifting in turn as if about to take a step. Tony almost cracked a smile. It was Sally who had found Tony drifting through the street after he'd left his mother standing in their gate. Tony had zigzagged from sidewalk to sidewalk, simultaneously searching but not wishing to be seen. Tony was sure that people were chuckling at him as he passed. When he'd felt an arm come down across his shoulders, he'd spun around quickly, fist clenched and cocked, expecting a Lombardi.

"Whoa, whoa, easy there, Ali," Sally had exclaimed, both his hands thrown up defensively.

Tony relaxed his fist, dropped his arm, and exhaled.

"C'mon," Sally said, and Tony followed his friend up the block.

Sally walked in front of him with his chin up and out, like he was his bodyguard. They marched all the way to the end of the block, where Sally lived in the walk-up above the corner bagel store. Sally drifted into the alley, the same alley where they'd spent many an afternoon playing when they were younger. It had always been an especially fun place to make a snow fort after a heavy snow. The two boys would pile a high wedge of snow in front of the alley. Insulated from attack on three sides, they'd won many a snowball fight. But at this moment, the alley was simply a place for Tony to hide.

Sally squeezed by Tony to walk to the alley's edge and peek his head out. He turned back over his shoulder and said, "I think the fireworks are about to start."

Tony shrugged.

Sally shook his head and came back over. "Since when are you some chooch sulking in an alley? C'mon! Let's get back out there."

Tony stared through the darkness at the brick wall opposite him. His mother had made him look like a fool, like a little kid. He imagined he was the joke of the block. Worse, he was sure Benny had carried the news of his humiliation to his own block, to Maria. Images of Maria laughing, laughing at him like those other girls had, tormented him. He was fine staying put.

"Boo!" Tony heard someone shout from the alley's entrance, and he and Sally both jumped. Sally spun around and cocked his fist. Tony saw two large silhouettes hovering at the alley's entrance, one taller, one wider. The taller one stepped forward and smiled. It was Chippy.

"You boys got a little powwow going on here?"

"Fuck!" Sally shouted. "You almost made me shit my pants."

"It's cool, it's cool," Chippy said, bowing his head slightly. "My humble apologies." Chippy looked around while he twisted his mustache. "So, what? You guys getting high back here?" Sally and Tony shook their heads no. Chippy arched his eyebrows and asked, "Ya wanna?" He took his cigarette box out from his front pocket, flipped the lid open, and extracted a rolled joint.

Without waiting for an answer, he lit it, blew out the flame, leaving a glowing tip, and took a deep toke. Chippy's companion entered the alleyway and walked over to the group. He held his hand out. Chippy coughed out a cloud of smoke and handed the joint to his friend. "This . . ." Chippy paused to cough several times. "This is Abe."

Tony looked at Abe. The man looked like he'd just escaped from prison. Regardless, Tony nodded his head to greet the bearded man, as did Sally; Abe nodded back in greeting and took a toke.

"Who's up?" Abe asked, holding out the joint. Sally, twitching with excitement, snatched it from him, took a deep hit, and began to cough violently. Sally's arms snapped back and forth as he coughed while trying to hand the joint back to Chippy. Instead of taking it back, Chippy gestured with his chin over to Tony. Sally began to shake his head, but when he turned, his eyes almost crossed in surprise at the sight of Tony reaching his hand out. Tony had never even smoked a cigarette.

"You sure?" Sally asked his friend between hacks. Tony took the joint without uttering a response; he avoided looking his friend in the eye. Tony spun the twisted paper in his fingers a few times before raising it to his lips and inhaling. He swallowed a small mouthful of smoke, which burned his throat. He quickly coughed the concoction back out. The joint continued to make several rounds, and Tony managed to hold the smoke in a little longer on each successive turn, though not as long as Chippy and Abe.

Tony waited to feel the effects, but he wasn't even sure how or what he was supposed to feel or how soon he would feel it. All he knew was that his throat burned and his mouth felt dry. On a final revolution, Chippy took one last toke, extinguished the lit end of the joint against the brick wall, and dropped it back into his cigarette pack.

"All right, time to go to work," Chippy said, and he and Abe walked to the end of the alley and began emptying black garbage bags from two large oil drums that served as trash bins for the bagel store. Once emptied, they each tipped a can on its side and began dragging them out from the alleyway, the steel edges scraping loudly against the concrete. Tony and Sally began backing out of the alley to make way.

As Chippy passed Tony, he asked, "Hey, you see your pop around?"

Tony shook his head no. "Why?"

"No reason," Chippy said as he continued to drag his drum over the sidewalk, then the curb, and into the middle of the street.

Tony was old enough to remember back to when the big fireworks finale was more of a multiblock collaboration celebrated in the public schoolyard. That had come to an unfortunate and abrupt end several years ago. The schoolyard's huge dumpsters had been overflowing with trash when the Fourth rolled around that year. The bundles of discarded school decorations, stacks of loose-leaf, and cardboard served as eager kindling for the pyrotechnics, and the fireworks display quickly turned into a three-alarm fire that blackened the entire schoolyard wall. Since then, the cops kept a squad car parked at the schoolyard entrance every Fourth. The unintended consequence, however, was that the one large celebration had splintered into multiple smaller versions occurring on residential streets—with Chippy's show alone traditionally almost as explosive as the original.

Tony turned back to look for Sally but didn't see him. He stared down the block and across to the opposite sidewalk, searching through the shadows for his friend's lanky frame. He squinted. Something seemed off with his depth perception—everything looked farther away from him than it should. He shook his head and turned his gaze back toward the street; in the few seconds he'd turned away, it seemed that the random clusters of people had massed into a large crowd.

Tony rubbed both eyes with his fingertips. He wasn't sure what to do next. He thought about stepping off the curb into the street to join the crowd or to search for Sally, but there were so many people now, he wasn't sure where they'd all come from. People kept coming and coming, and he thought about turning and running before the crowd could swallow him up. But when he looked around, he realized he had already wandered deep inside it, that he was surrounded by people on all sides. The realization frightened him. He had to get away from everyone. There were too many people. He tried to move his legs, but they didn't comply, as if they'd taken root in the asphalt. All he could do was turn his head to stare at the swelling masses. The crowd formed a huge circle, and at its epicenter, there was Chippy and his friend Abe. He spotted Sally with them and wanted desperately to call out to his friend, but he found himself unable to utter a word. Tony felt the crowd shift again, or maybe the street had shifted beneath his feet, two tectonic plates drifting out of place, and Tony was now on the outskirts of the crowd. He felt something soft press against his arm. He turned.

"Looking for me?"

It was Maria.

CHAPTER 35

As Dee lit a cigarette, she noted new movements in the crowd—clusters of people began drifting up the block. Before stepping onto the sidewalk, she turned and looked back into the gate, as if to remind herself that it was empty. Something wasn't right, she told herself. Something just wasn't right. She inhaled a throatful of smoke and began to follow the crowd.

She kept to the less congested sidewalk, proceeding in parallel to the swelling mob. In the shadows, the mob melded together, a singular amorphous entity lurching slowly up the street. Dee strained her eyes, trying to discern if her oldest had been sucked into the mass, or perhaps she'd stumble onto a glimpse of her husband. She spotted neither. As she passed Zizi's porch, she spotted Richie, leaning against its facade, one arm curled over some tramp with bangs and long straight black hair, her blouse unbuttoned down to her navel.

"Richie, you see Tony?" Dee asked, startling him.

Richie, clearly startled, and also drunk and stoned, struggled to answer. He looked over at the porch steps, the last place he remembered seeing him, but he wasn't quite sure when that was. Dee watched him bite his lower lip while he turned his head, clearly scanning the patio and immediate sidewalk for something lost.

Richie opened his mouth to speak, but Dee cut him off before he could utter a word. "Go back to your whooers," she growled and stormed off. Behind her, the girl with the black hair began to protest, but Richie tapped her on the shoulder. He shook his head to convey that it was best to say nothing.

Dee's heart raced. She was muttering to herself now, spitting out curses at everyone she could think of, with special attention given to Richie and her absentee husband. Dear Lord, what her children put her through, what her husband put her through. No one knew how she suffered, what it was like to be a mother. Only she knew.

Dee approached the massive crowd, now overflowing from the street onto both bordering sidewalks. It became increasingly difficult to navigate. Pressed tightly against the masses, almost impossible now to spot anyone who wasn't standing directly next to her. She looked left and right and then began to turn, spinning in circles, craning her neck in a fruitless attempt to see better. Not to be defeated, she jabbed out her elbows and continued to force her way through the crowd. She wouldn't stop looking until she found her children.

★

"This sucks," Vito yelled directly into Alex's left ear. "We can't see anything."

Alex flinched at the volume. His friend's observation was accurate, but while their view was less than perfect and larger people than they were constantly pushing past, Alex did feel sufficiently hidden from his mother's telescopic sight.

Alex just kept nodding as Vito protested, but then he felt Tommy's heavy hand tapping his right shoulder. He turned and looked up at his friend. Tommy bent down and said, "You're not going to be able to see Dennis, if he shows up."

Crap! Alex thought—Tommy was right. He couldn't afford to hide in the crowd. He needed to find a covert point where he could remain secluded but maintain a clear vantage point. Alex looked Tommy in the eye, nodded, and then gestured forward with his chin. Tommy read the unspoken signal, turned, and began to plow his way out of the crowd, with Alex and Vito following directly behind.

The three boys emerged from the crowd on the sidewalk opposite Alex's building. Alex heard people cheer, and the boys all turned, but nothing was exploding yet. The crowd swelled farther up onto the sidewalk. The boys were forced to backpedal and soon found themselves standing at the floor of a sunken driveway. Alex looked up and around. To his left was a tall, wide brick wall, and to his right was another wall that served as the base to a long stairway that led to the single-family home above the garage behind him. Unlike most houses on his block, Alex had no idea who lived here. He glanced up to see every window dark, shades drawn, which probably explained the empty driveway.

"Hey, watch it!" Vito shouted as the crowd pushed back again, and the boys were wedged against a row of three aluminum garbage pails that reeked of rotting vegetables. Alex found a small nook between Tommy and the cans where he had some elbow room, but unfortunately, he still couldn't see a thing.

Vito suddenly jumped up onto Tommy's back. For a second, it looked like Vito had started an impromptu wrestling match by locking his friend in the Chief Jay Strongbow sleeper hold.

"You're"—cough—"choking me," Tommy blurted. But with an

acrobat's finesse, Vito quickly climbed up Tommy's back, stood for a moment on his shoulders, and leaped sideways. In midair, he grabbed the outside of the iron railing that bordered the end of the stairway and caught the small edge of the concrete step that extended out below the railing. Delighting in his discovery, Vito held his hand over his brow, like a sailor that had scaled the mast of the ship to scan for distant shores. "I can see everything," he shouted down. "Climb up!"

Alex and Tommy exchanged looks. Tommy turned both palms over, locked his fingers together, and then signaled to Alex with a nod of his head. Alex stepped one foot into Tommy's palms, and his friend easily lifted him up, but Alex's leg immediately began to wobble. He teetered forward, then backward. Tommy grunted beneath him. Vito held onto the railing with one hand and, with one foot planted on the lip of the step, swung out to grab Alex at the elbow and pull him upward. Once within reach, Alex grabbed the railing for dear life and leaped off Tommy's sore palms. Vito, situated on the step above Alex, patted his friend on his shoulder.

Both boys then heard from below, "Hey, a little help." Tommy stared up, both arms and hands raised above his head. Alex and Vito's eyes widened, and they tried their best to plant their feet and tighten their grip on the railing as they each extended a hand for their friend. This wasn't going to be easy.

CHAPTER 36

Maria's kiss quickly dismissed Tony's worst fears. Tony stood there as she took him by both hands and leaned back so he was tethering her from falling backward while she smiled wide as they faced each other. Tony smiled back but was nervous staring Maria directly in the eyes, so he let his gaze lower. She wore a striped tube top and powder blue terry cloth shorts. He became transfixed by the smoothness of her tan skin and then the tiny slit of her belly button just above the waistband of her shorts. He was staring at her stomach, which he soon realized was a creepy thing to do. So, with some effort, he forced his gaze back to eye level. He wasn't sure if he was stoned, if Maria knew he was stoned, or if Maria was wondering if he knew that she knew he was stoned. Tony grew paranoid that the crowd's attention was suddenly directed toward him and Maria. He was scared to even glance sideways lest he be confronted with peering eyes, accusing stares. So he kept his eyes trained on Maria, and the more he stared, the more he felt like himself, like he was being poured back into the shell of his body. Maria tugged herself forward, wrapped her arms around his waist, and he felt her chest press against him. He felt his heartbeat then, and it began to race as she raised herself up on her toes to kiss him, and he felt her lips on his, her tongue slide into his mouth, and he pressed his mouth tighter against hers. He felt like himself again.

When the long kiss ended, Maria lowered herself back down against him, and Tony felt the fullness of her chest slide down over him. They stood there for a moment, belly to belly, arms clasped around each other's waists. Maria ran the palms of her hands over his arms, from elbows to shoulders.

She smiled slyly. "I heard what happened." Tony's breath felt stuck in his throat; memories of the humiliation suffered at his mother's hand began to flash in his mind. Then Maria asked, "Were you jealous?"

Huh? Tony thought. He wondered whether the details of the entire incident had warped over the course of interblock gossip, or maybe some details had fallen off. He certainly hoped so. But suddenly, all that seemed not to matter. Maria was smiling that smile of hers, and Tony couldn't begin to imagine anything that mattered more than that. He shook his head in response to her question.

"You sure?" Maria asked and pressed herself a little closer. "I heard you were really jealous." Tony cocked his head to one side and started to say something, but Maria kept talking, her tone suddenly angry. "Benny's a douchebag and a liar." Maria then smiled wide and leaned closer to whisper, "I'm all yours."

For Tony, everything then slipped away—the fight, the race, baseball, school, his parents, all of it. All that was left was Maria and how good she felt and how good she made him feel. He didn't think that he'd ever want to move from the spot where they stood until she playfully slid herself up to his other ear and said, "Let's find some privacy." Tony's thoughts raced. He scanned around with Maria still in his arms. His stare lingered for a moment on the alleyway he had recently sought refuge in, but when he looked at Maria, the slant of her eyebrows suggested that the alleyway wasn't what she had in mind.

"Are your parents home?" she asked.

"Well, maybe—" Tony started, but Maria interrupted him.

"Maybe what? Are you ashamed to be with me?" she accused, her expression suddenly severe. She watched Tony freeze up, mouth agape, a panic in his eyes. Maria smiled then, either in amusement, pity, or a little bit of both. She leaned in close again and whispered, "Don't you want your birthday present?" Before common sense had a chance to respond, *YES!* a voice inside him asserted. Yes, this was what *he* wanted. He took Maria's hand and began leading her in the direction away from his house.

"Don't you live that way?" she asked, pointing down the block.

"Trust me," he said over his shoulder.

CHAPTER 37

As a dejected Paulie turned onto his block and drifted into a large
crowd of people, he didn't notice Tony and Maria passing in the opposite direction, just several yards to his right. Robotically, he plod-
ded forward, stopping only when the person directly in front of him
did the same. He stood there staring at the back of someone's head
for a full minute until movement resumed, and the crowd surged,
splitting in half to encircle something just ahead. Through the split,
Tony spotted Chippy at the center of it all. Chippy! Like a moth to a
flame, he began to force his way through the crowd, barging between
people standing shoulder to shoulder, oblivious to their dirty looks
and angry protests.

He had almost reached the front, but the last ring of spectators
directly ahead of him happened to be kids, boys and girls maybe
eleven or twelve at most, that he could easily see over. Now he spied
Abe too. Both men were circling two rusty oil drums set in the middle of the street, side by side, like a double shotgun barrel.

Paulie watched the two men line the street with mats and mats
of fireworks that extended out from the oil drums like petals of a
flower. They both carried large brown paper bags from which they

continued to extract mat after mat, growing the mounds. Abe, who spun as he walked, alternated between steps forward and backward, tossing mats in a seemingly random pattern, while Chippy was much more meticulous in his craft. He never tossed a mat more than a few inches from where he stood, and once it had fallen, he tilted his head sideways to examine its placement as if he were an expert mason trying to build a level stone wall.

Paulie stared, almost trancelike, and soon was surprised that the impulse to confront (strangle) Chippy had faded as quickly as it had flared. Truth was, he didn't feel anything at all, his emotional pilot light extinguished. So he just stared, watching the two men dole out explosives. Paulie wasn't even annoyed when the crowd squeezed tighter around him or when a small boy dug his sharp elbow into his thigh, trying to wedge himself closer to the front. Only the smallest recognition registered with Paulie that Tony's friend Sally had emerged from the crowd and was now assisting Chippy and Abe with the setup, handing each another stuffed brown bag once they'd emptied the contents of the ones they carried; however, the sight of Sally did not tip any mental domino that led to thoughts of his own son. No, Paulie just watched and stared.

After the last mat had been placed on the ground, Chippy and Abe ran back to the sidewalk and pried open a wooden crate. Chippy removed a large black cylinder from the crate and handed it to Abe, then took another in his own hands. They carried the mortars into the center of the street, and each man folded over the rim of a drum to reach down and carefully place the explosive into its bottom. Chippy and Abe made another trip to the sidewalk and back, each carrying another stuffed brown paper bag. Both men flipped over their bags and spilled the unseen contents inside the drums.

The bags were emptied, and Chippy gestured with his chin to

Abe. Abe nodded and trotted over to the sidewalk and bent over a duffel bag. He fished around inside for something, then sauntered back, his feet sliding through the sloping piles of fireworks like he was trudging along a blizzard-covered sidewalk. Chippy shouted over to him not to mess up the piles, but Abe continued his stroll, his right arm swinging widely at his side. Paulie initially couldn't see what he carried with him, but as soon as Abe reached the oil drums, he raised his arm overhead to reveal a rusted tin fuel can. He tilted the can on its side and began spilling its contents equally, shuffling his feet like a dancer as he spun from drum to drum until the last drop of gasoline had fallen. Abe's pour reminded Paulie of the way Dee dumped olive oil into a salad bowl. She went through gallon-sized Filippo Berrio Extra Virgin Olive Oil cans like they were filled with water.

Once Abe seemed content with the saturation levels of both drums, he began walking backward, away from the dual barrels in an expanding concentric circle, a cascade of gasoline trailing along in front of him. Chippy shouted another complaint that Abe was messing up the evenly matted planes, but Abe just kept whistling and walking until every drop had completely spilled from the can. Abe looked at the empty can, looked at the drums, set his feet like he was at the foul line, and shot a perfect basket as the tin fuel can arced high into the sky and fell directly into the center of one drum.

"Two points," Abe shouted and high-fived whoever in the crowd was within reach.

Chippy shouted something to Sally, who shouted something to someone else; a chain of shouts raced down the block, and moments later, the DJ cut the music. The sudden silence was unnerving. Paulie's knees almost buckled; he felt suddenly untethered. The neighborhood had been exploding all day: muffled bursts and rattles were the ambient backdrop to every song and conversation. But now the only audible sounds were hushed whispers as the anticipation mounted. Even the whispers vanished, and an eerie silence stretched for several anxious seconds. Everything was now set: firecrackers, rockets, bombs, gasoline, fuses—an entire block huddled in a massive circle of wide eyes and gaping mouths, waiting. Someone just needed to strike a match.

★

Tony tugged Maria by the hand, hastily leading her down the block that ran parallel to his own. He walked at such a rapid pace that at a quick glance it looked as if he were trying to run away from her. Maria laughed, seemingly amused at Tony's eager pace. She wasn't dressed for bouncing down the pavement, though, and more than once she needed to adjust her tube top.

They turned left and continued down the avenue, only to stop abruptly in front of the three-story gray-brick building that sat on the corner of Tony's block. Tony sidled up close to the wall and peeked around its edge. He had a clear line of sight to his front gate and, as he suspected, saw no sign of his parents or brother. Briefly, it registered that he hadn't laid eyes on either his father or Alex for some time, but Maria squeezed his hand impatiently, so he double-checked again that there was no sign of light shining from his front windows. He stepped around the corner, tugging Maria along with him. He felt suddenly conspicuous as he turned up the empty sidewalk and crossed the street. He glanced up the street and saw that seemingly everyone, neighbors and visitors alike, now congregated at the far end of the block, awaiting the first spark.

Tony and Maria flew into and across his front gate. Tony pushed open his front door and motioned with his head for Maria to enter.

He nervously glanced up and down the block as Maria slid inside. Tony stepped away from the door, and it slammed shut behind him. They stood together inside the tiny foyer, and Tony hesitantly stared at the single flight of stairs that that led up to his apartment. He felt Maria squeeze his hand again, and he led her upstairs.

CHAPTER 38

Paulie jutted his elbows and rammed his hips into anyone who tried to usurp his spot in the crowd. He had ceded enough today. This would be his spot until he no longer wanted it. He watched Chippy circle the perimeter of his craftsmanship one last time. Chippy scanned the beds of mats and took a deep breath in through his nostrils, perhaps to confirm that a sufficient scent of gasoline fumes clung to the heavy night air. Paulie glanced up at the sky directly over the drums; there was no tree cover at risk for fire. The lone decades-old elm that had once cast its proud branches over this section of the street had caught fire in the '71 fireworks display and sustained terminal damage. It was cut down the following month and replaced with a narrow sapling that still struggled to fill its predecessor's roots.

Chippy stood directly opposite from Paulie now but still hadn't noticed him standing in the vast crowd. Paulie watched a look of satisfaction wash over Chippy as he surveyed the faces of those assembled: the masses had gathered to witness what came next, what he had crafted. A certain authority emanated from Chippy now; the crowd was wholly captivated, their collective gaze locked on his every move, and Chippy, fully aware that he held them in thrall, raised his right hand, calling for silence. The last hushed whispers quickly vanished. Chippy clenched his fist above his head, and the over-enthusiastic crowd circling the soon-to-be inferno suddenly constricted, drawing too close. Seeing this, Chippy's hands immediately shot up, palms facing them, commanding the masses to move back. Paulie, like the rest, obeyed, pushing backward without any mind to whoever was behind him. He felt his heart thumping against his chest, beating rapidly in anticipation. *Light the match, Chippy. Burn it all down.*

Chippy milked the mob's anticipation one last time. He raised his hand overhead. This time Abe emerged from the crowd, his right arm held high above his head, a rolled-up newspaper clenched in his fist. Abe dug his other hand into his pocket and pulled out a silver cigarette lighter. With a flick of the wrist, the lighter's cap popped open, freeing a bright-yellow tongue of flame. Abe grinned and raised the flame to the tip of the rolled newspaper; his makeshift torch blazed.

Paulie heard gasps from those closest to him. He held his own breath, waiting and wanting. He saw Abe look to Chippy, saw something sinister curl at the edges of Chippy's mouth as he swung his raised arm down, and Abe dropped the torch.

The flames raced left and right, two blazing streams that spiraled and spread. Immediately, a thick circle of fire surrounded the drums. For a moment it felt like the entire block had gathered, in solidarity, around a wide but low campfire. Then there was the first pop. An almost ridiculously small and insignificant sound as one fuse burned down and the first firecracker exploded. A second later, the drum-roll began, the rat-a-tat-tat of multiple mats igniting and exploding simultaneously. Paulie's eyes widened. His head, everyone's heads, began to nod subtly to the beat of the rapid blasts. Mat after mat exploded, a series of violent machine-gun bursts. But no one was running for cover.

★

Tony heard the kitchen phone ringing inside the apartment just as they reached the second-floor landing. The sound stopped him cold in his tracks. Even though he was sure the apartment was empty, Tony paused and held up his hand, instructing Maria to do the same. It rang and rang, ten times, before finally stopping. He exhaled and slowly pushed open the unlocked door. He pulled Maria inside. The apartment was pitch black; every light shut off. (Electricity wasn't free, his parents often said.) Though fainter, a trace of burnt pasta still hung in the air. He let Maria's hand fall and took several quick steps inside. He reached his hand out to intuitively find and flip on the kitchen light switch.

The halogen tubes flickered on, and Tony raced back past Maria to lock the front door. He again took her by the hand, and they both stepped away from the door, then paused. He stood once more at the nexus between rooms, the exact same spot in which, just hours ago, he'd tried to win permission from his parents to visit the girl who now stood beside him, whose hand he now held.

Tony looked left and right, not moving from the spot where he stood, unsure of what to do next. He became very aware of the thumping of his heart, the racing of his breath. This was crazy. They shouldn't be here. They needed to turn around and leave. Quickly. He could just make up some excuse, any excuse. Just as he became convinced that they should flee, go somewhere else, anywhere else, he felt Maria's hand on his arm. He turned and was immediately met by her lips on his.

CHAPTER 39

The noise from the fireworks display was so loud now that Alex crouched down and looped his arm around the iron railing so he could keep a finger in both his ears. Tommy pressed his large hands against the side of his head like earmuffs, while Vito, seemingly impervious to the sound, jumped and hollered at the top of his lungs. Just when the noise appeared to tail off, another section, another layer, exploded. It sounded like an unending parade made up solely of snare drum players, every drummer starting and stopping of their own volition, and when they all played simultaneously, the noise threatened to split his head in two.

Thick swirls of smoke began to rise from the flames and tattered paper, but the heavy, humid air resisted, and the smoke coalesced and hung suspended in a gray storm cloud just several feet above the flames. The outside of the oil drums then caught fire, as did the insides. A burst of red sparkles shot out from one of the barrels, and Alex, like the rest of the crowd, oohed as red embers streaked into the sky. Then the first mortar exploded, a thunderous blast so loud and sudden that Alex almost lost his grip and fell.

"I want to get closer," Vito screamed over the noise at his two friends. Just as Alex began to shake his head from side to side, Vito, not waiting for consensus, jumped down. He bolted a few steps toward the crowd but then paused and turned, waving his hand, urging his friends to follow. Alex looked over at Tommy, whose face was a fleshy mirror of trepidation. Despite his unease, Tommy began to carefully, and with great difficulty, climb down from the stairs onto the garbage pails below. Alex sighed, and once Tommy stood safely upon terra firma, he followed.

Just as Alex's sneakers touched the pavement—*bam!* He flinched; another explosion, louder than any before. Every instinct told him to turn and walk far away from the noise and fire, but he didn't. Instead, he followed his friends.

★

Animals. Fucking animals, Dee thought as she searched through the crowd and watched their faces contort as they hollered and cheered, and the flames soared above the tallest spectator's head. The detonated mats, blown apart into gasoline-soaked tatters, fed the blaze, and the inferno seemed to swallow the oil drums whole. The rockets that still launched appeared to burst from the very heart of the inferno but were completely ablaze as they shot into the sky and barely cleared the neighboring rooftops before exploding.

Dee watched the fire cast an unnatural orange glow over the crowd. Faces appeared and vanished into the shadows as the swelling flames flickered. She could barely breathe now. She held a hand to her breast, her gaze darting from side to side, desperate for a glimpse of Alex or Tony. Even though she stood at the far edge of the crowd, Dee could now feel the heat of the immense blaze across her face. She ignored the discomfort and continued to press forward, searching.

After pushing her way closer to the front, Dee's mouth fell open in disbelief as several males, teenagers, darted forward from the crowd, closer to the fire. Some tossed newspaper or cardboard boxes into the flames; others flung single packs of fireworks. But any small explosions were dwarfed by the dull roar of the fire and thunderous echoes of more powerful bombs exploding inside the oil drums. As the heat intensified, a mirage effect formed around the fire, warping all in its orbit. Dee couldn't believe her eyes—she spotted children, children now running at the fire, tossing whatever was in their hands. She gasped, watching one small boy, no older than her Alex, charge at the fire and then recoil back at the last moment, as if daring the flames to engulf him.

Sparks spewed from the center of the flames. Red and yellow fireballs erupted and shot overhead. They exploded in bright bursts, and a shower of colorful embers rained down over the crowd. Another volley shot from the barrels, and Dee watched in horror as, instead of soaring, the two fireballs collided several feet above the flames and ricocheted off each other. In concert with the horde, Dee recoiled. The blue streak shot sideways, flying safely above the crowd's heads, and careened off an aluminum awning and dropped harmlessly into an empty driveway. Dee's eyes followed the red fireball that did not fly sideways; instead, it spun once before launching itself back down toward the fire. Dee watched it slice through the flames and collide with a boy standing at the front of the crowd. Shouts and panic ensued as the crowd split apart, and a terrified Dee watched the boy lurch and spin, his shirt ablaze at the shoulder. He whirled and spun, his arms flailing about his head. A wave of fear enveloped Dee as the boy spun to face her, and instantly she recognized the yellow T-shirt, the one with the eagle stretched across it, the one she'd paid $4.75 for, and then she spotted the two buttons her son had so meticulous pinned onto it that morning. Her son was on fire; Alex was on fire; she screamed his name and ran to him.

★

Paulie stared into the blaze; the intense glow burrowed its way through his eyes and into his brain. He felt as if he were watching the entire day—no, his life entire—ignite and burn, disintegrating like strips of heated celluloid trapped in a projector; bits of Paulie flared and melted away. He drifted unconsciously closer to the fire, as the inner circle of the crowd broke apart and teenagers rushed to and from the flames. He stared deeper and deeper into and through the flames, and for a moment he thought he saw the apparition of his wife's face materialize inside the flames. But then something red and sparkling shot right past him, close enough for its cinders to sting his cheek.

A startled Paulie fell back. People were suddenly running and shouting, and over all their voices he could suddenly hear Dee screaming, "Alex! Alex!" Paulie turned, and next to him was a boy on fire.

Instinctively, he fell upon the child, smothering the flaming shirt with his body, roughly slapping a patch of the boy's smoldering hair. Dee stood directly over them, shrieking her son's name, and Paulie pushed himself back onto his knees, the boy lying prone beneath him, face down against the pavement. Paulie, confused, looked up at his wife. Why was she screaming Alex's name? He rolled the boy over. Paulie and Dee, husband and wife, stared down into the face of a boy, some boy they'd never seen before, who wore the burnt remnants of their son's shirt.

Others rushed to aid the boy now, and someone in the crowd

shouted, "I'm a doctor." For the second time today, the crowd began to chant Paulie's name, applauding his quick thinking and heroic actions. A bewildered Paulie stood up and took a step toward his shaken wife. Just as he reached for her, he heard a small voice calling, "Mom? Dad?" They turned to find Alex standing behind them.

CHAPTER 40

Tony made out with Maria in the shadows of his bedroom, away from the faint sheet of light shining in from the kitchen. When her tongue slid into his mouth to find his, he pulled her tighter against him and slid one hand down from the small of her back to grab her ass. He felt Maria's fingers dig into his back in response, and he reached around with his other hand too. The hand inadvertently slid into the gap between the small of her back and the band of her terry cloth shorts; his entire body tingled; and when Maria didn't protest, he slid his other hand into her pants. He heard a small gasp as he squeezed tighter than he ever had before. Her lips fell from his, and she began to kiss his neck. Tony was only vaguely aware of the muffled blasts continuing to explode from somewhere outside, only vaguely aware that the kitchen phone began to ring again. He tried desperately to keep some minuscule part of himself alert, listening for the sound of the front door slamming or footsteps in the hallway, but he was lost in her now. He took one hand from her pants and groped at her breast. After feeling the sensation of skin on skin, the ruffled material of her tube top was intolerable, and he slid his hand beneath it. She put her hand over his, and his grip relaxed. He let her move his hand over her, slowly. He pressed himself closer to her; he'd never felt this hard before. Then he felt Maria's hand sliding down his chest, over his stomach, reaching down into his pants.

★

Alex's mother dragged him by his ear down the block. He winced from the pain and feared his ear might tear off any second now. She screamed her admonishments so fast that he could barely understand what she was saying, and every time he tried to offer some explanation in his own defense, he felt her twist his ear farther. His father kept pace alongside, shouting at his mother to calm down. Alex could hear the continued explosions behind them, the sound of rockets whooshing and bursting in the sky; he heard the wail of approaching sirens. He was in so much trouble.

As if things couldn't get any worse for him, just as they marched over the sidewalk in front of Zizi's house, Alex turned and saw Zizi emerge from her front door—a ghastly apparition, wrapped in black silk, white hair undone, snaking down over her shoulders. Her bone-thin arms reached overhead, her hands clawing the air in front of her as she screamed down to them, *"Morto! Morto!" Dead.*

"Go back inside," his father screamed at the old woman. "Enough already!"

Behind Zizi, the front door swung slowly open. Alex saw Richie stumble out, staring down at the ground like he'd lost something. Richie looked up; his eyes found his uncle.

"Uncle Paulie," Richie said with tears in his eyes. "Uncle Frank . . . he . . . he had a heart attack."

★

Tony was afraid to open his eyes. Just the initial glimpse through the darkness of Maria reaching for him was almost enough to set him off, so he closed his eyes the moment she took him in her hand, and he felt her grip tighten. He tried to also ignore all his other senses; even the sound of Maria's breathing now threatened to overwhelm him. He just wanted to keep feeling how good this felt, the way the pressure of her hand was so different from his own; he wanted this not to end. He didn't dare reach for the soft skin of her arms or shoulders; that would be too much. He just let his arms dangle at his side, his fingers extended like they were reaching for the floor.

He didn't want it to end, but he had no real choice in the matter. He heard his own breath grow rapid, felt the muscles in his thighs clench. He teetered forward as he came and had to steady himself with one hand against the wall, and he heard something like a giggle from Maria, who still held him in her hand. Tony tried to catch his breath, but before he could even open his eyes, there was a sudden illumination. Maria gasped. Someone had turned on the light.

CHAPTER 41

Paulie was shaking as he fumbled for his keys. He couldn't see; his eyes stung with tears; he couldn't even think straight. Frank. Frank was dead. He could barely stand upright. Dee held her set of keys but was hesitant, for once, to speak. Alex, frightened, waited silently between his parents. He heard what Richie had said about Uncle Frank, but that didn't make any sense at all. Uncle Frank was big and strong. He was a cop.

Finally, Paulie found the right key. He turned the lock and pushed open the front door. He rushed forward to reach for the phone that hung on the kitchen wall. Alex followed, Dee just a step behind. Alex immediately spun left, intending to retreat into the safety of his room. He stepped into his bedroom as his hand simultaneously flew up to switch on the light. The light flashed, and he saw his brother standing there, the front of Tony's pants wide open, some girl holding him by his penis.

Dee saw it all, too, saw the girl with literally half her ass and one breast hanging out, saw what she held in the palm of her hand. She screamed, "Tony!" and the girl screamed, and Paulie dropped the phone and rushed into the room.

Tony leaped back and began stuffing himself back into his pants while Maria threw her arms around herself, trying to simultaneously right her clothes and shield her exposed parts from view. Dee grabbed Alex by the arm and pushed him out of the room.

"Go outside!" Dee yelled, and as her youngest ran out of the apartment, she fell back against the wall. Her face contorted, pressed sideways against the plaster, eyes clenched shut. Paulie clutched the sides of his head with both hands. He opened his mouth to scream or shout, but only a sick wheeze escaped, a death rattle. Despite the shock, Tony reflexively tried to step in front of Maria and shield her from his parents' view, but it was in vain. She was already running away, her head down, arms wrapped in front of her. She ran toward the doorway, and as she passed, Dee screamed again, and Paulie recoiled from her, as if she were an escaped zoo animal free of its cage.

Tony watched Maria run out of the room; he saw the twisted expressions of both his parents, shock, anger. But there was also something else, something worse. Then Tony bolted forward, following Maria's path. Although he wasn't sure if he was chasing after Maria or just fleeing from his parents.

His mother shouted his name as Tony rushed out of his room; his father tried to grab him by his arm, but he was too fast and slipped past him. Tony rushed out the door and down the steps, unsure why his father was screaming out his uncle Frank's name.

Paulie couldn't breathe. He didn't know which way to turn or what to do as he shouted his son's name, then his brother's. He shouted louder, to no avail, as if the increased volume might make either suddenly reappear. He turned desperately to his wife, who, even through her tears, glared back at him, accusingly, her mouth twisted, struggling to spit out words. Through the open doorway to their bedroom, Paulie saw flashes of light at the front window as rockets exploded outside. He ran. He ran past his wife, toward the window; he tried to toss his wife's rocking chair to the side, but it was too heavy and just spun sideways, slamming into his hip as it rocked backward. He flung open the window and spotted his son running out of the house, out of the front gate.

"Tony," he screamed, as loud as he could, sticking his head out the window. "Tony! Come back! Tony! Come back or . . ." Paulie climbed up with his knees onto the windowsill. "I'll jump. I'll fucking jump if you don't. . . ."

Dee couldn't move at first, couldn't peel herself from the wall. Her head dropped into her chest as she wailed; she wailed like she had when her mother had died and she was left all alone. Dee heard Paulie shouting her son's name, and she turned and saw her husband perched in the open window, heard him threatening to jump. Dee screamed, louder than she ever had before, and ran toward him.

"Paulie!" she shouted. "Paulie!"

Paulie hung halfway out the window, one hand pressed flat against the outside bricks, the other clutching the crown molding that framed the inside of the window well so he was precariously suspended, teetering on the narrow sill. Then something slammed into his back, and he lost his balance.

"Paulie!" Dee screamed as she clawed at his shirttail and the waist of his pants, trying not to let go of all she had. "Paulie!"

★

Alex's head spun. He didn't know what to do or where to go after she'd screamed at him to go outside, so there he stood, waiting in the gate, staring at the front door. Moments later, the front door flew open, and the girl who was upstairs with his brother burst from it. She ran directly at Alex as if he weren't even there. He had to jump out of her way, but he wasn't fast enough, and she shoved him by his face as she rushed past, her hand wet and sticky.

Alex wiped off whatever was on his face with the end of his tank top just as Tony ran out the front door and rushed past him, chasing after the girl. Above him, Alex heard his father's shouts. He looked up at his father perched on the ledge.

Skyrockets detonated overhead, shattering into neon bursts as the entire neighborhood seemed to explode around him. Even over the endless rattle of firecrackers and cherry bombs, M-80s and Roman candles, Alex heard his father shouting Tony's name. Then he heard people suddenly shouting his father's name, and he turned to see neighbors amassing along the sidewalk—some had witnessed his father dive onto the flaming boy or had, earlier that day, enjoyed his father's theatrics after winning the foot race. Seeing Paulie dangling out the second-story window, shouting and flailing, the flimsy gold medal still hanging from his neck, they again chanted his name, over and over, assuming this was all part of the festivities. "Pau-lie! Pau-lie! Pau-lie!"

Alex gasped as his father suddenly lurched too far forward, his entire upper body tumbling out from the window. His father's arms thrashed as his fingers frantically searched for a handhold.

"Tony!" Alex yelled for his brother. Tony, who had almost caught up with Maria, heard his brother's shout. He stopped and glanced back and saw his father dangling from the window.

"Pop!" Tony yelled. Alex turned and saw his brother rushing back as their father teetered from the window and their mother, screaming, held tenuously onto him.

"Pop! Pop!" Alex heard Tony call out, over and over, as his brother ran into the house and up the stairs. *Pop! Pop!* The same sound those little twists of white paper, which Alex still carried in his pocket, made as they struck the ground.

CHAPTER 42

Darkness. Paulie heard an unfamiliar, solemn voice, faint but nearby.

"I think you should go in alone."

Slowly Paulie opened his eyes. He was lying in bed, blankets neatly drawn up and over his chest. He tried to rise but couldn't. All he could do was turn his head. He looked around, trying to get his bearings. Something wasn't right. He was in a bedroom, but the bed, the walls: everything was colorless, just shades of gray. Across the room, standing in the open doorway, stood the ER doctor from earlier that day. Dr. Harpo faced someone in the hall and repeated, "I think you should go in alone." The doctor was abruptly pushed aside by Tony, who stormed into the room.

"I'm not letting anyone break up the act, Doc," Tony quipped. He wore a sharp pin-striped suit, a silk handkerchief neatly folded and tucked in his breast pocket, and, atop his head, a NY Yankees cap.

"Hey, Pop," Tony said, his smile barely concealing a look of grave concern.

"Tony . . ." Paulie struggled to speak.

"Don't worry, Pop. I won, Pop," Tony said reassuringly. "We won." Tony loosened his tie knot, reached down into the neck of his shirt, and proudly pulled out the two medals they'd both won earlier at the relay races.

"The crowds . . ." Paulie said, his voice barely above a whisper.

"I thanked 'em, Pop. Just like always," Tony said. "I told them, 'My brother thanks you. . . .'" Suddenly Alex popped his head into Paulie's frame of vision, grinned, and then vanished as if yanked away. Tony continued, "My mother thanks you. . . ." Dee suddenly came into focus, looming over Tony's shoulder. She shook her head disapprovingly. Tony, seemingly aware of her dissatisfaction, cleared his throat and continued. "I thank you. . . ." Paulie stirred in bed with almost a twinge of anticipation. Finally, Tony said, "And . . . and . . . my . . ."—his voice started to tremble—"my uncle Frank thanks you." Tony broke down in tears, burying his face in his hands.

Paulie, lying there, crushed, pleaded, "But . . . what about me?"

"It's too late for you," Dr. Harpo said, now standing at the foot of his bed. He shrugged and pulled a tall lever beside him. The bed vanished from beneath Paulie. He was falling, falling . . .

"Gaaaah!" Paulie awoke, screaming. Dee, sitting beside him, jumped back.

"Oh, Jesus Christ," she muttered, pressing one palm across her heart. Paulie tried to move, but everything hurt. Something else was off: he felt restrained. That was when he realized his left arm and leg were in casts and immobilized by wires and poles. His head was all jumbled; he struggled to focus, to remember, and suddenly he did.

"Frank?!" Paulie exclaimed, trying to prop half of himself up with his free arm and hand.

"Paulie, stop, lay back down." Dee leaned over from her seat to put her hand across her husband's chest and ease him still, but he squirmed. "We don't have any news yet." Her voice trembled. "Richie is waiting for someone to call." Seeing the agitation on her husband's face, she pleaded, "Please calm down. You have two sons."

Paulie turned and realized both boys were also standing there, huddled together in a narrow strip between the foot of his bed and a familiar blue curtain.

"Hi, Dad!" Alex said. Still snug in the ill-fitting gray tank top, he glanced to his mother as if unsure he still had speaking privileges. Tony stood beside his brother. He looked at up his father and started to say something but then dropped his gaze toward the hospital floor, his expression one of shame and defeat.

Paulie's memories began to crystallize. As he stared down past his suspended leg, wrapped tight like a mummy's limb, he spotted a mounted television through the half-open curtain. On its screen flashed images of fireworks bursting in the night sky above the Statue of Liberty. Paulie glanced around again and realized he was laid out in the same unit that Zizi had been. Just then, in strolled the one true Dr. Harpo.

"You liked it here so much, you came back, huh?" he said, more a taunt than a joke. Dee shot him a dirty look that he ignored. "You have a fractured left ulna and fibula." Noticing Paulie stared back blankly, the doctor said condescendingly, "You broke your arm and leg. That's the bad news. Worse news is all the rooms are full, so you'll be spending at least the night in the ER for observation."

Paulie had no words. He felt like he'd been split open and emptied out, like there was nothing left of himself, just a shell.

The doctor turned to Dee and said, "Sorry, but the rest of you need to leave soon. We don't allow overnight visitors for stable adults." The doctor turned and left.

Paulie turned to look at his wife. Her eyes were red and puffy, as if she'd been crying for hours.

"It's almost midnight. They should be in bed," she said, nodding toward their sons. "I need to get them to bed," she repeated. There was something absent in her voice. Then Paulie heard someone else speak.

"Can I get-a my rematch now?" Mario stepped through the curtain. He still looked crisp and fresh, like he'd just come from a salon. Paulie was almost relieved to feel a small rage manifesting inside himself. "I'm just a-kidding. Thank God you are okay."

This is okay? Paulie thought.

"Mario drove us here," Dee explained. "He's been waiting here the whole time."

"No worries. That's-a what neighbors are for." Mario shook his head and waved off Dee's words.

"Thank you, Mario," Dee said. She reached and squeezed Mario's arm. "Thank you." Dee then turned to her sons. "Say good night to your father."

"Good night, Dad," Alex quickly responded. Tony glanced up at his father and echoed his brother's words, then lowered his gaze again as he turned to leave with Alex.

Paulie watched his sons exit. Dee began to follow, but then paused, turned, and walked quickly back to her husband. She gripped his arm and kissed him on his forehead.

"I love you," she said, the words rushed but soft. As Paulie watched Dee trail after her sons, he saw Cronkite was back on-screen.

"Well, the party's almost over. . . ."

"What fucking party?" Paulie said aloud. Only Mario was left to listen, who nodded sympathetically.

"Feel better, Paulie. . . . I will say a prayer for your brother," Mario said.

"Thanks . . . thank you," Paulie said. Then he looked at his broken arm, down at his broken leg, and shook his head. "What am I going to do?" The question was posed more to himself than his neighbor. Mario nodded once, sideways, in contemplation, then looked Paulie in the eye.

"At least you're not a racehorse," Mario said, pointing to Paulie's leg. As Mario turned and left, Cronkite, hovering above, signed off.

"And that's the way it is, July fourth, 1976."

ACKNOWLEDGMENTS

First and foremost, thank you to my wife, Talia, for her unconditional love and support. I am happy because of you. And thank you to my amazing children—Anya and Eli—you are both my inspiration and my whole life.

I'd like to thank David Grand and Walter Cummins, whose mentorship and insight helped me mold a loose idea into a novel. My appreciation also to the rest of the FDU faculty and my MFA peers, whose camaraderie I enjoyed during my residencies. Also, thank you to Andy Hoffmann and Bruce Weigl, whose workshops helped shape a young Penn State writing student many moons ago. A special appreciation to my short-lived but productive post-FDU writing group—Elizabeth Jaeger, Anthony Truppo, Nicole Cirone, and Azly Rahman, whose feedback helped craft later revisions. And thank you to the creators of every comic book, film, television show, and literary work that has, through the years, inspired and fostered my love of stories.

I'd also like to thank all those who have provided their encouragement and support over the years. The list includes but is not limited to my brother, Michael Ausiello, and his family: Christina,

Michael, and Alessia; Elan, Tamar, Noa, and Asher Jacoby; Barbara Kipper; Carol Kloster; Scott and Tricia Lerner; Jeanie Pollack; Randy Varner; and John Orlando.

My sincere appreciation to Girl Friday Productions, especially Paul Barrett, Kristin Duran, Katie Meyers, and Karen McNally Upson, whose effort and talents were instrumental in bringing this novel to publication. Thank you to my developmental editor, Faith Black Ross, whose feedback and guidance helped me across the finish line.

This list would be incomplete without the two people truly responsible for me—my parents, Beatrice and Tony Ausiello. While both have passed away, I know they would have been proud to hold this book in their hands. Of course, upon reading, my mother also would have told me to go eff myself for the parts she took issue with. My father, on the other hand, would just be upset that Paulie missed out on the exacta.

And, finally, thank you, Brooklyn, the one I grew up in. And to those others out there fortunate enough to have ever called the borough your home—thanks to your Brooklyn too.

Where I grew up

ABOUT THE AUTHOR

Legend traces Anthony Ausiello's love of stories and storytelling to when, at four years of age, he received his first comic book, the latest newsstand issue of *Superman*, as a gift. To his parents' dismay, one comic led to another and another. Soon after, television reruns dug their hooks into him. *Batman*, *The Monkees*, *The Courtship of Eddie's Father*—it didn't matter; he loved them all. Before long, he moved on to *The 4:30 Movie* every weekday—especially during *Planet of the Apes* and *Godzilla* weeks. Saturdays meant watching professional wrestling and kung fu films, while Sunday mornings were spent with the Bowery Boys, followed by Abbott and Costello. And all the while, whenever possible, Anthony read. He cites *The Black Stallion and Satan*, *Dune*, and *The Amazing Adventures of Kavalier & Clay* among his literary inspirations. He graduated from the Pennsylvania State University with a BA in English. After a brief two-decade-long pit stop in corporate America, Anthony earned an MFA in creative writing from Fairleigh Dickinson University, where he began to work on his first novel. Thoroughly Brooklyn born and bred, Anthony now lives in Westfield, New Jersey, with his wonderful wife, Talia, and his amazing children, Anya and Eli.